LAST RITES

LAST RITES

PAUL SPIKE

NAL BOOKS

NEW AMERICAN LIBRARY

TIMES MIRROR

NEW YORK AND SCARBOROUGH, ONTARIO

Published simultaneously in Canada by
The New American Library of Canada Limited

NAL BOOKS TRADEMARK REG. U.S. PAT. OFF. AND FOREIGN COUNTRIES
REGISTERED TRADEMARK—MARCA REGISTRADA
HECHO EN HARRISONBURG, VA., U.S.A.

SIGNET, SIGNET CLASSICS, MENTOR, PLUME,
MERIDIAN and NAL BOOKS are published *in the United
States* by The New American Library, Inc., 1633 Broadway,
New York, New York 10019, *in Canada* by The New American
Library of Canada Limited, 81 Mack Avenue, Scarborough,
Ontario M1L 1M8

Library of Congress Cataloging in Publication Data

Spike, Paul, 1947–
    Last rites.

    I. Title.
PS3569.P53L3   813'.54   81–9440
ISBN 0–453–00410–5   AACR2

Designed by Julian Hamer

First Printing, August, 1981

1 2 3 4 5 6 7 8 9

PRINTED IN THE UNITED STATES OF AMERICA

To Alice Spike

WITH MANY THANKS TO:
Helen Brann
Bill and Lauretta Dean
Bill and Dorothy McGaw
Jim Stowe

Gods in the water, home for the night.
Who made the night so long?

—from a song by Teresa Tudury
Deyá, 1972

For here we have no continuing city,
but we seek one to come.

—HEBREWS 13:14

Monday
May 26, 1980

1

I BEGAN to read them Psalm 124. It was over one hundred degrees in the church and people were using the prayer books to fan themselves. At the seventh verse:

> Our soul is escaped as a bird out of the snare of the fowlers: the snare is broken, and we are escaped . . .

I glanced down from the pulpit. The books looked like redbirds beating their wings but going nowhere. I imagined Aaron's voice saying, "Watch yourself, Fernando." Perhaps it was just the girl's effect on me.

She was a beautiful girl. I had never seen her before Aaron's funeral. She was Mexican, no more than eighteen years old. She stood out in that crowd like a bonfire. She had jet-black hair and eyes the color of a tropical sea. But what was angering the crowd was her dress. It was yellow silk, expensive. Her breasts were bare under the fabric; you could see the shape of her nipples. Hardly the dress to wear to the funeral of the city's leading citizen. The crowd obviously thought a Mexican girl ought to know the color of mourning. But she had come to the funeral looking as gaudy as a Yucatán parrot.

Aaron Anderson had been shot in the head with a .38-caliber bullet. They had found his body in the front of his silver Mercedes, parked in the last row of the Colonia Drive-In. The gun itself had yet to be found. Nor were any useful fingerprints recovered from the car.

[3]

Some said it was a crude attempt to make Aaron's death look like a scandal, since the Colonia showed exclusively XXX-rated sex films. But I had never seen Holy Innocents Episcopal Church so full, nor so many leading El Sol families in one room before.

Present were all of the "old" Cottonwood Country Club crowd, Aaron's people, and many of the "new" crowd, best represented by young Joe Moore and his sleek wife in her black Halston dress.

Barbara Anderson, the widow, sat in the second row, flanked by her half-sister Lindy and by Dr. Elwood Munty, Aaron's best friend. I counted all my other fellow members on Aaron's committee in the front rows, notably Jamie Hillal, the city's controversial young criminal lawyer, looking very handsome and exceedingly angry in a seat on the center aisle.

Aaron had served Holy Innocents as warden of the vestry for three decades. He was the only perpetual deacon in our parish—in the entire state, as a matter of fact.

But at least half the crowd were neither parish members nor wealthy El Sol big shots, just ordinary folk. They had lived in this desert city on the Border most of their lives. They knew Aaron as neighbors, clients of his law practice, customers at his savings bank, and in many cases, as his loyal employees.

At the rear of the nave, crushed against the back wall, were many of Aaron's less fortunate neighbors. Mostly Mexicans, and a few Indians, they were afraid to sit down in the most exclusive church in Cottonwood. But they, too, had known the deceased as friends and clients, customers and employees. Aaron loved El Sol and its people. He loved the vast Southwestern desert that surrounded it, making it an island on an ocean of barren ground. The most isolated city in America.

* * *

[4]

I had been rector of Holy Innocents for only eleven months, but I had come to love Aaron like a father. I was thirty-two years old that May. I was not a native of El Sol, far from it. I had grown up in a small upper-middle-class town in central Connecticut, the son of an Episcopal priest whose guts I hated. Until my senior year at Brown, in the middle of the Vietnam war, the last thing I had ever dreamed of doing was following in my father's footsteps. But I had applied to Union Seminary in 1969, seeking to avoid the draft, and been accepted that spring. Thus had I embraced God to save my own ass. From the moment of my ordination, at St. John's Cathedral in New York City, in 1972, I had experienced what a Hollywood screenplay would call "grave doubts" about my vocation. It was no accident that I had chosen to accept positions farther and farther west, farther and farther from my Connecticut childhood and my father.

It was because of Aaron Anderson that I was still a priest that spring of 1980. My wife, Nancy, had left me six weeks after we had first arrived in El Sol. Afterward I had wanted to run too. But Aaron had talked me into staying, had even lied to his old friends in the church in order to cover for me. Now it was my job to bury him, and my debt. And I was afraid his funeral might turn into a riot.

But things went smoothly and I felt fine until the Eucharist was finished. The last of the hundreds had taken Communion from my hands and I felt the stab of old guilt. I believed in God. It was just that, too often, I wished I did not. What I had lost was not belief; my childhood indoctrination made sure I would always believe in God. What I had lost was faith. And my wife. And now Aaron.

I commended Aaron to Christ, and then, after nodding a signal to the leading pallbearers, I descended the three steps to follow the body as it was borne from the church.

"Into paradise may the angels lead thee," I chanted. "And at thy coming may the martyrs receive thee, and bring thee into the holy city Jerusalem."

The congregation rose and began to move out of all four doors of the church. The blue sky was as brilliant as acrylic paint: not a trace of cloud broke its monotony. No breeze stirred the cottonwoods in the Anderson family plot.

The grave yawned open next to the simple stone of his mother's grave. His sister Jane's stone was smaller, set off in one corner. She had died in an automobile accident in 1948. Of Aaron's father, I knew little. Only that he had left El Sol in the early years of the Depression and his family had never seen him again.

People crowded thirty deep around the grave. Members of the vestry tried to open a path to bring Barbara Anderson to the front. She had her arm hooked through Dr. Munty's arm. She wore a black suit and a veil, but no hat. Her tall, handsome half-sister Lindy towered above her.

I was midway through the committal when I sensed the disturbance. Someone was pushing through the crowd toward the grave. Heads turned. Whispers rose on the hot dry air. One voice cut above all the others: odd-sounding, excited, and foreign.

The Mexican girl in the yellow dress broke through the mourners. She was angry. A damp line ran down her right cheek. She was less than a foot from the grave. The great bronze casket was covered with a blanket of white cliffroses.

As they lowered it, the girl swept her black hair over one shoulder. Her hand fumbled in a small purse. The yellow dress blazed in the midst of all those somber clothes.

"The Lord bless him and keep him, the Lord make his face to shine upon him," I said. "And be gracious unto him, the Lord lift up his countenance and give him peace. Amen."

Nobody made a move to stop her. We all watched as she pulled out the salt shaker. It was a perfectly ordinary glass salt shaker with a twist-on cap, the kind you have seen in a thousand restaurants. She took it out and began to shake it over the grave.

I had already cast a handful of earth onto Aaron's coffin. Now, as the girl salted it, she chanted his name over and over in her border accent: "Airun, Airun, Airun . . ."

Suddenly Barbara Anderson unhooked her arm from Dr. Munty's and stepped forward. Someone reached out a hand to hold her back. But the widow pulled away from it. She planted one foot firmly on the grass six inches from the edge of the grave.

The Mexican girl turned and looked at her. Then glanced down at the salt shaker in her own hand. She threw the salt shaker into the grave. It made a clanging noise on the bronze.

Barbara Anderson lifted her veil with her left hand. With her right, she slapped the girl full across the face. I was behind Barbara a second later when she tried to slap her again. The crowd was in confusion, outraged. I put both arms around the widow and fought her away from all the turmoil. There seemed to be a hundred hands reaching for the Mexican girl. Somehow, in their midst, she disappeared from my sight.

It took five minutes to restore calm so I could read the final words of the service and dismiss them. This was not the riot I had feared. I had no idea what had happened to the girl. Nor why the widow was in such a rage she would not even wait to hear the benediction at her husband's grave.

2

It began a few minutes after the benediction. I had expected something like this but had seen no way to avoid it. When the shouting started out in the parking lot beyond the churchyard gate, I was listening to a group of parish women, led by Edith Munty, who were trying hard to gossip their way around the scene at the graveside.

I looked over at the lot and saw Joe Moore's reddish-blond hair towering above the rest of the men. I began to run. I heard the sound of a punch landing on a body, like a small firecracker going off in a can, and Jamie Hillal's angry voice.

Moore was over six feet three inches tall and at least 230 pounds. In his mid-thirties, the young millionaire could have been a college quarterback ten years out of shape. But Jamie Hillal was only average in height and wiry. He looked like he ought to be tough and fast. I was running without my heart in it, knowing I would have to stop the fight. I wanted so much to give someone a chance to beat up Joe Moore.

By the time I reached the crowd, a man I had never seen before had already separated the two fighters. He was quite tall, dark, not necessarily Mexican. He had on a tight-fitting black pin-striped suit and wore an elegant mustache on his face. He looked like an athletic criminal.

"Jamie, this is no way to settle anything," he said. He had his back to Joe Moore as he appealed to Hillal.

Hillal ignored him, looking beyond him at Joe Moore. "What are you trying to prove, Joe?" he demanded. "That you didn't have him killed? That you're man enough to do your own dirty work?"

"Man, I'm going to sue you. I'm going to kick your ass, Hillal," Moore shouted back, jabbing his finger, his cheeks flushed with anger. "You people don't have a chance to stop us next Tuesday, no matter how dirty you want to get."

"Don't talk to me about dirty, Moore. You're nothing but a high-class speculator, you're dangerous, and you should have stayed out in California where you belonged."

"I'll see you in court, Hillal. After Election Day. That's next Tuesday, remember? Don't you forget to vote, hear?" Moore bent down and picked up his suit jacket. Standing nearby was his burly Chicano chauffeur, glaring at Jamie Hillal. The Rolls-Royce that Moore had brought to town several months before was across the parking lot. His wife stood beside it with her arms akimbo, trying to see what was happening over the heads of the crowd of men.

"You bet, Joe. We'll all see you in court. We'll see you in the electric chair, you motherfucker."

Moore suddenly whirled and began to move back at Hillal. But the stranger with the mustache intervened and pushed him back with both hands. "Look," the stranger said, "I thought this was a funeral. Let's have a little respect for the man's family." He turned his head. "That goes for you too, Jamie. Knock it off, gentlemen. Or I'm going to lose my temper."

The crowd murmured its approval and began to move away. Everyone knew, of course, that Jamie Hillal had

[9]

been quoted in the El Sol *Post-Examiner* on Friday as blaming Joe Moore for "creating a climate of hate" that made Aaron's murder inevitable. We had all seen the TV commercials, both Joe Moore's and Aaron's committee's.

Aaron had spent the past two months fighting to defeat the two Propositions that Moore had put on the ballot for the coming June 3 election. Propositions which Moore believed would bring El Sol to glory, and Aaron contended would turn the city to ruins. Jamie Hillal was on Aaron's Committee to Save El Sol, and so was I, and we both had received death threats only days before Aaron was shot. So had everyone else on the committee, which had been characterized by Moore's TV ads as "a group of anti-American reactionaries opposed to progress and the economic rebirth of our great town."

I saw the man with the mustache trying to talk to Jamie, holding on to his upper arm. Jamie ripped his arm away and kept walking toward his red Porsche 928. Meanwhile, Moore had settled in the backseat of his Rolls beside his wife. They drove past me, and Moore nodded at me through the glass.

I turned and walked back inside the churchyard. Johnny Attlee, our sexton, was half-finished with his shovel at the grave. The work made a mournful racket. The heat was vicious. A small group of parish people lingered near the front steps. One of them, Carl Tooman, now separated himself. I could tell Aaron's law partner wanted to talk to me in private. We both began to move toward the side path.

"How can it be, Fernando?" Tooman asked. "How can the man be dead?"

His funeral on May 26, 1980, came at the end of the Ash Spring. A volcano had filled America's sky with billows of ash, a symbol of all the other ashes that shrouded us those first months into the new decade. Riot ash. Refugee ashes. Ashes in Iran. The worst drought since the Thirties had just begun. On the ashen horizon was November's national election, which seemed to offer many a limited a choice: one disaster or another.

I had buried Aaron. Cremation would have carried the metaphor too far for us that Monday. At age sixty-seven, Aaron had joined his mother and sister under the cottonwoods. It was better than ending up in a made-in-Hong Kong urn. At least Aaron would end up worms. Or whatever lived under our desert.

In eight days, we faced the local election. El Sol would elect a mayor for two more years and decide, in the process, if there was a "Murder Wave" in town or not. According to the incumbent, Mayor John Castillo, there was no such thing. According to Leo Mulcahy, U.S. Army colonel (retired) and candidate for Castillo's job, there certainly was a "Murder Wave" in town. Ironically, Aaron had made fun of the entire issue for the last eight weeks. The only issues Aaron recognized were Propositions 3 and 8.

Aaron Anderson was a tall, silver-haired Western gentleman with indigo eyes and long, tapered fingers. He appeared to be conservative: he was. But he was never stuffy or false. He judged on the facts, not on a formula he carried around in his head. Aaron had a fine sense of humor. He loved to shock people, especially people who refused to take it. I thought we got along so well because we were both cynical idealists. He was very rich. He believed in God. He had been married three times, and for the most part, he did exactly as he pleased.

On the surface, the confrontation between Aaron and Joe Moore looked like a classic battle between "reactionary" old man and "progressive" young newcomer. Except that Joe Moore had been born in El Sol and grew up there before he went off to college in California in the Sixties, then Stanford Business School, and eventually made a fortune speculating in land up in the Napa Valley of northern California. Joe Moore was one of the first to persuade big American corporations that they ought to invest in vineyards and quality wine for the consumers of his own generation who wanted to drink "light" and stay young forever. He had made millions through his land deals, and then something had gone wrong and he had decided to leave California all at once, to return to his hometown and—why not?—"develop" it. He had personally written both Propositions 3 and 8 and financed the write-in campaign to put them on the ballot.

Joe Moore was not long in El Sol before he had decided to turn it into the next Los Angeles. In the first place, as he saw it, the Northeast and the Midwestern sections of America were doomed. Their frigid climates, organized labor, and the cost of oil had combined to force the migration of American industry and population toward the Southwest. Joe Moore was a prophet. El Sol was going to be his sacred tablet.

Moore proposed to transform El Sol from a Sun Belt city of half a million people, one already ranked the fourth-fastest-growing city in America, into a human explosion: a starburst of a city with a population of twenty million by the year 1999! According to his own estimates, Joe Moore wanted to increase the population by 4,000 percent in a mere twenty years.

His Proposition 3 called for the development of the northern zone of El Sol County, most of it public land: six hundred empty square miles of sand, greasewood, and rattlers. On those thousands of acres Moore proposed to build the most modern city in the world, what he called "a city for the next century." He would finance this utopian development thanks to Proposition 8 and the taxes it would ultimately bring the city. Proposition 8 called for nothing less than the total razing of El Sol's *barrio* and the relocation of its 250,000 Mexican-American citizens to the "new city" in the desert. In their place, Moore would build the nation's largest ultramodern industrial park, on the Border.

Aaron detested both ideas. He wanted his city to grow, not to explode. The Mexican-American *barrio* was, in fact, a collection of small villages that had been in existence, and occupied by Spanish-speaking residents, long before the first Anglos had crossed west of the Mississippi River. Aaron couldn't find dirty-enough words to curse Joe Moore's plans. He had formed his committee. He had begun to raise money to finance TV commercials to defeat the Propositions.

Joe Moore had his own TV commercials, and some people said he was prepared to spend a million dollars, if necessary, to get his Propositions approved by the voters. But most of the polls showed the voters almost evenly divided between Joe Moore's camp and Aaron's. Next Tuesday's election was going to be excruciatingly close.

One thing I had never completely understood was how Aaron felt about Jamie Hillal. He had asked him to join the committee but had confessed to me that he didn't trust Hillal. "How can you defend all these drug smugglers and not be involved yourself?" Aaron had said. He called Hillal a "Cadillac liberal" and hinted that his chief motive for opposing Joe Moore was jealousy. "The Hillals are land-rich," he said once. "And some of us will never forgive 'em for it." Yet Aaron seemed to get along well with Jamie at the committee meetings. They would joke together and Aaron would insult him. I had assumed Jamie Hillal was Mexican at first, because of his dark handsome looks, but Aaron had called him an "Arab son of a bitch" too many times. Still I refused to ask if Jamie was part Mexican because of my own predicament. I was also rather dark, my first name was Spanish-sounding, and people thought I must be Mexican when they first met me. How many times had I explained about my

Puerto Rican mother who had met my father at a country-club dance in San Juan his first year out of seminary? They had been married six months later and spent their honeymoon in, of all places, Westport. My mother rarely ever got back to her island. She died of cancer, when I was seven years old, at a hospital in Hartford. But that has nothing to do with Jamie Hillal, I know. Nor the murder wave. Nor Aaron's death.

"It's the water." Maggie Endicott had said that to me the afternoon we got the news about Aaron. Maggie had been the church secretary at Holy Innocents for sixteen years. I was sorry when she said that. The phrase was driving me crazy. "You watch, now," she'd continued. "We're getting to be a regular New York City jungle. We had those chemicals in the water all these years. But now they're gone and poor Aaron Anderson is shot dead. Who'll be next? Can you imagine?"

El Sol was not famous for many things. Two of them happened to be its low murder rate for a city of its size and the lithium found in its water supply. The city's water was drawn from natural reservoirs deep below the desert surface. It had been found rich in the element lithium. The lightest metal known to man, lithium had been proved an effective medicine when used in the treatment of psychotic patients, especially manic-depressives. There were psychiatrists who claimed lithium was *the* miracle drug of twentieth-century psychiatric medicine. So the taps in El Sol were gushing with lithium. But the fact that they were gushing at all, that was the miracle.

A rumor had surfaced that spring. People said the lithium was gone, that it had suddenly disappeared from the water supply.

This rumor happened to surface at the same time as a sharp increase in the number of murders in the city. The police blamed these murders, not on any missing lithium, but on two facts. First, it had been one of the hottest springs in living memory. Second, there was a gang war taking place on the streets of El Sol. A power struggle between the Mexicans from across the Border in El Sol's "sister" city, Gomez—Mexicans who had always controlled the prostitution and drug-smuggling activities in the region—and a group of newcomers. These newcomers were soldiers in our new all-volunteer U.S. Army. They were stationed at Fort Ricks in the southeastern part of El Sol. These soldiers had volunteered to join the Army from some of the toughest, poorest neighborhoods in the nation. While there were people who said the GI's were really working for the Mafia or some other shadowy syndicate, in fact the GI's involved, perhaps no more than 3 percent of the total Army, were too tough to work for anybody but themselves. Their America the Beautiful was the South Bronx or the South Side of Chicago, Appalachia or East Los Angeles. It was no secret in Washington that our all-volunteer Army was a disaster. The Soviets' invasion of Afghanistan had provided a welcome excuse to introduce a new draft-registration law that spring of 1980.

Twenty-seven people had been shot in cold blood in El Sol since January. Many were small-time gangsters from Gomez. Many others were GI's. Leo Mulcahy's "Murder Wave" issue was well chosen: he hoped to build his mayoralty on it. Not coincidentally, it had helped produce a sharp rise in the *Post-Examiner*'s circulation. The newspaper was vigorously supporting Mulcahy's candidacy.

"It's the water" was *the* slang expression of that spring. But I had seen no evidence to prove the lithium was, in fact, missing. Only rumors—and that phrase. Every time another GI was shot, or there was a bad accident on the Interstate near one of the malls, or someone's grandpa cut a fart at the counter in Sambo's, you heard it. "It's the water."

Nobody with any sense took it seriously—except for Aaron. It *was* the water for him. Water was the key issue involved in his fight against Joe Moore's Propositions for developing the city. Not lithium, but the water needed for humans to live in the middle of a huge desert.

Aaron would tell everyone he met that there was only a limited amount of water in the deep wells under El Sol County. If the Propositions passed, he said, in ten years there might not be a drop of water left. El Sol would not be the first ghost town born when its wells ran dry in that part of the world. "In the desert," Aaron said, "water is God's own hospitality. Man has no lasting claim on it." And he added, "If the water ran out here, this town would just blow away in three weeks' time."

The picture Aaron painted was grim. He said he had seen evidence that proved the water supply was running out under El Sol at an alarming rate. But Joe Moore didn't care about any of that. He was after profits, enormous sums of money that would not wait for anything as mundane as water. If we didn't stop Joe Moore, Aaron said, he would turn the small oasis that El Sol had always been into a desert of sand, displaced lives, and unspeakable greed. But, of course, Aaron loved to preach in a style old-fashioned by today's standards. Still, I believed what he said was mostly true.

"How can he be dead?" Tooman asked me.

I looked at Aaron's law partner and shook my head. Tooman was everything Aaron was not: pompous, meticulous, sly. He was a fat man who waxed his thin mustache and who always wore a vest. He did the hard work in their law practice and was smart enough never to discuss it with Aaron. "How can he be dead?" was Tooman's way of feigning grief in front of a preacher.

"I have the feeling Aaron would have enjoyed his funeral," I said.

Tooman dropped his unctuous expression and grinned. "I reckon he would have. A cat fight over his grave and a kick-ass brawl in the parking lot. Aaron would have been tickled."

"It's almost as if he wrote the script in advance. By the way, what happened to the widow? She left just before the benediction. Was she all right?"

Tooman shrugged his shoulders. "I don't think she's feeling too well in this heat. Barbara called me this morning about his will again. I'm afraid I can't give exact details until we all sit down together. I was wondering if you would be available next Wednesday afternoon, Father O'Neal?"

"Available for what?"

"To come down to the office and hear Aaron's will read."

"Sure, but why me?"

"Holy Innocents is the major beneficiary of Aaron's estate, Father. Or didn't you know that?"

"No, I did not."

"I thought Aaron must have discussed it with you. I certainly wish he'd made it a little plainer to his wife. She is very upset by what I've told her. I fully anticipate some sort of challenge from her before this is finished. Did you happen to catch the name of that Mexican gal who started all the fuss?"

"No. I've never seen her before this afternoon."

"Pretty little gal, but a shame about her dress. I wonder if she could be a Miss Hernandez. I'll have to find out." He took a handkerchief out of his pocket and wiped his moist forehead.

"Who is Miss Hernandez?" I asked.

He shook his head. "You'll have to wait until Wednesday, sorry." Tooman's expression darkened. "I spoke to Detective Dorfman on the phone just before I drove over here."

[17]

"Yes? Anything new?"

"That Dorfman is a smart cop. He was in Philadelphia before he moved out here for his wife's asthma. Philly cops are supposed to be damn tough."

"What did he say?" I insisted.

"He believes Aaron was shot by a close friend. Even a relative. He says Aaron must have trusted this person a good deal to go to the dirty pictures with him. Or her."

"That's an interesting theory."

"Dorfman also said we ought to all be careful. He said there was something 'wrong' about the killing. What could be right about a killing, though?" Tooman said, raising his eyebrows. "Anyway, I got the impression Dorfman was worried. Maybe we're all in danger these days, like this fellow Mulcahy claims."

"Maybe we are," I told him. I thought of the ugly hate letters I had recently received in the mail. "What do you think?" I asked.

"Me?" He laughed. "Father, don't ask me that."

"Why?"

"I'm too dumb to think anymore. Too dumb and too old."

"Like a fox, is that it?"

He laughed and his fat hand smacked me on the shoulder. "I've got to get moving along back to my office. Father, can I count on seeing you about two P.M. next Wednesday?"

I told him he could, and we went our separate ways. As I started down the rest of the side path, I saw Johnny Attlee had finished with his shovel.

3

MAGGIE WAS crying at her desk in the outer office. Tears rolled slowly from underneath her glasses as she tried to type on her coral Selectric II. I insisted she take the rest of the afternoon off. She handed me a fistful of white addressed envelopes and made me swear to drop them in the mailbox on the corner. I gave her a peck on the cheek and walked her to the front door.

After changing out of my stifling hot robes, I had collapsed in the chair behind my desk when Johnny Attlee came by and said he was leaving. The grave was filled. He'd locked all the doors in the church. He would come back the next morning and do the mopping-up in the nave. Johnny liked to do all his janitorial work in the dawn hours. He had several other jobs besides being our sexton, and Aaron's funeral was the first time I had ever seen him around the premises in the afternoon. Usually the undertakers would provide a man or men to handle the gravedigging. Mexicans, invariably. But Johnny had come to me soon after Aaron's murder and told me he wanted to dig the grave himself and would require no outside help. He shut my office door behind him when he left.

I put my stocking feet up on my desk and stared at the Dali print on the opposite wall. It was a reproduction of a line drawing of Christ as seen from above, arms spread, trunk and legs severely foreshortened. The Cross was missing. It looked like Christ was soaring in pure white space. It was signed and dated 1951 and I had bought it in a shop on the Rue de Seine in Paris at the end of the summer of 1971, the day before Nancy and I flew back to New York after two glorious months in Europe. I could remember the restaurant where we had eaten dinner on the Rue Git-le-Coeur that last evening, and even what we had each ordered. The taste of the chilled Brouilly was suddenly as fresh in my memory as the taste of bread. And the envelopes . . . ?

I suddenly remembered the envelopes Maggie had handed me. While I had changed out of my clerical garb, I had put them down somewhere. Now I couldn't recall where. Searching through the clutter on my desk, then on top of the bookshelves, I was back looking in my closet when I heard the knock on my door.

The church was supposed to be locked.

"Yes? Who is it?" I called. "Come in."

The door opened slowly. She stood with one foot slightly forward, her hands clasped in front of her waist. The yellow dress was wrinkled and there was a smudge of dirt on the lower part of the skirt. She was all eyes: vast blue. At first I thought she was trying to look the waif. But then I saw that her eyes not only were exceptionally large and clear but also shone with obvious intelligence. There was something defiant in them, too. But that first moment, as we met at close range in my office, I did not see the defiance, only felt it. And I mistakenly thought it was directed just at me.

"Hello."

She only nodded.

"Please come in. Would you like to sit down?" I nodded at one of the modular chairs. She moved in that direction as I looked back at the closet, confused. "Excuse me," I said. "I misplaced something and I can't seem to find it now. I've been doing that a lot lately."

"I am sorry," she said. I knew from her voice that she was not talking about my lost envelopes.

"Sorry?"

"Yes, for this trouble outside. I can't explain to you why I did what I did. I can tell you that Aaron would have understood. He would have laughed. I wanted to make him laugh one more time."

I nodded and moved to sit in the chair facing hers. "You knew Aaron well?"

She shut her eyes quickly in a gesture of slight embarrassment. I realized what a thoughtless question I had asked. "I'm sorry," I said. "I meant . . ."

"No, don't be. Aaron and I were very good friends. He told me about you."

"He did?"

"Yes, he told me how much he liked you. About your wife leaving. He told me if anything ever were to happen to him, that I should get to know you." She smiled again. "Actually, he said that wasn't likely. Aaron planned on living forever."

"I wish he could have."

"So do I." She touched her hair. "Do you have a car?"

"Yes."

"I need a big favor. And one smaller one. Could you give me a ride to my apartment? I have to work at six o'clock and I'm afraid to be late. It's not too far."

I looked at my watch. It was 4:13 P.M. "Where do you live?"

"Haynes Drive. Behind the Sandman Motel."

"You can direct me."

"Thanks. It's not hard."

Once we were in my Fairmont and out on Desert Hills Avenue heading toward the Interstate, I asked, "What kind of work do you do?"

"I dance."

I should have guessed. She had a sublime figure. "Where do you dance?"

"A club called Rainbow. You know it?"

I shook my head. Perhaps it was one of those which advertised in the entertainment pages of the *Post-Examiner*. A topless club. But I wasn't sure. "How did you get into the church just now?" I asked. "I thought it was locked."

"After all the trouble with his wife, I ran inside and hid."

"Throwing that salt, I don't understand. Can you explain?"

"No," she said. "It is a personal thing."

We drove in silence for a while. I wondered if driving her back to her apartment was the "big" favor or if that was still to come. I glanced at her from time to time. She was so young and beautiful, it was difficult to concentrate on driving. And I wanted to ask her where she had learned to speak such good English, but of course, I would never ask her that. One thoughtless question was all I wanted to risk with her.

The city of El Sol spread out for miles along the Border. Contrary to what she had said, the Sandman Motel on Haynes Drive was a long way from Cottonwood. But the drive wouldn't take too long, thanks to the Interstate. It pierced the whole body of the city, threading together all the various neighborhoods and *barrios* with eight lanes of fast concrete.

Cottonwood was one of the oldest sections: four square miles of fertile land nestled in a bend of the river. Centered around the country club, it was the part of town where residents tended to divide themselves into sets: the "golf set," the "horse set," and the "tennis set" all folded neatly into a master set: upper-middle-class, Anglo, and Protestant.

Holy Innocents was the oldest church in Cottonwood.

We were surrounded by the largest homes in the city: extravagant colonial or sprawling ranch-style, landscaped on several acres with pools, stables, tall shady trees, and white-fenced paddocks of emerald turf where the quarter horses grazed oblivious to the arid wasteland not far away.

The Sandman Motel, where I was driving the girl, was located in a no-man's-land of gas stations and motels, furnished apartments and bargain stores. It had grown up as a buffer between Fort Ricks and the *barrio*. The local nickname for this district was "the Station," because it was where a once-busy (now abandoned) railroad station was located. The enlisted GI's who lived off-base rented their furnished apartments in the Station. When high-school boys talked of getting drunk and losing their virginity, it was to the Station they drove when they got tired of just talking.

On the way from Cottonwood to the Station, the Interstate passed through downtown El Sol. We were lucky to be missing rush hour. You could see from the highway that most of downtown, built in the 1920's, was decaying. There were two modern towers of glass and steel that broke the low city profile: a mining-company headquarters and the Sheraton. Like many small cities in America, El Sol's downtown had ceased to be a shopping center for most of its citizens. They had been attracted to the three regional shopping malls stationed at intervals alongside the Interstate, while downtown shopping was almost exclusively the domain of Mexicans who crossed the river from El Sol's "sister" city, Gomez. Thus downtown El Sol was more Mexican in feeling than American these days.

After the Interstate left downtown, the highway itself became a kind of border. On the south side were the crowded flat-roofed tenements of the *barrio*. On the north began the tract homes of middle-class El Sol.

[23]

Anglos had been arriving here in increasing numbers each year since World War II.

The *barrio* was wedged between the Interstate and the Border, bursting with its Chicano population and with thousands of illegals from across the river. The middle-class tracts, on the north side of the Interstate, stretched leisurely up to the edge of the desert, and beyond. Every day the desert succumbed to new asphalt roads, to more model homes thrown up by the developers. But what Joe Moore wanted to do with the hundreds of square miles of empty, county-owned desert that remained was far beyond the local developers' wildest imaginings.

"It is very nice of you to drive me home," she said finally. "Can I ask you another favor now?"

"The big one?"

"I'm afraid so, Fernando."

"Go ahead." I liked the way she said my name, with a Spanish pronunciation.

"I have Aaron's briefcase. He gave it to me last Wednesday evening before he was killed. By the way, I don't understand why Aaron would have gone to this sexy movie last Wednesday. It makes no sense. . . . You know what I am trying to say?"

"Yes." I wondered if Aaron had "given" her the briefcase, or simply forgotten it? Perhaps he had meant to pick it up later? Of course he had.

"He was with me Wednesday evening for two hours. He left a little after eight. His briefcase contains many papers. They must be important, I think. I think his wife would want them back. Don't you?"

"Yes, she probably would."

"Do you know his wife very well?"

"No."

"This is our exit." We were approaching the turnoff that would lead to Haynes Drive.

"I know."

She took out a pack of cigarettes. Winston. She put one in her mouth and lit it with a gold cigarette lighter shaped like a lipstick. I had the feeling she smoked rarely, for effect.

The Interstate was built twenty feet off the ground, so that I always felt like I was flying low across the city, not driving. At night, with the stars stretching out to the horizons above, and the city lights running to the same horizons below, I felt like I was in the Milky Way. Not the heavens, but a desert fairyland. Now, coming down the exit ramp into the Station, was something else entirely. It was like waking up after a late-afternoon nap and finding yourself in a cheap furnished room with a radio blaring somewhere and a pain behind your eyes and a water glass full of stale whiskey with a cigarette butt floating in it. That was how driving into the Station affected me. Except for this strange young girl on the next seat.

"I think his wife killed Aaron," she said. "She must have found out about us."

"I don't know about that," I said. "Are you sure?"

"No, but who else could it be?"

"Aaron had enemies. We all do."

She nodded. "You like this dress? He bought it for me. He was going to take me to Las Vegas this week."

"Have you . . . have you talked to the police about what you think?"

"Police? No, I can't talk to police. I'm illegal in this country."

"Your English is excellent."

"You think so? Thank you. Aaron said so too. I have lived on the Border most of my life. But I studied English on my own, too. It is necessary, don't you think, if you want to have success?"

"Yes."

"For reasons that are obvious, I don't want to speak

to Aaron's wife. I think she would like to shoot me. I know she would. But I thought you could speak to her for me."

"About the briefcase?" I asked.

"Yes. I want two thousand dollars for it. I think she might pay this much, don't you?"

"It seems like a lot."

"That's it up ahead," she said. The large motel sign loomed in front of us. "You go in the first entrance, then all the way around to the back, and you'll see the apartments. I don't think two thousand is too much."

"What's your name?"

She looked at me and smiled as if she knew a secret about me that even I myself didn't know. "In Spanish, they call me La Muñequita. In English, I am Doll."

"I speak Spanish," I said.

"My real name was nothing special: Maria." She ignored what I had said. "You can call me Doll. Aaron did."

It was hard to tell where the yellow-painted cinder blocks of the Sandman Motel ended and the ones of the apartment complex began. The apartments looked like an afterthought, an excuse to get rid of building materials and fill up some land at the back of the lot.

"Okay, Doll."

"Can I call you Fernando?"

"Sure. Aaron did."

"I loved Aaron," she said. "I wish he was still alive."

"Where can I reach you? Here?"

"No. Please don't come here. You can call me at the Rainbow Club. Or even come to see me . . . if you want."

"And you want me to ask Barbara Anderson for two thousand dollars for Aaron's briefcase? Which belongs to her by all rights."

"He gave it to me. Will you do it?"

[26]

I hesitated for a minute. Finally I asked, "Why am I going to say yes to you?"

She thought this was mildly amusing as she opened the door of my Fairmont and got out on the pavement. She leaned back inside and put her blues eyes, full force, straight into me. "Don't you know why you do things?"

"I wish I did sometimes. Do you?"

"Always," she said. "I'll see you soon."

I wanted her to say something else, to invite me to come inside with her, to continue this mysterious conversation, to give me a signal. I was bewitched. Who was she and why had I just driven her to the other end of El Sol? She said nothing. She shut the door and gave me a little wave, turned, and walked away.

She was too damn sure that she would see me again. And there was nothing I could see that would change her mind.

4

I DROVE with the Fort Ricks traffic against the flow of
rush-hour cars coming out of downtown. On the car
radio they played "Against the Wind" by Bob Seger.
There was no wind. Just traffic and the waves of heat
rising off the asphalt. They made the distance look like
a mirage. On the news, the announcer was excited about
an earthquake in California, over six on the Richter
scale. Aftershocks continued to jolt Yosemite. But California was over five hundred miles west of El Sol. I tuned
to another station. No more earthquakes or volcanoes—
and I didn't want to hear about California. That was
where Nancy had gone.

Alone in the Fairmont, I now remembered that I had
forgotten to mail Maggie's envelopes. This made it easy
to recall all the other mental lapses I had noticed in myself. Not the least of them was the previous Wednesday
night's blackout. I had gotten utterly drunk, for no
specific reason, plugged into the earphones of my stereo
and a bottle of Jack Daniel's. It was the same night Aaron
was shot in the Colonia Drive-In. Even if I had been
sitting in the backseat of his car that night, I wouldn't
have remembered a thing that happened. Before that
night, I had actually gone nine straight evenings without
getting drunk. I had been reading books again. It was
impossible for me to watch the TV without drinking
heavily—and the TV and booze always ended with my

listening to music in a drunken haze until I passed out. Blackouts scared me, but not enough to quit drinking.

I came up on an enormous truck, and the Fairmont gradually worked its way past in the left lane. I waited to be demolished every time I passed one of these amphetamine-crazed lunatics babbling CB slang and paying scant attention to their side-view mirrors. When it didn't happen, I was always grateful. But I hated my car. Ever since the day I had read that it was the best-selling car in America, I had hated it. A majority of us could elect Nixon and Carter; a majority could buy the wrong car. And I was part of that majority.

I was tired and longed for a whiskey. But I had already decided to postpone my return to the rectory and head over to Aaron's house first.

Aaron had built his house on six acres of riverfront land, the choicest to be had in all Cottonwood. Each time he married, Aaron built his new bride a house. But this time he must have been either too busy or too bored with the "dream-house" experience. What he had built was a kind of monstrosity. He knew it, of course. He blamed it on the architect, who had been heavily influenced by the latest in franchised highway architecture.

The house was all gray with black trim: four towers around a circular core of glass. It would have been perfect if Aaron had intended to sell fast food from his living room, but was bizarre as it stood. Aaron had trucked down about thirty pines from the Arizona mountains and planted them as camouflage around the walls. At least it had a good view out the back across the river. There was a small barn for the horses back there too. And a little white cabin where Vicente, Aaron's caretaker, lived with his wife, Mimi, and their dogs.

It was only the third time I had ever been to Aaron's house. The driveway was full when I arrived. I was amazed to see Joe Moore's Rolls-Royce parked there, with the burly chauffeur picking his nose in front. There was also Dr. Munty's white Continental and a red Trans Am with Texas plates which I didn't recognize. It was about six o'clock in the evening. The heat had decided to stay forever, and it was hard to draw a breath. The sun was spreading golden orange over the western mesa.

I took the path around the front. Suddenly I heard voices ahead of me. Then I heard a door shut. In a second, I was face to face with Joe Moore.

"Well, hello, Father O'Neal. Say, I thought your eulogy was just brilliant. I mean it. It's a shame about that girl. And then your friend Hillal had to show up there."

We were standing on flagstones set into the thick turf. I did not say that Hillal had every right to be there, while it was something of a surprise that Moore had come to the funeral. "Aaron wouldn't have minded, I think."

"A really great man, and this city will sure miss him," Moore said, showing no sign of having heard what I had said. "If Aaron and I didn't usually disagree, we would have been close friends. I know it."

I looked at this young, ruthless man and understood that words meant nothing to him. He could say anything, the worst gibberish, the biggest lie, if he thought it would please you. And if pleasing you was necessary to get what he wanted.

"So long, Moore," I said, and pushed past him.

"Father, if you aren't too busy, I'd like to talk to you—"

"I'm much too busy," I shouted without turning around. Then I climbed the steps up to Aaron's double doors and pressed the bell. What had Joe Moore wanted here with Aaron barely in his grave? It made me shiver, my back to the man who was Aaron's sworn enemy.

The door was soon opened by Lindy, Barbara Anderson's half-sister. She was an attractive woman in her mid-30's, quite tall, with long straight hair tinted the same shade of chalky blond most women in El Sol seemed to favor. She had only recently come home to El Sol from Chicago after divorcing her husband, a dentist. The rumor was that she had received almost three hundred thousand dollars as her share of the property settlement.

"Come in, Father. I guess you ran into Joe Moore. Elwood Munty is here but says he's leaving too. Maybe you can talk him into staying."

"Lindy, what did Moore want here?"

"Nothing, really. He said he just wanted to express his sympathy to Barbara. A friendly man. It was nice of him to come, after all the bad feelings. Don't you think, Father?"

"I suppose it was. By the way, Lindy, how many times do I have to ask you? Just call me Fernando. No more 'Father,' okay?"

"I keep forgetting."

"How is your sister?"

"Barbara's . . . she's okay. She's in her den."

I followed her across the tiled foyer. Its white walls were covered with some of the examples of Aaron's priceless collection of native American art: beautiful carved tools, intricate baskets, some of the finest silver and turquoise jewelry in the world. She took me down two steps into the main living room. Long and wide, it stretched to a curved eighteen-foot wall of glass. Here the view was of the river, of Mexico on the far side, its chamois-colored mountains vivid against the blue sky.

Dr. Elwood Munty raised himself from one of the soft armchairs. He drained his whiskey glass, set it down, and we shook hands. "Glad you've arrived to hold down the fort, friend. I was just on my way out." He shook his head. "That was a bad dream at the graveyard. Who would have thought that little Mexican gal would put on such a show in front of half the city?"

"How is Barbara?" I asked.

"She's doing all right, I guess. I wouldn't really know. I've been sitting out here talking to Lindy. Lindy, the doctor prescribes a stiff drink for the Reverend Father Fernando O'Neal here."

"What can I get you, Fernando?" Lindy called from the wet bar.

"Jack Daniel's with a splash of water, please. Not too stiff."

"Did you see Hillal or Father Ortega afterward?" Munty asked. "I had to leave with the ladies."

"Then you didn't see the fight," I said. Of course he wanted to hear all about it. I gave him as brief a description of the events in the parking lot as I could get away with. I watched him as I talked. He was drunk but he hid it well, as usual.

He had been Aaron's best friend since they were both schoolboys. They had shared their bikes and their hunting trips, their whiskey and their countless secrets: they had shared much over the past sixty years. Yet one of the first things Aaron ever told me, soon after I arrived in El Sol, was, "Elwood Munty is the best friend a man could want in a saloon or a whorehouse. But never in that clinic of his. Don't go to Elwood if you're sick. People think he's my doctor, and I let them think it, but I go to Dr. Eli Silverstein on Overlook Drive. Elwood knows it. He doesn't mind, either. Elwood hates doctoring, and the less patients he has, the happier he is. I've helped make him a millionaire. He's satisfied with that. His only patients are too blind to see he's drunk all day. And his wife, Edith, is one of the most loyal creatures God ever put on the earth. Elwood is frightened of new patients, but he sometimes is too scared of offending them to turn them away. I suppose he's got no more than a baker's dozen left these days."

"I'm sorry I missed that," Munty said when I'd finished describing the fight. "You don't know who broke it up?"

"I didn't recognize him."

"Sorry he did. Let those two boys hammer each other till the sun goes down, that's my opinion."

"Do you know about the meeting Hillal has called at his office for tomorrow morning?"

"What meeting?"

"He called me about it this noon. All the committee members are invited."

"Where's his office?"

"On Clay Street, just off the Interstate. A new building."

"I reckon I'll find it. What time?"

"Ten o'clock."

"I'll be there. Got to go now. The old woman will be wondering where I am." He always called his wife, Edith, "the old woman," despite the fact that she was at least ten years younger than Elwood. She was actually a sweet woman with lots of energy, one of my favorites down at the church.

I shook Munty's hand, and Lindy showed him out. I took my drink over and stared at Aaron's Picasso for a while. It was a still life from the mid-1930's. God knows how much Aaron had paid for the painting. "Somebody told me a rich man has got to have one of these Picassos," he once told me. "So I bought myself one. It's uglier than a hound dog's backside, isn't it?"

I knew Aaron bought the Picasso to shock folks in El Sol. Just as he told me how ugly he thought it was for shock effect. I didn't tell him that I half-agreed with him. (I wondered if someone had sold Aaron a fake Picasso? It would have served him right.) He talked to the painting like a pet. "Hey, now," he'd sometimes say to it.

[33]

"How you doing today? Sure don't look like you feel too well. Frame too tight? Sorry 'bout that, Mr. Picasso."

"Do you like that picture?" Lindy had returned and was standing just behind me.

"Not really."

"I used to hate it. I sort of like it now. Each time I look at it carefully, I see more things. They're having a big show of Picasso up in New York. Did you read about that in the paper?"

"Yes. Ever been to New York, Lindy?"

"Oh sure. Marty—my ex-husband—used to like to go there every December. Just before Christmas. We'd shop and see the theater."

"Did you like it?"

She thought for a minute. "Yes, it was nice. It was really nice sometimes."

I nodded. Lindy was an inch taller than I was. I suspected she had a crush on me. It would have been easy to start something with her when she first came back to town after her divorce. I assumed she knew the truth about Nancy. Aaron had probably told Barbara, I guessed. And surely then Barbara had told her half-sister that my wife was *not* in New York City nursing her mother through a terminal illness. The truth was that Nancy had left me to run off with a hippie six weeks after we'd arrived in town.

Nancy had met Flipper in the K Mart parking lot. Her Rabbit was parked next to his Econoline. She had told me all this during a phone call she made to me at the Sheraton, where I was sequestered with the bishop in a ridiculous meeting about Eskimo missions. I'd raced home at eighty-five miles an hour on the Interstate to find them packing the last of Nancy's gear in her car. He had a dirty-blond ponytail that hung down to his belt in back. And there was a bumper sticker on the back of the

Econoline that sent a chill of nostalgia mixed with nausea down my spine: "Keep on Truckin'!" After fifteen minutes of heated argument, and then some shoving, it was the message of the bumper sticker which Nancy chose to obey. . . .

"Do you ever miss the East Coast?" Lindy asked me. I looked at her and thought how glad I was that I had not started something between us. Not with a woman who thought everything, including New York City, could be adequately described by the word "nice." Still, that was probably the only word for Lindy herself.

"I miss it sometimes, yes. Do you think I could talk to Barbara now for a few minutes?"

"Well . . . sure." She looked slightly dubious, however. Nervous. "She has Roy with her right now."

"Roy?"

"Her son. I guess you haven't met."

"No."

"You knew Barbara was married before?"

"Yes. I didn't know she had children from that marriage."

"Just Roy. I'll take you in," she said. We went through a side door and down a hall. The floor was beautiful maple, lighted by spots on the ceiling, the walls covered with Navajo rugs. This was Barbara Anderson's wing of the house.

Lindy opened the carved oak door. We stepped into a cozy room with a fireplace, many baskets of cut flowers from the garden. The air conditioning was turned higher in here. I was stopped in my tracks by the large oil portrait which hung over the fireplace. It was of Barbara, flattering in the extreme. A terrible portrait: garish, dishonest.

She sat behind a huge antique Spanish table in a high-backed Mexican chair. On the sofa to her right sat a

[35]

man in his early twenties, dressed in jeans and a cowboy shirt, with a very short haircut that made his ears stick out.

In her fifties, Barbara Anderson was still a beautiful woman—although the portrait distorted her actual beauty in a vulgar way. She had a regal air, or so I always thought, with her perfect posture and her long graceful neck. She was rather plump, but it was part of her character. Her hair was tinted a warm honey blond and piled high on top of her head. She had changed out of the black dress she'd worn to the funeral.

Her son, Roy, on the other hand, looked like a hard case. He seemed to be taking great pleasure in just sitting in this house. I wondered if Aaron had liked him; had perhaps forbidden him to come around? Roy was handsome, but there was something sour about his mouth, and vacant in his eyes. His clothes couldn't have fit any tighter. I decided he was a vain young man.

He stared at me with amusement, as if it was a joke to see someone dressed in a clerical collar.

"Elwood just left, and Fernando wanted to—" Lindy began. But her half-sister cut her off before she could finish.

"Fine, thanks, honey. Hello, Fernando. This is my son, Roy. Meet Father O'Neal."

We put out our hands and shook with less than acute enthusiasm. I suddenly realized what was all over the table in front of Barbara. Silver coins. A flood of silver coins. And large sacks at her feet on the floor stenciled with the words "U.S. Treasury."

"It's a pleasure," said Roy.

"How do you do," I said. "How are you, Barbara?"

"I'm doing all right, thank you. What brings you by this evening? I'll bet you're missing Aaron tonight. We all are."

"I wanted to say how sorry I was about this after-noon."

"Oh, that," she said in a distracted voice. "I'm sorry too. Best to forget it."

"If I had known about that girl, I could have asked the ushers to keep an eye on her. But I had never seen her before. Did you know her?"

She shook her head. She was holding a silver Morgan dollar in one hand and a small blue coin book in the other. "Never saw her before in my life. Know what I'm doing?"

She laughed. I saw the half-full whiskey tumbler on the table near her hand. Roy grunted. He was drinking a highball, and he rose to freshen it. Suddenly his mother looked up at him. "Roy, I think Father O'Neal would like to talk to me in private."

I shook my head. "Not at all . . ."

"My intuition says you would, Fernando. I'm very sad tonight, and when I'm very sad, my intuition is very strong. Roy, honey, would you leave us alone for a bit? Thank you so much."

He looked annoyed, but he turned for the door with-out any protest. Lindy cleared her throat and said, "I thought I would see how Mimi is doing with dinner."

"You do that, sis. Just close the door behind you."

I was left standing in front of the long table covered with thousands of dollars' worth of silver coins. "May I sit down?"

"You go right ahead. I see Lindy fixed you a drink."

"Yes."

"Did you know that Aaron would have terrible insom-nia? Not every night, not every year, but sometimes he did. Know what he used to do when he couldn't sleep?"

I shook my head.

"He'd go down to the bank. He'd go back into the

safe and take out the big coin bags." She kicked one of the gray lumps beneath the table. She laughed. "I'll bet you never thought of Aaron like that. An old scrooge. A miser counting his filthy money. But it used to relax him, he said. He didn't count it. He went through it looking for old coins, rare ones, flawed-up coins like the ones that get hit by the same die and come out double-stamped. Aaron had a tremendous memory, as you know. He didn't need one of these"—she held up the blue coin book—"to see what was valuable. He was damn lazy, though. He couldn't be bothered to sort things out. If he found something valuable, he'd just throw it in a bag or one of his own safe boxes. He had about twenty safe boxes down at the bank. Did you know that?"

I shook my head. "What did Joe Moore want here this evening, Barbara?"

"You saw Joe, did you?"

"Yes."

"He wanted me to tell you people on Aaron's committee to stop fighting him. I told him to jump in a lake."

"Did he offer you anything?"

"No, I told him to jump in a lake before he could start offering me things. He's a slimy man, that Joe Moore. But I'll bet he's a good lover." She smirked after she said this. She was drunker than I thought.

"I wouldn't know about that."

"No, you wouldn't," she said. "See what I'm trying to do here? Somebody has got to organize all these coins. There's twenty years' worth of Aaron Anderson's insomnia in these coins. I think they must be worth a few dollars."

"I'm sure they are."

She stared at me hard suddenly. "Did you speak to Carl Tooman? Is that why you're here?"

"I spoke to him after the funeral. But that's not why I'm here."

"Aren't you happy with everything? What's wrong? Does that stinking little church of yours want even more?"

"Of course not. Listen, Tooman wouldn't tell me any details. He just asked me to come to the office on Wednesday for the reading of Aaron's will."

"What the hell are you doing here, then? Did you come to stare at a sinner? To gloat?"

"Don't be crazy," I told her. "I came here to see how you were."

"This is not a community-property state. That's how I am. He leaves one will, and he's written more wills in his life than Bob Hope has told jokes, and that will gives me nothing but this house and these damn coins. You'd be crazy too if you were in my shoes."

"I talked to that Mexican girl."

She glanced up sharply. "You did what?"

"The girl came to my office after everyone was gone. She says she has Aaron's briefcase. It contains, quote, 'important papers,' she says. She said Aaron left it with her the evening he was shot. I don't necessarily believe any of this. But I felt I should—"

"Why don't you believe it?" Her voice was suddenly very serious. "I knew about Aaron's habits. Didn't you?"

"No, I didn't."

"You were such pals, you and Aaron, I thought he must have taken you along on his escapades. Your wife was gone, after all. How *is* her mother, by the way?"

I didn't answer. Perhaps Aaron had never told her the truth about Nancy. Finally I said, "I don't want to upset you any more. But this girl wants two thousand dollars for the briefcase."

"Does she? Maybe she killed Aaron."

"I don't know. Somehow I doubt it," I said, although it had occurred to me, too.

"She wants a lot. They always do. You go back and

tell her I'll give her three hundred for everything, sight unseen. If she wants any more, she'll have to show me exactly what's in there. And risk my not buying altogether. You tell her I'm in no mood to bargain with one of his whores."

"Perhaps you should ask Carl Tooman to handle this," I suggested.

"No. I don't want Carl Tooman near me, or my house, ever again. You handle this. You can, can't you?"

"I suppose I can. What about the police? If you think this girl is a suspect, don't you want to call them?"

"No no no. She'd run back across the river so fast, and we'd never see that briefcase again."

I could see she was extremely interested in this briefcase. In fact, she looked better now than at any time since I had entered her study. I had brought her some hope. A new will. It was obviously her last chance, and although she was trying to hide it from me, I could see the excitement in her eyes.

"All right. I'll tell her three hundred dollars is your limit."

"My limit until I get a look at what she has."

"Yes."

"Don't you louse this deal up, Fernando. It's unlikely. But it just could be important."

"Yes, of course."

"Good. I'm glad you understand." She ran her hand across her eyes. "I have a migraine coming on. I've been waiting for this migraine for three days. It's finally here. I'm going to my bed now, if you'll excuse me?"

"By all means."

She didn't rise. She only put her hand across the silver coins, and we shook hands quickly, avoiding each other's eyes.

"Please shut the door behind you," she said. I went down that maple floor in the hallway trying hard not to count the cracks. I felt dizzy, as if I had just been through some kind of physical ordeal.

Neither Lindy nor Roy was to be found. I let myself out and walked back to my car. I drove out onto Desert Hills Avenue. Passing the familiar landmarks of America's indigestion on both sides of the highway, I found myself turning in under the Dairy Queen's red-and-white demented eye of a sign. Inside, the place was empty except for a girl behind the counter in a red-and-white uniform with a matching jockey's cap which bore a red pom-pom on its peak. She was trying to fix the broken spout on a plastic tub of "tropical" punch. I waited until she gave up. Then ordered the daily special: three fried burritos for a dollar and a medium root beer. Ten minutes later, my dinner mercifully over, I drove home and got the new bottle of Jim Beam from under the sink.

I sat in the living room and drank, thinking about Nancy, listening to Ricki Lee Jones and Jackson Browne through the earphones. Later, I put on my standards: Dylan, the Stones, Otis Redding. Sixties music. Finally, I went into my study, undressed, and lay down in my sleeping bag on the floor. Since Nancy had left, I had gone back to my old college habit of sleeping on the floor.

I was drunk, but I knew what I had done. I had made myself Barbara Anderson's messenger boy. Now I would have an excuse to see the Mexican girl again.

Tuesday

5

THE TELEPHONE woke me at 8:35 the next morning. I stumbled into the bedroom and held the receiver to my ear. A voice shrieked over the wire. I didn't know what it was. I couldn't understand a word.

"Maggie?" I asked finally.

The noise could have been "Yes."

"What's wrong? What's happened?"

She said something that sounded like "flowers" and "body" and "God" and then she broke down into steady sobbing. She wasn't even trying to talk anymore. Whatever it was, it was registering in the deepest part of her.

"I'm coming right down there. Okay?"

She only sobbed.

"Are you hurt? Call an ambulance. Call the police. You hold on, okay?"

I hung up and staggered into the bathroom. I took a ten-second shower, scalding hot, and dried my hair as I ran back to the study and started to throw on my clothes. I was hung-over and my brain was not working very well. Out in the kitchen, I drank two spoonfuls of instant coffee mixed with hot water out of the tap. I washed that down with a swig of cold apple juice. Then I drove down to the church.

Two El Sol police cruisers, black and orange, were parked in the lot. I was trying to fix my collar as I ran from the lot to the front steps.

In the outer office, a Mexican sergeant and a young Anglo officer were trying to talk to Maggie. She was shaking her head and holding a handful of Kleenex to her face. The sobbing had given her a bloody nose. When she saw me, she dropped her hand, started to speak, but got nothing except a red dribble out of her nostril.

I tried to comfort her. I made her move into one of the easy chairs in my office and put her head back. I stroked her frail shoulder under the thin cotton blouse and stared at the wiry gray hair that lay stiff and close to her skull.

"What's going on?" I demanded of the police officers.

"Father, there was a man found dead in your graveyard this morning. She reported it to us a few minutes ago. I've got a call in, and homicide is sending down detectives right away."

"What do you mean, a man found dead in the graveyard?"

"The name in his wallet is Attlee."

"Johnny Attlee? He's our sexton here."

"Sexton?"

"The janitor. He's dead?"

"Yes, Father. Dead and . . ."

"And what?"

The Mexican sergeant shook his head. "And nothing, Father. I think the ambulance will be here in a second. This poor lady could use a pill or something for her nerves."

"I know she could," I said. "What did they do to poor Johnny?"

"Father, I'm sorry. He's real bad. Worst I ever saw."

Maggie took the Kleenex away from her mouth. "I wanted to put flowers on Mr. Anderson's grave. I brought some lovely cowslips from home, and first thing I got here and . . ." She couldn't finish. You could see her eyes were still brimming with the horror.

I started for the door, and the sergeant put his hand firmly on my upper arm. "This is my church, Sergeant. It's my duty to—"

"No, Father. I can't let you go out there. No point in it. Maybe Dorfman will say it's okay, but I don't think it's right. That's not your job. We get paid to look at these things, you don't."

Later, after Detective Dorfman and his men arrived, and the ambulance had taken Johnny Attlee's body away, it was determined that he had been found on top of a fresh grave. Aaron's grave, of course. He was shot once through the side of the head. Somebody or something— one detective said it looked like a "wild animal"—had tried to do something to the body. But Dorfman gave orders to his men not to talk about that. After an hour of answering their questions, I decided the cops were both shocked and smug with their secret. It was their horror. They felt possessive of it, like small boys with something nasty.

I sent Maggie home. She had my firm orders to call her doctor and not to come back to work for at least a week. (I guessed she might take the next day off.)

By the time I left for the meeting at Hillal's office, I had answered dozens of the same questions for Dorfman. And I had learned that Johnny Attlee was forty-one years old (he'd looked ten years older); that he had served eleven years in prison for sexually molesting a child; that he was a devout Seventh-Day Adventist. From me, Dorfman had learned that Attlee was a hard worker, an early riser, and a man of exceptionally few words. Together, what we knew was pitiful.

"Why do you want to know?" Dorfman asked. We were standing next to his unmarked car in the parking lot. I had just asked him straight out for the first time. "What's your need to know, Father?"

"This is my church and he was my employee. There

are going to be hundreds of rumors. A lot of frightening talk. I think it is my right to know."

"That's the point. We don't want it to get around. Talk about rumors, what if it did get out? It is always good for us to know a few things the public doesn't know. That's standard homicide procedure."

"Okay, but how am I going to be able to understand my secretary's mental anguish? She's an older woman, and I've got to somehow get her through this . . . whatever 'this' is."

He thought for a moment. "All right, but promise me you won't tell anyone else. Swear on the Bible?"

"Yes, okay."

Dorfman grinned uncomfortably and said, "It looks like they tried to take his heart out."

"Take his heart out?"

"Yeah. First they shot him. Then they cut him open with something crude and ripped at his heart. That's about all I can say until I see the coroner's report. That enough so you can deal with the old lady?"

"Yes," I said. "But who would ever do something like that?"

"Father, if you think of someone, would you give me a call?"

6

JAMIE HILLAL's building was an elegant fortress of russet-colored concrete and black-tinted glass, two stories tall, with a brass sign set beside the front entrance which read simply "Hillal & Co."

An armed guard, a young Black in a gray uniform, sat behind a desk in the foyer watching three small TV monitors. A TV camera hung off the ceiling in one corner, staring at me like some kind of sci-fi reptile. There was only one other door: solid steel with no window and no knob, just a lock.

My name was on a clipboard, and once the guard found it, he hit a hidden switch that opened the steel door with hydraulic precision. It was my first visit to Jamie Hillal's office. I left the Mission Control air-lock atmosphere of the foyer for a comfortable reception area and a breezy young receptionist. She wore a name-tag that read "Mary Ellen" and she said they were expecting me upstairs. She went so far as to press the button that opened the elevator's sliding doors and admitted me to a lift swaying with the palsied rhythms of Muzak.

On the second floor, I found yet another windowless antechamber. Anonymous abstract art hung on polished rosewood walls. Behind a perfectly antiseptic desk, an even lovelier young receptionist with strawberry-blond hair smiled at me. "Father O'Neal, go right on through, down the hall and it's the last door on your right. If you have any trouble, just open any door and ask one of the girls."

"I'm sure I can manage." I wasn't sure. Hillal & Co. was a bank vault full of beauty queens. But I was quite badly shaken by what Dorfman had told me about Johnny's murder.

The last door on the right opened directly into Jamie's office. In keeping with modern executive practice, there was no desk. Only an arrangement of leather-covered furniture and a vast circular conference table. One long wall was covered with green drapes to match the sage-colored carpet. Hillal stopped in mid-sentence when I opened the door and rose from his seat at the table to greet me with an outstretched hand.

Behind him sat the other three surviving members of Aaron's Committee to Save El Sol: Dr. Elwood Munty, Professor David Snow, and Father Jose Ortega of Mission San Juan el Bautista.

There was one other person in the room. A fat man in a salmon-colored knit shirt and baggy khaki trousers, he was holding some kind of electrical gear and staring at the far wall. There were sweat stains creeping out of his armpits despite the coolness of the air-conditioned room. I couldn't imagine who he was or what he was doing there. But Jamie Hillal ignored my questioning look as he guided me to one of the empty chairs around the big table.

It had been Aaron's committee from the start. He had chosen us, financed us, held us together. How would it change now? Jamie Hillal was obviously hoping to fill the vacuum created by Aaron's absence. He had insisted that we hold this meeting at his office.

"I'm sorry I'm late," I said. "But I've got some very bad news."

"What's that?" Jamie asked. The others all lifted their heads to stare at me.

[50]

"There's been another murder. Johnny Attlee, our sexton at Holy Innocents, was found shot to death this morning. His body was lying on top of Aaron's grave. There's one other thing. I don't understand it, just as I don't understand anything these days apparently, but the body was mutilated in a terrible way."

"Johnny?" Elwood Munty said. "What would anyone want to harm him for?"

"Mutilated?" Professor Snow said. "What do you mean?"

"My God," Jamie cried, "what do you think he means? This is the last straw."

"What does it mean?" Father Ortega asked. "It sounds like a madman's work."

"Joe Moore is no madman, Father. He's trying to make the police think Aaron was killed by a crazy person, that's all. God, he is cold-blooded, though."

"Excuse me," Father Ortega said, "But there is no proof Joe Moore had anything to do with Aaron's death. Or is there?"

I had to speak. "No, Father Ortega, there's no proof."

"You don't believe that, Fernando, surely?" Hillal said. One thing I liked about Jamie Hillal: he called me Fernando. I am as low-church as one can get. Being called "Father" in front of a Roman priest irritated me.

But one thing I didn't like about Jamie: his arrogance.

"Boys, hold on a second here." It was Elwood Munty. "Is this committee ready to change its name? Are we now the Committee to Solve Aaron Anderson's Murder? Or are we the group trying to stop Joe Moore's propositions on next Tuesday's ballot?"

"The fact remains that Aaron's murder and this latest atrocity are typical of Moore's level of business," Jamie said. "He will stop at absolutely nothing. He'll call us Reds, call us faggots, threaten us in public, on TV, in those letters we all received last week. Now he's gone to the point of killing Aaron. And he's even killed an inno-cent bystander to cover his tracks."

He was such a good speaker, I almost wanted to nod my head in agreement. Instead, I said, "But you don't know any of that, Jamie. All our lives may be in danger now. But we can't get hysterical and blame everything on Joe Moore."

"The man hopes to terrorize us. Frankly, I believe we have to fight fire with fire. We have to destroy Joe Moore, or we'll never stop him and his plans for the city. We have to expose him."

"You're such a fine lawyer, I don't understand how you can talk like that," I said. "We have no proof that Moore had anything to do with Aaron's murder. As for Johnny Attlee, he dug Aaron's grave. He spends hours every morning out in the churchyard doing the gardening there. I don't think we can read too much into his mur-der, without proof. I hate to keep harping on the word, but proof is the key word here."

"Might I speak for a moment?" Professor Snow asked. "I believe Dr. Munty addressed the crux of the issue. Are we going to allow this unforeseen tragedy to change our association into a deviation from our original mission? I hope not."

"Aaron didn't want this to be a popularity contest," Munty said. "We've got to show people just how Joe Moore wants to turn this city into one giant housing tract for twenty million suckers from up North and back East. We've got to educate folks here about the water issue. I believe Aaron knew what he was talking about. There's no shortage of water. There's just a surplus of thirsty people. That's a surplus Joe Moore is ignoring. If we show that to our folks, if we prove it, then they'll defeat those two propositions next Tuesday."

"Yes," Father Ortega said. "This I believe too."

"Nonsense," Jamie said. "People can't understand there

might not be any water in ten years. Not when they can go into their kitchen right now and let the tap run for hours. People in this city are falling for Joe Moore's talk about progress and the future. We've got to show them the blood on his hands."

"It is a very disturbing dilemma," Snow said. "You still haven't told us what you mean by 'mutilation,' Father O'Neal."

"No, and I can't tell you. The police wouldn't elaborate. And I didn't see the body."

"It's not necessarily a madman's work," Snow said.

"What do you mean?" Hillal asked him. "Of course it isn't."

"I mean that many different tribes of people, including the Indians, have used all sorts of rituals for inflicting death on their enemies."

"Aren't you going a little far afield?" I asked now.

He stared at me with tolerant condescension. "I don't see why. The murder remains unsolved, I take it? Both murders. As a scholar, I have undoubtedly studied more bloodshed and murder than all the detectives in the local constabulary put together. Actually, all I was doing was pointing out a simple truth. Not all violence is insane. Not when viewed from the context of the violent party's own set of cultural assumptions."

"Okay," Jamie Hillal said. "But we do have to keep up with our own reality, Doc. History is fine. But reality talks."

"History is as real as you or I, Mr. Hillal," said Snow. "And more eloquent than both of us perhaps. Although I am tempted to except myself, of course."

It was hard not to laugh when Snow was abusing the English language in your presence. His sentences were ropes of ungainly verbiage: ideal equipment to send his listeners climbing right up the walls. What just saved him was that he seemed to suspect how awful he sounded.

He couldn't help it, but at least he seemed to want to joke about it.

Professor David Snow was the author of over twenty books, all historical studies of the Southwest. His most famous title was *The Aztlan Empire*, which was a 450-page study of the early desert peoples who had lived in the area which stretched from Los Angeles to the Gulf of Mexico, along what eventually became the border. Snow (along with many other experts) believed they were the original Mexicans. Snow had taught at the state university in the capital until his retirement several years before; then moved down to El Sol, where he had maintained a home for many years.

He was a small man with a windburned face and a full head of silver hair. He smoked a briar pipe and usually wore Mexican-style shirts under an old canvas sport coat, and baggy slacks above brown sandals and white socks. He was regarded by many people in El Sol as wildly eccentric. In fact, he was a fairly typical academic in appearance and manner. He was unmarried, but I didn't know if he was a life-long bachelor, a widower, or even divorced. I didn't really care. He was the kind of man you did not easily picture with a sexual life.

As for Father Ortega, he was shaking his head. He did not approve of Snow's historical attitude to murder. Obviously Father Ortega believed murder was a sin. He seemed to be holding back a sermon on the subject just behind his firmly shut brown lips.

Father Ortega was undoubtedly the most popular priest in the *barrio* and the least popular priest in much of the Anglo community. Many saw him as a "radical" Mexican. To his own people he was a voice of moderation and wisdom. I had learned to respect him in our past meetings and to admire Aaron for risking Anglo disapproval when he asked Father Ortega to join his committee.

"How much do we have left in our account down at the bank?" I asked.

Father Ortega was our official treasurer, although the account was held at Aaron's bank. "I have the figures here. There is thirty thousand, two hundred and twelve dollars, and fourteen cents left in our account."

"That'll buy us a lot of TV time," I said.

"Yes. And we have those three commercials already rolling from time to time. I think we should step up our media blitz," Munty said.

"I think we need new commercials," Hillal said. "Much tougher ones. We've got the money to make at least one new one. Especially if we use a local agency instead of that San Francisco outfit."

"Face it, Jamie," I said. "You want to turn this into a personal crusade against Joe Moore. If I had any proof that he was involved in Aaron's murder, or this terrible thing someone did to Johnny Attlee, I would probably agree with you. Do you have any proof, though?"

"It's obvious, Fernando. Come on! Do you want to save this city? Who the hell do you think we have to save it from? Dr. Munty? Professor Snow? Me? Or is it Joe Moore?"

"We all know you hate Joe Moore, boy," Munty said. "But I think you're beginning to protest a mite too much."

"What do you mean by that, Doc?"

"I reckon you can figure it out for yourself."

"No, give me some help."

"Well, those of us who know our history real good may recall Joe Moore wasn't the only one who had a feud running with Aaron. Some of us recall there was bad blood between the Andersons and the Hillals long before Joe Moore was ever born."

Jamie's face flushed dark red. "Are you serious, Munty?

Come off it with that shit. That's a TV game you're talking about, right? Family feud? You think I killed Aaron, now?"

"I never said that," Munty said. "All I know is that you and Aaron were never the best of friends, nor were Aaron and your father on particular speaking terms. Maybe you think you have to prove your loyalty to the man now. Maybe you think that by screaming the loudest about Joe Moore, you'll prove it. Of course, I don't know for sure. I'm just talking."

"You should stick to drinking, then," Hillal snapped. "Your talking leaves a lot to be desired."

"Gentlemen, please," Snow said. "Let us not tear at each other this way. This is our—"

"Shit!" The fat man in the salmon-colored shirt shouted. "This ain't no stud. Mr. Hillal, here it is. I found it!" He slammed his fist on the wall about ten feet behind where Snow sat.

Jamie jumped up, and together he and the fat man stared at the device in the fat man's hands. Three meters were built into what looked like a camera with no lens. Jamie said something under his breath.

"Do you want to just . . . ?"

"Yes. Do it."

"What about your meeting?"

"Fuck it. Get that out of there right now."

"I don't really have the tools to do a clean job."

"Clean it up later. Get it out of my wall," Jamie ordered.

The fat man proceeded to walk to the far end of the room and exchange his electronic metering device for a small metal chest. Out of this he produced a hammer and chisel. He had marked a spot on the wall; now he put the chisel there and began to hammer into the plaster with short hard blows. They sounded like pistol shots in the room.

[56]

We all sat in stunned and baffled silence around the table, watching this drama unfold. Jamie stood close to the fat man, following each hammer blow with intense concentration.

Suddenly he turned and said, "You still think I'm just paranoid about Aaron's murder? How about this? I have my office swept once a month. I've been in here four months now. Suddenly I find this. What do you think? What about you, Munty? You think Joe Moore is a nice guy? This is what I mean when I say reality talks."

"To the walls?" Munty joked.

"You're goddamn right, Doc," Hillal said.

The fat man was digging in the plaster with his finger. He said, "Got it," and pulled out his fat digit. "Right there."

After Hillal had his turn, we all passed it around from finger to finger. It was perhaps an inch long, three-eighths of an inch wide, plastic, with a tiny metal thread hanging off it. That was the antenna. The fat man said it could pick up every word said in Hillal's office and broadcast it 250 yards to a car equipped with tape equipment. "Whoever he was, he's miles away by now," the fat man said.

"What about the Government?" Jamie asked. "Are the feds using this kind of bug?"

"Sure. The feds have got it all. It could be them."

Jamie took the bugging device off Father Ortega's finger and held it up to the light to examine it. "Gentlemen, I think we had better call this meeting to a close. I've got some calls to make."

"May I remind everyone that the candidates for mayor will be coming to the Mission on Thursday. If you wish to come, we will start the questions and answers at noon. You should bring your own sandwich," Father Ortega said.

"Or taco," Dr. Munty joked.

"If you wish," Ortega said. He glared at Munty.

"I don't think I'll have the time to make it down to the Mission, Father," Munty said. "But I will be over at the city supervisor's meeting tomorrow. They've put aside an hour for an open debate on the Propositions."

"I'll try for both meetings," Hillal said. "But I've got the Garza brothers' appeal tomorrow at ten in front of Judge Melner. That could last a couple of days."

"I'll try to make both," I said.

"So shall I," Professor Snow said. "By the way, Father O'Neal, could I have a word with you after this?"

"Of course."

We all stood up. I felt terrible, depressed and still shaken by the events of the morning. I wiped my hand across my forehead and found that, despite the air-conditioning, I was sweating.

On the way down in the elevator, Professor Snow offered to buy me lunch across the Border.

7

"MAY I recommend the margaritas and the quail," Professor Snow said. "Or, if you prefer, the Gulf shrimp are delicious in a piquant tomato gravy."

"The quail sound great," I said.

"If you prefer beer, the Bohemia is my personal favorite."

"Perhaps I'll start with a margarita and have a Bohemia with my food."

"Excellent. I think I shall simply have a Bohemia and one of their avocados stuffed with fresh crabmeat."

We were sitting in a window booth at Nando's on the Avenida de Cinco de Mayo in Gomez. I had never been to Gomez's most famous restaurant for lunch before. It was a shock to see that hodgepodge of naugahyde booths, glittered mirrors, and linoleum floors in the daylight. Nando's food was always a shock because it was so good. No restaurant in El Sol could touch it.

After we had ordered, Snow said, "I have been most anxious to talk to you, Father."

"Yes?"

"I am very disturbed. It is difficult to know where to begin. This murder and that murder . . . so many murders. Among men we once knew so well. I can trust you. You are educated and I have watched you. You are sensitive."

"Thank you, Professor. But lately I really haven't been

at my best. And this murder thing has made me just as anxious as you."

"Where did you attend college, by the way?"

"Brown."

"Very good. And your major was religion?"

"No, it was English literature."

"Oh, did you want to teach?"

"No, write. Like about ninety percent of the other English majors, I had delusions of being the next Hemingway."

"Do you still write?"

"No. I occasionally tell myself I will get around to a novel one day. But my excuse is always that I need to collect more material first."

"That is no excuse," Snow said. "I have spent my life gathering material."

"Yes, but you are a scholar."

"Have you ever studied history?"

"Biblical history. And the usual high-school history courses."

He nodded. "Biblical history is fascinating, even if one is not a believer. Are you happy here in El Sol, Father?"

I stared down at my glass. How much did I want to tell this old man? How much of myself did I want to expose? "No, I suppose I am not very happy here," I said. "But I don't blame it on El Sol. This is not a good period in my life, I guess. But I'm sure things will pick up before too long."

"Do you think you could trust me the way you trusted Aaron Anderson?" Snow asked.

"Well, I suppose so. Trust you how, exactly?"

"Can you believe me when I say that Jamie Hillal must not take control of our committee?"

"Could you be specific?"

"Yes, I want to be specific. You do know Jamie Hillal is an Arab?"

"Yes, so I gathered."

"Are you familiar with my book *The Aztlan Empire*, by any chance?"

"I've seen it in the bookstores here, yes."

"We live in an ancient and legendary part of the earth, you and I. This is Aztlan. Long before the birth of Christ, this land was inhabited by civilized men. I believe that El Sol is, in fact, built on the ruins of the Seven Cities of Cibola, or Chicomoztoc. The river here contains water from both the ancient Gila and Colorado rivers. And those of us who live here today, on this Border, are only the latest of the tribes to have settled on this arid but rather magical ground."

"Yes, I know what you mean by magical. It's so stark and yet it seems to get more and more beautiful the longer I live here. I must say that I didn't expect to like the desert nearly as much as I do."

"Jamie Hillal is a member of a different tribe. What do you know about Jamie's father?"

"Nothing, actually."

"Robert Hillal is the single wealthiest man in this city. Richer than Aaron Anderson, or Joe Moore, or any other three men combined. In many ways, he owns this city."

"Really? I had no idea."

"Yes. He is in his mid-eighties now, but he remains a vital man. He arrived here almost seventy years ago. A young beggar who gradually worked his way up to smuggler. Prohibition was his Golden Age. He made a considerable fortune. When the Depression ended, Robert Hillal owned roughly thirty percent of the best land in downtown El Sol. He owned the land our new City Hall is built on, for example. And the land where the Sheraton stands. On the other hand, he owns none of this desert which Joe Moore wants to develop. Can you see why the Hillals might wish to stop Moore from replacing them as the most powerful landowners in El Sol?"

"Yes, perhaps."

"Let me give you another example. Robert Hillal lives today in a secluded but luxurious villa overlooking the third fairway of the Cottonwood Country Club. Perhaps you didn't realize that an Arab owns the country club? He leases the land to them on a ninety-nine-year basis. But he has never even bothered to apply for membership."

I was amazed. There was no more exclusive or wealthy enclave in El Sol than the Cottonwood Country Club.

"He is the leading member of the Arab tribe in this city."

"The Arab tribe?"

"We have over fifty Arab families in El Sol, who date back to the early part of the century. Christian Arabs. But Arabs all the same."

"Still, if they've been here that long, aren't they just as native as you or anybody else?"

"You would think so. But the Arabs do not assimilate like Italians or Irish or Greeks. The Arabs are ancient wanderers, like the Jews. They do not lose their old customs, no matter how modern their dress, how expensive their homes. The Nusayriyyah of northern Syria, the Akery of Akar, the Druze from Haurian and southern Lebanon—these were some of the clans who crossed the ocean between 1899 and 1920. If they were turned away in New York, they would return via Veracruz. Robert Hillal was one who came up through Mexico, along with his brother Jamil. His brother was later killed smuggling whiskey across the river in 1926. Jamie Hillal is actually named after his uncle Jamil."

Our food had arrived. The three quail on my plate looked perfectly roasted to a crisp gold. There were slices of green avocado and saffron rice and refried beans on the side. I should have been starving, but what Snow was saying was fascinating. I did not want to insult him by digging into the food like a hungry oaf. Still, I wondered exactly what he was driving at with this lecture on the "Arab tribe" in El Sol.

"I did not want to say this in the meeting, for obvious reasons, but mutilation is common among Arabs. They are brutal with their enemies, with infidels and criminals."

"You can't believe an Arab killed Johnny Attlee?"

"It is not impossible. Let me tell you something else. During the Depression, when the Anglos in this city could not afford to pay the lowest property taxes, Robert Hillal was quietly stripping them of their land."

"Stripping or buying?" I said. "Surely he didn't steal the land from them?"

"There was little difference. He took their land for nothing. I know that Aaron Anderson put Robert Hillal's son on his committee in order to keep his eye on the Arabs. I know Anderson was opposed to Hillal's desire to turn this campaign into a personal slander on Joe Moore—a man who frightens the Arabs even more than he offends men like you and me."

"Okay, but wait a second. Why would anyone want to kill poor Johnny Attlee?"

"Perhaps the motive was not logical. Perhaps it had emotional significance, rather than the usual things like revenge or jealousy or theft."

"You mean a ritual murder?"

"Call it a warning," Snow said. "Did Aaron ever mention his own father to you?"

"No."

"His name was Walter Anderson. I knew him only slightly. I was very new in this area, coming down for weekends from the college to do my research here. I do know that Walter Anderson sold his ranch to Robert Hillal back in 1931 for one dollar an acre. He gave the money to his wife and left the city, and later committed suicide in a WPA camp in Oregon in 1934. He was a hopeless alcoholic by then. Of course, Anderson hardly ever mentioned his father."

"I didn't realize that."

"The feeling of mutual distrust between the Hillals and the Andersons ran very deep."

"I see."

"Although he was a wealthy man, Aaron never had a grip on the land like the Hillals have. Like Joe Moore wants. Aaron was in the middle. In History, it is often men in the middle who are crushed to death. Now, let me ask you something else. Do you know this Pointer Report which Aaron constantly talked about?"

"Yes. The report on the water supply in El Sol." According to Aaron, the Pointer Report was a study undertaken by a Major Pointer in the U.S. Army Corps of Engineers which had been completed in the early Sixties. It showed that the water located in El Sol's underground reservoir, the water which supplied 100 percent of the city's needs as it was pumped up to the surface, was severely limited. Or at least running out faster than it should. Aaron referred to the Pointer Report often. But when I'd once asked him if I could have a copy of it, he'd said that he was "looking into that" and would get me a copy as soon as he could.

"Have you read the Pointer Report?" Snow asked. "You know you can get it down at the public library?"

"No, I haven't seen it."

"I'm afraid that Aaron was rather misleading on the Pointer Report. It was directed toward cataloging drilling locations, both existing and promising sites for the future. But Pointer said nothing about the size of the actual supply, nothing about the water running out too fast in the El Sol–Gomez Aquifer."

"I don't understand."

"Aaron, you see, believed there was a special appendix. He claimed he had read this appendix when the Pointer Report was first issued. Now I have done extensive research and I have not been able to find this appendix. Neither the Pentagon nor the regional files of the Corps of Engineers in Denver has any copy of it. Moreover, Major Pointer died in Iowa in 1977 of a cerebral hemorrhage. I told this to Aaron. He would not accept my findings. He *had* to believe in the Pointer Report."

"Why?"

"Partly because he was getting old and did not like to admit it, like all of us. But also because such a thing, an appendix with plain facts proving that Joe Moore's plans for expanding the city were dangerous, was just what Aaron needed. Or so he thought."

"Tell me, Professor, why exactly do you oppose Joe Moore's plans?"

"It should be obvious that I love this part of the world. I do not want to see it turned into junk, a million bucks in some huckster's back pocket."

"But you think Aaron invented this appendix?"

He nodded his head. "Let me tell you something else. I think that the Hillals would like to see Joe Moore defeated next Tuesday. And they would like Moore to give up and leave El Sol. So that then *they* could try to develop the land in the empty half of the county. Joe Moore has opened up the Hillals' eyes to the possibility of much greater exploitation than they had seen before."

"If that's true," I said, "then the Hillals would not be any happier about Aaron's evidence, this appendix, *if* it existed, than Joe Moore. But, of course, you say it didn't exist." I did not add that I suspected Snow's failure to locate the appendix through his research had been enough to convince him that it could not exist. Snow had a scholar's pride, of course.

[65]

"That's true. And all this talk of appendices and proof is based on an interesting but rather dubious assumption," Snow said.

"Which is?"

"It assumes that the voters, if they were shown proof of some sort, would necessarily know what to do about it."

"You sound rather cynical, Professor."

"I know my own tribe, Father. By the way, how do you find your beer?"

"Exactly as you said."

8

AFTER LUNCH, I said good-bye to Snow and drove back across the Border over the Morales Bridge. Was Jamie Hillal the suspect Snow wanted me to believe? I didn't know. How could I? I was full of doubts about my vocation, my ability to get along with women, even my sanity. Judging what Snow had just told me, including the vague slurs on Aaron's mental capabilities, was too hard for me. It was a stinking hot afternoon in the desert. And as shabby as downtown El Sol surely was, it looked like Fifth Avenue compared to the view of the outskirts of Gomez I got from up on the Morales Bridge.

The river snaked through a series of curves here. On the U.S. bank, Cyclone fences and a few warehouses sat on acres of smooth black asphalt. On the Mexican bank, everything was dirt. A number of small hills, bumps really, rose from the trickle of the river, carrying shacks and huts in every possible direction. These shanties seemed to ride the bumps, as temporary as fleas on a hairless dog. They were built of adobe and cardboard, scraps of tin and plastic. You could see the ruts of tire tracks that marked the "streets" and the ancient Chevies and Fords parked in front of every fifth one. Some lucky ones could afford not only transportation but also paint. These stood out like false hope, in shades of pink or blue or yellow, pastel bunkers on the brown dirt. The others did not stand out; they were lucky they stood at all. From a distance, they looked like small heaps of rubbish dotting the hillside. You could see the children wading at the edge of the river. Brown kids in brown water. Everything was the color of the desert except for the sky, its cool relentless blue lifted overhead like a taunting sea.

I had the Tuesday-evening New Testament study group coming to my house at seven P.M. We were to discuss II Corinthians. It had been years since I had looked at it. Some called it "the hard letter" because Paul decided to use it to unload a long list of his sufferings and doubts. How we would get through ninety minutes on it, I did not know.

Located in a development called Cottonwood Estates, the rectory provided rent-free to me by the church was nearly indistinguishable from the neighboring houses. Only a few details were different: the white gravel in the yard (instead of the Astroturf on both sides of me) and the Spanish "style elements" on the garage door. The vestry of Holy Innocents had invested in this new rectory in order to attract a sharp young rector—me, as it turned out—with a brand-new home. And I had taken the job despite the rectory. And despite Nancy's warning me that, after three years in a small city in Colorado, she was not ready for years in the desert.

I had taken the job because Aaron, as Holy Innocents' most important layman, had flown up to Denver to interview me. Over dinner at Brown's Palace, he charmed me into saying I would at least fly down and look at El Sol. Aaron struck me as a caricature at first. But very quickly I realized that he was not playing a role; he *was* a Southwestern gentleman with easy manners and a whiskey voice and clear blue eyes. Once he got down to El Sol, it was the desert more than anything else that convinced me. So strange, yet I sensed the beauty there. Like the ivory yucca flower growing out of a nest of spikes, it was an earned beauty.

Had my telephone been ringing all day in the empty house? I picked it up as soon as I came home and heard Carl Tooman ask, "Father, what the hell's going on out at the church? Do we have a madman loose?" I didn't know any more about Johnny Attlee's murder than he did, I explained. Tooman said El Sol was full of all kinds of rumors. But his chief reason for calling was to say he'd postponed the reading of Aaron's will until next Wednesday. Barbara Anderson had requested this. She had a terrible attack of migraine. I said that was okay with me, and after ignoring several more of his questions, I hung up.

I dialed Maggie's home number to see how she was feeling. My secretary sounded very far away. Her doctor had given her some strong sedatives. But she was glad I had called. "That poor man," she said. "It must be the water, Father. He was so quiet and gentle. Why else would someone want to harm Johnny?"

For the next few hours I wandered around the house trying to straighten up, and occasionally I sat down and read a few passages from II Corinthians. By the time evening arrived and the study group filed into my living room, I had read all of it. But everyone had seen the local TV news and nobody wanted to discuss II Corinthians. We talked for ninety minutes about Aaron's and Johnny's murders, about Propositions 3 and 8, and about the campaign for mayor. It seemed most of them were very impressed by Leo Mulcahy's anticrime image. Of course, they were all Anglos and all rather conservative. Mayor Castillo had never been their man.

There was a jar of herring in sour cream in the fridge. After everyone had left, I ate this, standing up in the kitchen. I washed it down with a bourbon and water. Then I turned off the lights, went out, and climbed into the Fairmont. It was a thirty-minute drive under the stars on the Interstate to the exit. Then minutes later, heading north, the sign rose eighty feet high in front of me. This was the edge of the city, the start of the barren flats. Four arcs of bright-colored neon framed the words:

THE RAINBOW CLUB

and in baby-blue neon:

Fancy Ladies
On Stage

The parking lot was full of Detroit models, everything from Corvettes to a 1953 De Soto. The building was one-story, flat-roofed, obviously a converted showroom of some kind. You could see where the display windows had been filled with cinder blocks. The door was covered with a steel sheet, painted black, flaking where it wasn't scratched up with curses and a few lewd drawings.

I opened the door. The roar of disco music was staggering. It was very dark. A large shadow emerged out of the blackness to loom above me and ask for two dollars. As my eyes adjusted, I saw he was at least three hundred pounds, with snake tattoos all over arms that stuck out of a sleeveless denim jacket. Mexican.

There were two stages, each backed with a mirror on the wall. I pushed my way through a narrow aisle between round tables and many pairs of cowboy boots. Two women danced in white streams of light in front of the mirrors. One was a pretty Anglo girl with blond hair and a crude tattoo somebody had scratched into her thigh that read: "FREE RIDER." It meant she'd crossed a biker. The other dancer was Doll.

She had her back to the crowd. She was peeling an electric-blue body stocking down her front. Then she put her hands on the mirror, moving her ass, encased in thin latex, to the beat, and stared over her shoulder at the crowd of cigarette tips glowing in the darkness.

I found a seat at the center of the bar. Doll had turned and hitched her thumbs in the sides of her leotard. She was inching it down as she pumped to the music. I saw the lipstick mark where she had kissed the mirror. Her blue eyes threw off glints of light. Her breasts were larger than I had realized, with small pink areolae and thick nipples. Her waist was tiny and her thighs looked very strong. She pumped and wriggled and the leotard became no more than a blue line. Stretched across the top of her thighs, it widened to cup her vagina in front, was all but invisible behind. She wore a stylized expression on her face, like a mask.

The bartender was a Korean woman who looked tough as broken glass. I heard someone call her "Tiger." I waved a ten-dollar bill to get her attention.

The song ended. The two girls climbed down from their stages. The blond walked straight to the back of the room, finished. She passed me, holding her costume against her breasts with no real attempt to cover them. Doll walked to the stage she had just vacated. A new dancer, a plump girl in a pink chinz shortie nightgown, took the other stage. "Hot Stuff" hit the sound system: Donna Summer demanding it to a vicious beat. My eyes were gradually adjusting to the darkness in the place.

On my right was a young white GI in civilian sport clothes: T-shirt and jeans. He caught my eye and nodded. "Hard to get a drink, huh?"

I looked at the ten-dollar bill. "Seems that way."

"Tiger is a bitch."

I nodded, looking around at the rest of the crowd. There were plenty of young white soldiers off-duty. At a table in the corner, four bikers sat with two dancers and many pitchers of beer on the table. Other dancers were doubling as waitresses. A sign over the bar read "Table Dances $2 Minimum."

The place smelled like gangsters, although I was hardly an expert on the aromas of organized crime. But there was some kind of heavy restraint obviously built into this place: all these men were docile as sheep in the midst of blatant provocation from a dozen almost-naked young women.

Up front, four Mexicans in business suits sat drinking brandy. They looked like Gomez salesmen with their slick hair and formal attire. Mexican-Americans dressed more casually, just like the Anglos, in pressed jeans and plaid cotton shirts. But these were true Mexicans, stiff and proud, concentrating on Doll.

She had a way of stalking the audience, controlling her muscles so that just to look at her, you could imagine her against you. She turned and bent over low, grasped her ankles, stared upside down straight into our eyes. It was dirty, somehow childish, and very seductive.

Donna Summer's song ended and Doll climbed down. I had chosen a place to sit where she would have to pass me on her way to the back of the club.

But first she went and stood over the table of Gomez businessmen. I felt a nudge in my back and turned to face Tiger. She had finally decided to wait on me. I gave her my order and a moment later she put the bourbon on the bar and took my ten-dollar bill. In a minute she brought me six dollars change.

Doll was laughing, trading remarks with the Gomez men. Then she said something with a straight face. They nodded and she began to walk in my direction.

She was a pro. She knew how to scan the faces at the bar as she walked past without turning her head. How to smile without focus. How to generalize herself: a sexy young woman. How to keep you in your seat, drinking, fantasizing, but never crossing the line beyond control. It was a narrow line and she walked it like a star.

[72]

She was an actress, I told myself. This place was her theatre. Look at it that way.

She almost walked right by me, then stopped. She turned and met my eyes with a cool appraisal. "Hello. How long have you been here?"

"Not long."

"How do you like it?"

"It's interesting."

"You saw me dance?"

"You're a fantastic dancer."

This pleased her. She pushed to the bar, brushing her breasts against my arm as she did so. "Tiger, a vodka-tonic please."

"I'll bet you're thirsty."

"Yes," she said. "We don't get many priests here. You might be the first one."

"That's possible, I suppose. I saw Barbara Anderson."

"Oh?" Her drink came and she picked it up and stared at the strings of tiny bubbles.

"I told her you had the briefcase. And how much you wanted. She wants to see what you have. Or else her highest offer is three hundred dollars. She says that you're taking a risk if you show her the papers, since she may not be interested after that."

I thought she might be upset by this bargaining, but she only nodded as if she had expected it. I told myself I was very naive when it came to business matters between two determined women. Then she said, "I have something you can show her."

"You do?"

"Yes. I brought it tonight. I hoped you would come by tonight, and you did. It's back in the dressing room."

"Very good."

She nodded and sipped her drink. "Aaron told me your wife left you for a hippie. You must want to kill her."

[73]

I winced. "No, I don't."

"Do you still love her?"

I shrugged. "Who knows? It's been eleven months."

"You look like the kind of man who likes to love women."

"What do you mean?"

"Perhaps you like to love more than you actually love. Do you understand?" she asked. She was searching my eyes with her blue flashing stare.

"I understand," I said. "I don't know what to say. Have you been observing me or something?"

"You've been watching me. But you think I might be right?"

"I don't know."

"You are sexy, you know. Do you have many girlfriends since your wife left you?"

"No."

"What do you think of me? Do you think I am sexy?"

"You know you are. Why ask me?"

"I want to hear a priest say it."

"You're perverse."

"What is perverse, exactly?"

"Worse than silly."

She laughed, shook her head, and picked her drink off the bar. She walked away down the bar. There were two doors in the back wall. One read "Rest Rooms" and the other read "No Entrance." Doll disappeared into the latter.

I stared at the door for several minutes. My glass was quickly empty. The shots at the Rainbow were not exactly generous. I caught Tiger's eye and pushed my glass toward her for a refill.

The GI on my right leaned over and said, "You know what my buddy told me?"

"What?" I asked loud enough to be heard over the music.

"He said this place was owned by an Arab."

"Really?"

"That's right. He swore it was an Arab. By the way, she's some fox you were talking to there."

I nodded, forcing a smile onto my face. So an Arab owned the Rainbow. Snow had said there were over fifty Arab families in El Sol. Why shouldn't an Arab own the place?

"Man, I'd like to be in your shoes tonight," the GI continued. "She gave you the eye. I know the eye when I see it. She gave it to you real sweet."

"I hope you're right," I said. My drink came and I took a large swallow.

"Is he bothering you?" Doll whispered in my ear. I turned around abruptly. She laughed and put an envelope against my chest. I took it from her. "Show his wife this and tell her two thousand dollars is my final price."

"What is it?"

"Look if you want."

"Okay. Frankly, I doubt if she'll pay you that much."

"Why?"

"Aaron didn't leave her as much money as she expected."

"No?"

"No."

She thought for a moment. "That's good, in a way. Perhaps she thinks I have a new will in his briefcase."

"Do you?"

She looked at me with an amused defiance in her eyes. It was so much stronger than anything visible in the faces of the other dancers. I abhorred the place and I hated what she was doing. And yet I was falling for her.

"Listen," she whispered. "Tonight is no good for me. Perhaps you will come back tomorrow. If you brought the money, we could celebrate together. Just be careful of that woman. She is very dangerous."

[75]

"You think she is?" Was this the pot calling the kettle a cliché?

"Very."

"Tell me, who owns this place?"

"Someone," she said. She shrugged as if it was hardly important.

"An Arab?"

"Yes, I think so."

"Is it Jamie Hillal?"

Her eyebrows raised in a brief sign of recognition. But she shook her head. "I have to go now. Those men are waiting for a table dance. I think they will pay me a lot of money. Are you going to stay?"

"No, I'm leaving."

"Tomorrow night I get off work at one o'clock." She didn't say good-bye. Just turned and walked away in the direction of the men from Gomez. Suddenly she stopped and came back. She was smiling as she leaned down to whisper in my ear, "I like perverse."

I said nothing. She walked away looking pleased with herself. She didn't know what she was talking about. "Beast of Burden" came on the stereo system. I walked out of the nightclub as she began to pump in front of their hungry faces.

I opened the Fairmont door. It wasn't locked. I never thought of locking my car doors in El Sol unless I was parked downtown. But now I smelled a strong odor of cheap booze as I sat down behind the wheel. Had someone been drinking in my car while I was inside? Or had they just opened the door and tossed a glassful on the upholstery? It must have been very strong for me to notice it after the stench of whiskey and cigarette smoke in the club.

I turned on the overhead light. Nothing seemed out of the ordinary. Then I took the envelope Doll had given me and looked at it carefully for the first time. It was marked with the logo of Aaron's bank. Inside was a ticket issued by United Airlines. A round-trip ticket from El Sol to Denver on May 21. It bore Aaron's name and it had been used the day he was murdered.

Wednesday

9

FOR SEVERAL minutes I sat in the Fairmont and stared at the ticket carbon. I remember thinking it was too late to call anyone. It was obvious that Aaron had kept his trip to Denver last Wednesday a secret. Otherwise the newspapers would surely have mentioned it by now. If anyone knew, I thought, it was probably Elwood Munty.

I put the key in the ignition and started the car. Shifting into reverse, I backed slowly out of the parking space and then dropped the stick into drive. I left the bright neon arcs of the Rainbow's sign behind me as I drove onto the highway.

The road was very new, well-illuminated, and absolutely empty out here on the northeastern edge of the city. It was after midnight. I was cruising along at roughly fifty, heading toward the Interstate three miles away, when it happened.

The car suddenly took off. I hit the brakes but got no response at all. I pumped the accelerator pedal: this had no effect on the racing engine. The needle on the speedometer was steadily passing sixty-five, seventy, seventy-five. I was standing on the brake now. No response. Somebody had cut my brake line.

The engine was screaming as the carburetor blasted a richer and richer mixture down the manifold into the hammering cylinders. The accelerator return spring must have been cut. Once I had reached a decent speed, the pressure on it had caused it to snap. All I knew then was that I was in a runaway automobile going over eighty miles an hour. It was late and the road was empty. There was only one thing I could do. I reached down and tried to turn the ignition key off. It was stuck. I tried again. Nothing happened.

I watched the needle hit eighty-five on the speedometer.

I ripped at the key, to no avail. Someone had tampered with the starter key lock. Cursing, I couldn't even pull it out of the lock. I let go and pounded the steering wheel with my fist in rage.

The Fairmont roared through the empty crossroads under the flashing red light. I clenched both hands on the wheel and pushed myself back into the firm support of the bench seat. I tried the emergency brake, as hard as I could, but it didn't do a damn thing. They'd cut all the brake lines. The car had run amok. I had to go with it, steering for my life.

I had a third of a tank of gas, or a little less. That and the desert were my only hope. Otherwise I was going to hit something. At eighty-plus mph, my chances of surviving a crash were nonexistent. There could always be a miracle, of course. Someone could have planted a hundred-foot-thick haystack in the middle of the highway. Or the car might spontaneously rebuild itself. Sure. And I had lots of time for macabre jokes as I shot down that empty highway.

Suddenly I had run out of all time. Ahead, two big trailer trucks were rolling side by side at a ponderous fifty-five mph. I could see their red and orange lights getting steadily larger, brighter. I was going so fast that I couldn't get a good look at the right side of the road. There were some stores; a car dealership?

I threw the Fairmont across the double yellow lines onto the wrong side of the road. In the distance, for the first time, I saw headlights approaching. They were running directly at me. Less than one hundred yards away was the next intersection. It was Summit Avenue, a main thoroughfare running east to west. I watched the yellow lights pop off, the red lights come on ahead.

As I came up past the two trucks, the driver on the outside hit his horn and swerved angrily across the double lines. He wasn't really trying to hit me. Just outraged. I saw two cars cross ahead of me on Summit, and the headlights of another approaching from the west. It was a Chevy Blazer. I swung hard right as it entered the intersection. The back wheels of my Fairmont moved out from under me and I started to spin, just missing the back of the Blazer. I was suddenly facing the two trucks again. Their foghorns cut hideously through the sound of my own tires screeching on the pavement. But the spin lasted only a second. Suddenly I was jumping the curb into the parking lot of a Piggly Wiggly market. Fortunately, it was shut and empty.

I pulled hard on the wheel and got back on the road. The light had gone green. The spin had cut my speed. But I had the two trucks ahead of me again and I was quickly picking up speed.

I couldn't try the wrong side of the road this time. I had seen the oncoming headlights. By now the cars were almost level with the two trucks. I had to leave the highway again, hitting the curb, landing with a crash. I straightened out and shot down through a series of parking lots belonging to a Dunkin' Donuts, a car wash, a hair salon, All State Insurance (they insured me!), a Chinese restaurant, a Church's Fried Chicken place. Each lot was separated from the next by a low concrete curb. I hit these at speed, bucking and lunging across, mauling the suspension system of the Fairmont brutally. But each time I hit one of these would-be speed bumps, I was glad.

Each one kept me from accelerating back up to the terrifying realm of eighty-plus mph. And I was almost past the two trucks again.

Directly in front of me, built at the edge of the highway, not recessed like the other places, was a branch of the El Sol Federal and County Bank. It was a low, square pillbox of brick and concrete. I was heading straight for it. I had no choice but to jump left back onto the highway, just scooting ahead of the enormous front tires of the nearest truck. The great diesel engine roared in my ears. I picked up immediate speed back on the smooth asphalt.

There was another major intersection half a mile ahead. If I could make that safely, my next worry would be getting up on the Interstate. In the meantime, I saw the taillights of a car ahead in the right lane rapidly growing brighter as I continued to gather speed.

It was an El Sol police cruiser, black and orange, leisurely patrolling this stretch of highway. I saw the two officers in the front seat whirl to look at me as I bolted past in the outside lane. The siren began to whine. Red lights flashed in my rearview mirror. They were much faster than my Fairmont. They were amazed when I didn't pull over.

I had rolled the window down and put my left hand outside. How did you signal if your automobile was out of control? I simply waved my hand around crazily. No doubt "crazily" was the operative word in the minds of those two cops.

They increased their speed until they were hanging right off my tail. I thought they might ram me. Or shoot! But then I saw the intersection at Wright Brothers Drive ahead. Down to my right, to the west, a flashing red light on the roof of another police cruiser sent a new shudder through my guts. Too many cops were coming

[84]

after me now. This was worse than the trailer trucks. They would see me running and think I was trying to escape something even worse than their bullets. At eighty-plus mph, I was bound to look armed and dangerous.

The police cruiser pulled to a stop blocking both lanes ahead of me in the center of Wright Brothers Drive. I had a few seconds to make up my mind. Then my hands on the wheel made the decision for me. I swerved right, around the back of the black-and-orange cruiser, up into a Gulf gas station. I was terrified of hitting the pumps. Instead, I cut sharply between two rows of pumps and then plowed through the back end of a Toyota Corolla that someone had left parked there. The Japanese model went flying and I was slowed a bit, but not too much. Behind me, the first cruiser split the pumps okay, but met the Toyota where I had knocked it, head-on. The cruiser spun sideways and into the side of the parked tow truck. I was already one hundred feet up the highway, aiming for the Interstate, praying for my gas to run out soon.

Who did this to me? My mind was racing as fast as the car. This was no accident. This was an attempt to kill me. I was fighting a murderous machine. Someone had done this to *kill* me. I flexed my fingers over the plastic steering wheel. In a moment, I would have to face, at more than eighty miles an hour, a curved approach ramp onto the Interstate that was designed to be taken at no greater than thirty mph. My initial fear was gone. The surge of adrenaline had dried up in my blood. Now all I had left was my anger. Fortunately, it was growing.

I swore I would kill the person who had done this to me. If I lived, I swore, I would track down that person. It was the same murdering bastard who had killed Aaron and Johnny, I believed. But why me? What had I done? It didn't matter. I had gas left in the tank and nothing left in my nerves except this rage. I would kill the person and then run over his dead body with my car. I swore I would do it.

Driving that last part, I must have lost my mind. The whole thing became a blurred film, and so it remains in my memory. After the Gulf station, I somehow made it onto the Interstate. The tire marks show that I must have done two complete spinouts before I made it. One at the bottom of the ramp. The other halfway up, where the angle of the curve was the greatest.

I ran alone for over thirty more miles, straight through El Sol and out into the desert. I saw the red lights flashing behind me, drawing closer, but the Fairmont had a long lead. It was not as fast as the cruisers. But it had a mighty will of its own. The car earned my respect that night, shooting across that flat asphalt under the blanket of desert stars. Somewhere inside its economy chassis was a mechanical heart that could beat at over one hundred mph. It carried no malice, just six cylinders that would not quit. And when they stopped, it was as unexpected as when it all began.

A sputter, a cough, followed by loud empty gasps from the engine compartment. The Fairmont began to lose speed rapidly. I pulled off the road onto the asphalt shoulder. As I did so, I heard the sirens. We coasted along the shoulder for another two hundred feet or so, then simply came to a halt. Out of gas. The best feeling I had experienced in a long time.

All the killing rage suddenly left me. In a stranded automobile, in the desert, I looked up at the sky. Alive, but I could not explain why. Nor why someone had just tried to kill me. Nor who that someone was. I just felt happy. The sirens were almost on top of me. It was wonderful to hear them coming. I could never kill anyone, it seemed at that moment. I looked down at the dashboard between the empty fuel gauge on the left and the dead speedometer on the right. Seeing my mistake, I began to laugh.

The transmission indicator bar was in the drive position, where it had been ever since the parking lot back at the Rainbow. I was laughing harder now.

For the last eleven months, I had wallowed in self-pity and bourbon. Celibate. "Rejected." I was going to put all that away now. I was going to . . . if only I could stop laughing. I was sitting there with my head back, eyes closed, feeling the laughter rolling up through my chest, my throat, and out to the stars.

"Out of your car with your hands up!" The cop spoke through a loudspeaker, standing behind his open cruiser door. "One wrong move, your head is blown off."

Later, after being spread-eagled across the Fairmont's trunk, with my pockets emptied and my hands on the roof, two cops spoke almost simultaneously.

The first said, "No wonder it smells like a distillery. Here's an empty gin bottle under his front seat."

The second said, "Hey, this guy's a fucking priest."

10

At 3:50 a.m., Detective Dorfman came back into the interrogation room in the basement of City Hall. A thin, ferret-faced man in his late thirties, Dorfman was going gray in the temples and mustache. He wore a yellow-and-black sport shirt and checked trousers, both completely out of style. His eyes were red and he carried yet another Styrofoam cup of coffee.

"One more time, Father. I want to hear it one more time, if you don't mind."

"Hear what?"

"Why didn't you throw it in neutral?"

"I told you, it never occurred to me. When the brakes didn't work, and then the key was jammed, I just panicked."

Dorfman nodded. He stared at the other detective, who sat with his back against the cinder blocks at the far end of the table. Dorfman smiled and the other detective shook his head. Dorfman turned back to me and said, "Your blood test says that you weren't drunk. Not according to the law in this state. Drinking, yes. Drunk, no. So I can only conclude that, in order to tell me what you just did, Father, you must be nuts."

"I'm sorry."

"Don't be sorry. You're nuts, right? Not me. Okay, one more time on the gin bottle."

"I told you—"

"One more time, Father, please?"

"I have no idea how it got there."

"Thanks," Dorfman said. "Did I tell you the charges?"

"The charges?"

"Yes, Father. The charges start with reckless driving, endangering the life of a police officer, speeding, leaving the scene of an accident, numerous counts of trespass in a motor vehicle, and so on. And so on, right, Sergeant Downey?"

The other detective smiled. "Right."

"You don't care, do you, Father?"

"What do you mean? Of course I care."

"What were you doing at the Rainbow Club? Once more. I like to hear your voice, Father. It's inspiring to me."

I frowned at Dorfman. I wanted to tell him what I thought of him, but I was not going to do that. Not since I had realized, during the last hour, that Dorfman thought I might have killed Aaron and Johnny Attlee. So, instead of telling him off, I said, "I went there out of curiosity."

"Was your curiosity satisfied, Father?"

"Yes."

"You were researching sin or something, that it?"

"No, not at all. I just wondered what it was like. I'd seen the ads in the paper."

"Where were you last Wednesday night?"

"At home."

"Alone?"

"Yes."

Dorfman looked over at Sergeant Downey. Then back at me. "You and Johnny Attlee were pretty close, weren't you, Father?"

"Not at all."

"Did you ever invite Attlee over to your house?"

"He occasionally did some maintenance at the rectory. He raked the lawn every two weeks. Socially, he never

[89]

came to my house. Listen, Dorfman, I'm not a homosexual, if that's what you're implying."

"I never implied any such thing, Father. God forbid. Okay?"

I just shook my head.

"How do you figure all this, Father?"

"Somebody tried to kill me. I don't know who. But obviously somebody has something against my church. There've been two murders connected with Holy Innocents in less than a week. Now this."

"You think somebody wanted to kill you and make it look like a drunken accident?"

"Of course. What do you think, Dorfman?"

He stared at Sergeant Downey, then at me. "You know what I think, Father? I think your lawyer's outside waiting to see you. I think maybe it's time you two had a nice talk. As for me, I think I've had enough inspiration for the moment. How about you, Downey?"

Sergeant Downey wrinkled up his nose. "It wasn't all that inspiring."

"Oh?" Dorfman said. "You were disappointed, Downey?"

"Yeah. Sort of."

"Well, I'm sure the good Father has given better, more inspiring sermons. But, in the meantime, his lawyer is busy raising hell out there. So I suggest we let the two of them get together. Maybe you and I can go back to my office, Downey. By the way, Father, one more thing."

He was at the door, Sergeant Downey standing next to him. They both stared down at where I sat with my elbows on the table under the harsh fluorescent lights. I stared back at them. "What's that?"

"I had a little talk with the arresting officer a few minutes ago when he came off duty. He told me something interesting. You know what he said?"

"What?"

"He said that when you got out of your car, out there in the desert after it was all over, he said you were wearing the biggest shit-eating grin he's ever seen."

I just stared up at the two detectives.

"Well, Father?"

"What do you want me to say?"

"Do you think this is funny, Father?"

"No. Of course not."

"That's good. Father. Take my word for it. This is not funny."

"I'll take your word for it. Somebody tried to kill me tonight."

Dorfman frowned. "Thank you, Father O'Neal." At that, the two of them left the interrogation room.

There was no clock on the wall, but they had let me keep my watch. Of course they had, I told myself. They hadn't booked me for anything yet. I wasn't in prison, just "helping the police with their inquiries," as they said in the British Isles. I sat at the table and glanced from the cinder blocks, which were painted a shade of creamy green, quite revolting, to the brown steel door and back again, over and over, until the door opened and Jamie Hillal entered the room.

He looked very sleek in a mustard-colored summer suit and dark mahogany-hued loafers with tassels. He didn't look like I'd gotten him out of bed, which I had, nor as if he was insulted. When I had called him, before I had said anything else, I had asked, "Do you own the Rainbow Club, by any chance?"

He'd laughed. At 1:35 A.M., having been woken up and asked this question, point-blank, I thought it showed considerable grace on his part to laugh. Then he'd said, "Of course not. Al Mirabi owns the Rainbow. Why do you ask, Fernando?"

So I had explained. I was calling from police headquarters and I needed a lawyer because . . . and so on.

[91]

"Hello, Fernando," he said now, as he pulled out a chair at the table. "How do you like Detective Dorfman?"

"Not particularly."

"I've got Norm Jatlow working on your bail. He's getting Judge Smith out of bed, I think. Should come through any minute now. Are they treating you rough?"

"It's okay. They think I'm crazy."

"Don't worry about that. I stopped by the garage before I came down here. The cop down there said your car was clearly messed with. They had cut your accelerator return, whatever it's called, in two spots. Also, there were marks on the steering wheel where someone got into your key lock. This is attempted murder. Forget whatever Dorfman's been telling you."

"I think he thinks I killed Aaron and Attlee."

Hillal laughed. "That's what Moore would have liked everyone to think. You killed them, then cracked up, got drunk, and ran your car into a wall or something. That's how it would have looked."

I shrugged. "I suppose. You still think it was Joe Moore behind all this?"

"It's got to be. He hired someone to fuck up your car. Someone who knew what they were doing. By the way, your car has been impounded as evidence. You have another one?"

"No."

"Why don't you rent one?"

"I guess I'll have to."

"They must have followed you out to the Rainbow." He leaned across the table. "Who did you go to see out there? Was it Doll?"

"Yes. I didn't know you knew—"

He nodded and put his finger to his lips. "We'll talk about this in a little while. Once we get you out of here. But I'll tell you something right now. You should stay away from that place. The Rainbow isn't safe these days.

Also, whatever your reasons were, you should stay away from her. I know her and I know Montoya even better. There are too many fish in the sea, Fernando—"

"It wasn't that. Look, I want to show you something. I got this from her tonight." I reached into my pocket and started to take out Aaron's Denver ticket stub. But Jamie reached across and put his hand on the outside of my jacket to stop me bringing it out.

"Later, okay?"

I nodded.

It was an hour later that they finally released me on ten thousand dollars' bail. The charges were essentially as Dorfman had outlined them. But Jamie had held a private meeting with Dorfman before we left. As we walked down the basement corridor a few minutes later, Jamie said that Dorfman would probably drop all the charges by noon. He would be forced to do so, Jamie said, by the evidence in the car. Now he was just being stubborn because he was angry about staying up all night and getting nowhere with the cases which were really on his agenda: the two murders.

We had to walk up a set of wide stairs to get to the main foyer of police headquarters. From there, we could exit into the street. Jamie said he was parked just outside.

We reached the top of the stairs and Jamie held open one of the swinging doors. I stepped forward and was immediately blinded by the lights. That's why later it would look like I was trying to hide my face out of shame or something.

The TV people had been allowed to set up right in the foyer. "Come on," Jamie said, "Just follow me." Behind his blocking, I moved through the TV cameras and the reporters with their outstretched mikes, saying nothing, shaking my head. They flung their questions at me like so many insults, but, thanks to Jamie, we were soon on the sidewalk and dashing across the street to his red

Porsche. Once inside, he gunned the engine and we took off in a screech of rubber.

"Please," I told him. "Not too fast. I've had all the speed I need for one night."

"You exhausted? Or do you want me to take you out to the airport? You can rent a car there twenty-four-hours. You might want one in the morning."

I said that sounded like a good idea. On the way, we could talk. I noticed my hands were shaking.

"That prick Dorfman must have called the TV people," Jamie said. "Apparently that cop car that crashed at the Gulf station was pretty well totaled. Cops hate to lose their cars."

I didn't care. The idea of bad publicity hadn't really sunk in at that point. It was too late and I was too shattered. "I'm just happy to be alive," I told Jamie. "Look, this is what Doll gave me tonight. It's a cancelled ticket showing that Aaron flew to Denver and back the day he was killed."

"Doll was Aaron's little friend, I knew that. But how did she get this ticket?"

I explained.

"Okay, okay," Jamie said. "But I still don't get it. Why do we care if Aaron went to Denver last Wednesday?"

"The Pointer Report?" I said. "Does that ring a bell?"

"The report on the water? The one Aaron was always hyping? It rings a bell now."

"I think somebody might have killed Aaron for a copy of the Pointer Report. An original copy."

"You mean somebody like Joe Moore?"

"I knew you'd say that. Look, what if somebody thought I had gone to see Doll tonight to get that copy?"

"Who knew that Doll had this briefcase?"

"So far, I think, I've only told Barbara Anderson and you."

[94]

"How about Elwood?"

"No."

"You know Barbara is related to Joe Moore's wife?"

"No."

"Yes."

"How, exactly?"

"It's a long story. Ask Elwood if you want the grisly details. Can I see that ticket?"

"Sure." I put it in his hand. He examined it as we drove. A few minutes later we were parked in the bright glow of the airport terminal. "We've got to get this briefcase from the girl. That's the whole ball game," Jamie said.

"What should I do?"

"You like the girl, don't you, Fernando?" He laughed. "I can see it in your eyes. But remember, Aaron liked her too. Stay away from her."

"I'll try to take your advice."

"And stay out of the Rainbow Club. Why the hell did you think I owned that cesspool, anyway?"

"I'm not sure," I lied.

"I know. Al Mirabi is an Arab and so am I. How many Arabs do you think live in this town? I'll tell you. Too fucking many."

"Sorry."

"That's okay." He flashed me all of his perfect white teeth.

"Now, don't worry. I'm going to get you off this thing, okay? Don't worry about anything."

"Thanks." I wasn't worried about the police at that point. I was worried because somebody clearly wanted me dead.

"We'll talk tomorrow. And take it easy on the way home. Don't run any red lights; keep below fifty-five all the way home. A second time, even I couldn't get you out of Dorfman's jail."

I laughed weakly. He put his Porsche in gear and shot away, leaving the pavement smoking and my ears ringing. The way he drove, he must have gone through a new set of radials every six months. Of course, Jamie Hillal could afford them.

11

"AARON ALWAYS did have a little Mexican gal somewhere," said Elwood Munty. "At least one."

The way he said it, you might have concluded a "little Mexican gal" was just another part of the El Sol gentleman's basic outfit, along with his yellow ostrich-skin boots, fourteen-karat-gold flask full of Wild Turkey, and air-conditioned golf cart.

It was three o'clock the next afternoon. I had gotten a few hours' sleep before Hillal called me, about noon, to say Dorfman had been forced to drop all charges. The evidence of tampering with my Fairmont was clear-cut. Instead of charging me, a new case had been opened regarding the incident. It should have been attempted murder, Hillal said. Instead it was much less serious.

Munty and I were sitting on a bench in the plaza outside City Hall. It was hot as blazes in the old plaza, with its six dying palms offering no shade to the sullen Mexicans, the young white drifters. There were far too many young children with their hands out for coins.

I had met Dr. Munty in the supervisors' chamber, where an "open meeting" was supposed to allow the public to question the board on the upcoming Propositions. Instead, the chamber had been packed by a group called Citizens for Decency, led by a grandmother with orange hair and aviator sunglasses named Ruth Nypes. She and her followers were there to shout about Proposition 6.

This was a law which would ban all alcoholic drinks from public parks.

Unfortunately, Proposition 6 had been getting far more play in the newspaper and on TV than any other Proposition. It was a nice safe issue. The supervisor's eyes had glazed over as Ruth Nypes sent one follower after another up to testify, to build a mountain of moral indignation out of a few beer cans.

Munty finally had nudged me and said, "There's no reason we have to put up with this. Let's go while the going's good."

After we had settled on the bench, Munty had spent a good ten minutes questioning me on my nightmare ride of a few hours earlier. I explained and told him all charges had been dropped. He said I was lucky they'd been dropped before the evening news on TV. And lucky, too, that the incident had taken place in the early hours of the morning, long after the *Post-Examiner*'s deadline had passed.

I decided to tell Munty why I had gone to the Rainbow. At least the official reason. When I told him about the briefcase, and Doll's efforts to sell it to the widow, Munty had only nodded and said, "Sure, they'll get what they can. Nothing new about that."

I told him about the ticket. His response was rather cautious. "Aaron took a lot of airplane rides. He did business all over the West. Why should he tell people if he had to hop up there to Denver for a couple of hours? Are you sure about this Pointer Report?"

"No, I'm not sure. Professor Snow told me that he never agreed with Aaron on the Pointer Report. Snow has searched for this so-called 'original' report, for the appendix which Aaron always talked about, but he couldn't find it."

"Dave Snow is a good man," said Munty. "But he's a social misfit. He gets along with books better than with people. That's why he talks like the dictionary and an overdose of diet pills. Sometimes, when I listen to Snow, it's enough to make me want to get drunk."

I nodded. From the smell on Munty's breath, it seemed he didn't need Snow to encourage him in that direction. Undoubtedly Munty had taken his first snort before breakfast and had been coasting along from drink to drink all day.

"But sometimes Aaron could get carried away," Munty said. "I trusted Aaron with my life. Many times. I wouldn't place my life in Snow's hands, of course. But I would be inclined to trust him when it came to books. Or reports."

"You may be right."

"You told Barbara about this briefcase, didn't you?"

"Yes."

"She wants to buy it?"

"Yes."

"Why do you think?"

"I think she hopes it will contain another copy, a later copy, of Aaron's will."

"But you want the briefcase because you think it contains the Pointer Report?"

"Yes."

Munty laughed. "You think you're any different than Barbara Anderson?"

"What do you mean?"

"It's damn hot and my throat is baked dry. You want to take a walk over to the Sheraton with me?"

"Okay."

"By the way, what did you think of Barbara's son, Roy, the other day?"

I paused for a minute. "Well, I was going to ask you about him. He seemed on edge, hostile."

"He just got out of federal prison. La Tuna, down in Texas."

"Why?"

"He did something while he was in the Marines. Drugs. Old Jamie took his case. Didn't win that one. Roy got four years' hard labor."

"I see."

"I like Lindy, Barbara's half-sister, more than I like Barbara herself," Munty said. "I didn't like the way that Roy looked at Lindy, his half-aunt."

"Why not?"

"Didn't like it, that's all. Here, what the hell is this?"

We had reached the edge of the plaza. A very dark woman, either Indian or a Gypsy, dressed in rags and holding an infant, ran at us. Her eyes were jaundiced and one tooth stuck through her lips. The infant had no diaper; there was excrement caked on his bottom. Flies were thick around them. "Get out of our way!" Munty shouted. "*Vaya!*" Extending her palm, she bent over directly in our path. "Look at this. She keeps her poor child in that condition to get our sympathy. You can't encourage her," he said.

In my pocket I found some change. It was about two dollars' worth and I handed it to the woman. She mumbled something in Spanish. I was glad she made no big show of gratitude. Perhaps Munty was correct. This was his city, not mine. Still, perhaps a doctor's notion of charity was different from a priest's.

The Sheraton loomed ahead of us, the color of aluminum with turquoise-blue trim, everything you would expect. There had been talk of completely "renovating" the plaza, but aside from the hotel, nothing had been done.

"What I think we should do," Munty said, "is buy the briefcase ourselves. If there's a new will inside, we can always give it to Carl Tooman to do as he sees proper. But if the Pointer Report's in there, I would not want to give it to Barbara."

"Doesn't it belong to her? She's the widow."

"I don't know. I'm a doctor. Aaron was the lawyer. Did you know Barbara's maiden name was Peebles?"

"No."

"Her first cousin is also a Peebles. Emily Peebles Moore. Mrs. Joe Moore, actually."

"I didn't realize."

"This is a small town if you limit yourself to the old Anglo families. Let me tell you something. I don't think Aaron trusted his third wife too much while he was alive. Otherwise, why would his will leave everything to the church instead of to her?"

"How did you know that?"

"Everybody in town knows."

"But the fact remains that I told Barbara I would try to get this briefcase for her."

"Did you swear to her?"

"I gave her my word, in a sense."

"You're ready for Joe Moore to win big on both his Propositions next Tuesday? Ready for him to turn this city into desert again? To shove people out of their homes? To bring in millions, *millions* is his word, of strangers and all that will mean? Are you ready for that?"

"Of course not."

"You think on it, then," Munty said. "Come on, let's go in here and get us a drink." He held open the glass door to the hotel and I felt the air-conditioned air being burned up just in front of my face.

"No, I have to go," I told him. "Didn't realize it was so late."

"Come on," he insisted. "Have just one with me."

I didn't like him. There was something soiled and selfish in this man. He wasn't just an alcoholic, a victim of his social illness. Exactly what he was, I didn't know. Parasite. That was one word that came to mind.

"I really can't stay," I told him. I did not want to drink

with him, and it hit him as hard as a slap across the mouth. "Let's talk soon." I turned my back on him and walked away. I decided to skirt the edges of the plaza rather than take the shorter route back across its middle. I was tired of watching little children beg and older children nod out.

Two blocks away, at a meter, I had left my rented tan Mustang. I expected to find a ticket under the wiper, since the meters downtown were only good for forty-five minutes and I had neglected to pay another quarter. Instead of a ticket on my rented Mustang, however, I found a white VW bug with a "F**K THE AYATOLLAH" bumper sticker. I searched up and down the block. I tried the next block, even though I knew that was ridiculous. I had parked in front of the Hi-Fashion Dress Shop. Automobiles don't change parking spaces on their own. Nor did the El Sol police tow cars that were parked illegally, not in 1980 anyway.

They had stolen my car.

Whenever you are robbed, it is always "they" who did it to you. If someone attempts to kill you, it is more likely to be a "he" or even "she." But it took me a few minutes to understand, thanks to the afternoon furnace and the exhaust fumes and the lack of sleep, that "they" had finally found me. It was the first time in my life I had ever been robbed of anything of value. It was the day after "he" had tried to kill me.

I hated coincidences. Almost as much as I hated having to walk the two blocks back to City Hall and enter the side door of police headquarters. It took me another ninety minutes to go through the red tape with an officer from the stolen-car squad. We had to call Avis. I had to sign dozens of forms. The only person at all surprised by any of this was me. Avis was blasé. The stolen car squad said the Mustang was probably already across the Border. It would be shipped South, or broken up and returned north of the river to be sold as spare parts.

I left City Hall and took a taxi out to the airport. Fighting a strong urge to get on an airplane, any airplane, I discovered that Avis was perfectly willing to rent me yet another Mustang. A red one. The skinny blond behind the desk with the spray of freckles across her nose put it succinctly: "If you'd stolen it, why would you want to rent another one, right, Father?" That was El Sol logic. I was awed.

Wondering why I had not boarded that airplane, any airplane, I drove slowly back to the rectory.

12

I WAS too late for the TV news. The first thing I did when I arrived home was go into the kitchen. I opened the freezer, took out a frozen Swanson Mexican-style dinner. After staring at the picture on the front of this for several seconds, I changed my mind and threw it back in the freezer. I took a glass full of ice and the bottle of Jim Beam out to the living room, turned on the TV, and poured myself a drink. Just in time to see Aaron.

It was the last fifteen seconds of one of our committee's thirty-second spots. Aaron was wearing a red-and-white-striped rep necktie and a white shirt as the camera closed in on his strong face.

> Save El Sol for your children, and their children. Save it for yourselves, not for the land barons, who care only about high profits. Save this city for progress, not for chaos. Vote No on Proposition Three on June third.

Suddenly Aaron's wonderful worn features were replaced by a young Black boy holding a telephone to his ear, saying, "Mama, it's me." It was a Bell Telephone advertisement I'd seen too many times already. The key line, the annoying fishhook they planted in your mind was, "But, Mama, I *am* calling. . . ." Black or white, the actors were just there to grab your attention and destroy your mental privacy. Hopefully to an extent where you decided to forget whatever you were doing and go pick up your telephone. Instead, I poured cold bourbon down my throat and switched off the TV.

I missed Aaron so much. He had been my best friend. Seeing his videotaped ghost on the screen, I had to fight back tears. A friend and a kind of father, Aaron had been holding me together ever since Nancy had left town.

The hysteria of surviving that ordeal in the Fairmont had gradually changed into a heavy depression. I felt very nervous. My life was in danger. But I had been drinking so hard, acting so self-destructive ever since Nancy had left, it was a shock to feel how much I wanted to live. The empty house suddenly had me spooked. I had locked the Mustang in the garage.

Was it the church: Holy Innocents? Was that the link between Aaron's murder, Attlee's, and my murderous Fairmont? Who had something against the church? Was it Barbara Anderson? Doll had called her "very dangerous," and, it struck me, her son, Roy, looked like the kind of man who knew the intimate details of automobiles. Still, that just didn't seem right. What about Joe Moore? I could see, as Jamie kept insisting, why he would have a motive regarding Aaron, and even me. But why would he have killed Attlee, and in such a brutal way?

Then there was Jamie Hillal himself. Snow didn't trust him because he was an Arab. Certainly Munty didn't trust him. But I had found Jamie, despite his reckless style, the one potential kindred spirit on the committee after Aaron's death. I had even called Jamie, with my only phone call, to be my lawyer. No, Jamie Hillal did not strike me as a murdering, savage Arab. Yet, I reminded myself, there was so much about a man like Jamie Hillal that I could not know, only sense beneath his flashy exterior and his bright words. Finally, there were Professor Snow and Father Ortega. Were they murderers? Did they cut the spring on my accelerator return, and my brake lines—and mutilate poor Attlee's body in such an unthinkable way? It was too crazy, too unthinkable. But who, then?

I tried to clear my mind by staring around me in the living room. How unnecessary it all looked: couch, easy chairs, dining-room set, my stereo, the Sony TV. All had once seemed necessary. All these things were evidence of earlier days when Nancy and I had caught the buying influenza out in the Real World: fresh out of seminary, serving as an assistant at the cathedral in St. Louis. That was before Colorado. And long before El Sol.

To my neighbors, I was sure the rectory looked bare, sadly lacking in American household charm. Where were all my latest appliances: my automatic popcorn popper, my Fry Baby, my color prints of big-eyed tykes and the Desert Sunrise? Where were my giant table lamps from Levitz, my gas-fired barbecue, my coordinated rug and towel sets to match the commode covers in my bathrooms? My house lacked these goods. It had the feeling of being inhabited, but not settled. It was more like a motel room than a warehouse stuffed full of the bounty from a dozen Labor Day sales.

Yet, if I felt like such an outsider, why didn't I just get out of El Sol? Because, unlike Nancy, I knew that Freedom was a notorious two-way street. If I ran away, out into the desert, I could find freedom there. Only the sun and the empty scorched terrain would limit me. I would be free, but free to do what? Free to die. Back in El Sol, caught between Fry Baby and TV news, between Sambo's and Levitz, my limitations were seemingly infinite. But so was my freedom to match them, even to rise above . . .

I had lost faith in my ability to rise above anything at that moment—when the telephone rang. Even before she spoke, I knew she was calling from a public phone, outside, and that she wanted something urgently. I don't know how, but I knew that immediately.

"Fernando? This is Doll."

"Yes, Doll. Is something wrong? You sound upset."

"No, everything is okay, but I have to get out of this city. I have to go away. Have you shown it to her yet?"

"The ticket?" I had to think quickly. In the end, I decided to lie. "Yes, I did."

"What did she think?"

"She was . . . impressed. But she wants to see more. If she's going to pay you two thousand, she wants to see everything she's getting. I'm sorry, but that's what she said."

She cursed in Spanish. "That's too bad. I can't do that. You tell her I'll take one thousand. I cut it in half. But I want to get the money tonight."

"That will be very difficult."

"I don't care. Now, look, you do this. Go and tell her. Get the money. Then you come down to the Sandman Motel. Remember it?"

"Yes."

"Take a room there. Take a room and wait. Don't ask for me and don't come back to my apartment."

"What's wrong, Doll?"

"Nothing. Just a lot of people I have to avoid seeing. This city is finished for me."

"You sound very upset."

"Don't worry about me. You just tell his wife that if I don't get the money tonight, that's it. I can sell it somewhere else. I can throw it in the river. But she'll never see those papers."

"Okay. I'll tell her."

"You get the room and wait for me," she said. "Is it agreed?"

"Agreed."

"I'll see you." She hung up.

I have to admit that the first thought which crossed my mind was that she might spend the night with me.

Why else did she want me to rent a room? I saw her body, with that thin turquoise line cutting into her loins, in my mind's eye. But I wasn't that drunk yet.

I took out my address book and looked up Jamie Hillal's number. I dialed and it rang twice before a female voice answered. It was his answering service.

I left my number and hung up. I poured more amber whiskey onto the dregs of ice at the bottom of my glass. It was clear that Barbara Anderson ought to be called. But I had already decided I wasn't going to call her. If it came down to it, I would take full responsibility for that. All these people were acting to a script I couldn't begin to understand yet. But outsiders have certain advantages. The freedom to ignore scripts you don't understand, for example. Still, I wanted Jamie to call. He had been very convincing when he told me not to see Doll again. I wanted to ask him why.

I had also decided to ask him what the truth was about the feud between his family and Aaron Anderson.

An hour passed during which I had to resort again to the TV. Jamie didn't call. I found I couldn't watch another Monty Python rerun at that point. I didn't want to be amused, only diverted. A good old American situation comedy was just the thing. Halfway through it, I got a sick feeling in my guts and began to search the house. Where was Aaron's ticket stub? I had forgotten where I had put it.

I was afraid of falling apart again. I kept thinking about Doll's naked body, her thick nipples and those small pink circles, as I searched. It was easy to fall in love. Something a college friend once told me flashed through my head: "Fernando, you walk around with an invisible pedestal on your shoulder. You can't wait to fall in love with any girl you can worship." It looked that way. But I had chosen to marry the one girl I could never worship.

And now Doll was waiting for me to check into the Sandman Motel. . . .

Wrong. She wasn't waiting. After an hour, I had gone out and climbed in the red Mustang and driven to the Interstate, across the city, to Haynes Drive exit. Soon the Sandman's sign stood out clearly ahead: the Sandman himself, a neon-lighted figure, looked curiously like Howard Hughes with his long white hair and white beard, tossing yellow neon "sand" over the road. I parked in front of the office.

A Mexican woman, plump, in her early forties, came out of the back room. I had been staring at the large glass-fronted cold chest behind the counter. She said it would cost me nineteen dollars for a single with twin beds. I paid her. "You want something to drink? I sell pints and half-pints too."

"Give me a half-pint of Jim Beam. And a six-pack of Coors."

"You been driving all day?" she asked as she got the beer. "Need to unwind, huh?"

"Yeah."

"That's a good TV in your room. Or maybe you'd like some company? I could send up a nice girl."

"That's great. But I'm really kind of tired."

"Anything you say. You a salesman?"

"Yes."

"Where you from?" she asked, taking my money. "I'll bet you're from L.A., right?"

"That's right. How did you know?"

"I know a lot." She laughed, and gave me back the change.

"I'll bet you do. Good night."

I was a much better liar these days. When Nancy left me, it was Aaron who came up with the plan to tell the parish a lie. "Tell them her mother was sick and she went back to nurse her. The ones you want to believe it, they will. The others will just be glad you're smart enough to lie about it."

Doll never showed up. I fell asleep in front of the TV, a late movie with Richard Widmark and a lot of uniforms blurring in front of my eyes until I couldn't see to open another beer. The whiskey was all gone. The mattress was rutted down the center. All night I had dreamed of knocks on the door, of doors opening, of Monty Python inviting me onto their show. The only mercy the next morning was the lack of a cigarette butt floating in my half-full water glass of stale beer. I knew there had been a reason to quit smoking that first year in Colorado, although back then I thought it was the Rocky Mountain altitude.

First thing, I reached for the phone.

Thursday

13

"I GOT your message," Jamie said. "Where the hell have you been? I must have called you ten times last night, this morning."

"What time is it?" I asked.

"After eleven."

"In the morning?"

"Of course in the morning. Where the hell are you?"

"In a motel."

"What happened?"

"Doll called me last night. She was very nervous, upset. She wanted a thousand dollars right away. I was supposed to come down here and check into the Sandman Motel and wait for her to show up and bring the briefcase."

There was silence on his end for a long moment. Finally he said, "You don't mess around, do you, Fernando?"

"What do you mean?"

"I thought I warned you about Doll."

"You did. This sounded important."

"You spent the night in the Sandman?"

"Yes."

"You've got adventurous blood for a clegryman. Look, don't worry about Doll."

"Why?"

"She was uptight last night because of certain pressures

[113]

I put on her boss, Al Mirabi. Now I've got Doll on ice. She's fine. She's not going anywhere yet."

"You've got Aaron's briefcase?"

"No. But I will have it. Very soon. Look, can you come to my office this evening, say, about seven o'clock?"

"Yes. Can't we meet earlier?"

"I've got to be in court all afternoon. I've got this appeal. New evidence. It's a narcotics case, and my clients, the Garza brothers, collectively face about eighty years. How about seven tonight?"

"I'll be there. There's one thing, Jamie . . . ?"

"Yes?"

"What is this feud between your father and Aaron's father all about?"

Silence. Finally he said, "It was a long time ago. My father didn't invent the way the system works in this country. He didn't invent the Depression, either. Aaron's father was a bad lawyer, and a drunk. But you have been talking to Munty, haven't you?"

"I did see him yesterday afternoon, yes."

"I could tell you some things about Elwood Munty that would shock you. But I don't want to play that game. Take my word for it, there is no feud between my family and Aaron's. They weren't friends, but Aaron and my father respected each other."

"I'm sorry if I sounded suspicious. It's just that I'm new in El Sol and—"

"See you tonight," he said, cutting me short with a voice that sounded strained. "Okay, my friend?"

"Yes. Just one more thing, Jamie?"

"What is it?"

"Did I give you Aaron's ticket stub the other night? It was a wild night and my memory is so lousy these days . . ."

"Yes, I've got it."

"Great. See you at seven tonight."

We both hung up. I looked down at myself. Some-time during the night I had gotten up and undressed, hung my clothes neatly over the back of the chair under the window. But the TV was still running. I shut it off.

I looked at my watch: 11:25 A.M. Strapping it on, I thought of going back to the house, changing clothes, and going down to my office at Holy Innocents. A thought struck me. I picked up the phone again and dialed the church. Maggie answered on the first ring.

"What are you doing there? I told you to take a week's rest, didn't I? How are you?"

"Oh, so-so, Father. I just can't sit at home on a Thursday when I'm not sick. You must have been out early this morning. I tried you when I came into the office."

"Yes, I was. What's up?"

"Only that Father Ortega called and wanted me to remind you the candidates would be at the Mission this noon. I told him you wouldn't forget something like that. He hopes you'll attend."

"I see. As a matter of fact, I'm down near there right now."

"Very good. Will you be coming by the office later?"

"I have quite a few calls to make around town," I lied. "I may not come in at all this afternoon."

"That's fine, Father. I'll see you tomorrow morning, I expect. Unless you do come by."

"Let's talk on the phone later, Maggie." She agreed, and we hung up.

I stopped at a *taqueria* and picked up a chicken-and-avocado tostada and a Pepsi to go, then drove down to the mission. I ate in the Mustang, listening to the radio news. The President's chief aide had been cleared of snorting cocaine after a five-month investigation. People were afraid that shifting so many Border Patrol officers to Florida, to handle the Cuban refugees, was going to allow Mexican aliens to "overrun" the river into El Sol County.

And there had been sixteen more earthquakes out in California. I shut off the radio and stared across the street at the Mission San Juan el Bautista.

Built in 1809, it was the oldest building in El Sol. The Mission stood in the heart of the *barrio*, two blocks from the river, ten blocks from the Anglos' downtown. On the same street, small bungalows alternated with tin-roofed tenements, with vacant lots, auto wrecks, cottonwood trees, and abandoned iceboxes.

The Mission was not a simple building, but it was easy to miss. Adobe was always easy to miss if you weren't accustomed to its dusty beige shades, blending so gracefully with the desert, since it *was* the desert. Dried earth. The Mission consisted of the main building, its *espadaña*, or false front, rising three stories tall. The main doors were wood, uncarved pine stained black by time, and above them was a triangular window cut in the four-foot-thick wall. Behind the false front, a roof of red-clay tiles was supported by visible log beams. To the left, the campanile stood even taller than the main church. This bell tower contained only one bell, a very large one of melted-down Spanish cannon, and ended in a simple white cross at the apex of the roof.

Inside the long whitewashed nave, perhaps eighty people were listening to the mayor when I walked in and found a seat. The dark carved-wood *reredos*, or altarpiece, shone with gold-flecked saints, with silver candlesticks, and a silver crucifix. Off to the left, Leo Mulcahy and Father Ortega sat on folding chairs. Mulcahy had a yellow legal pad on his knee and was taking notes.

Mayor Castillo was attacking Proposition 8, the one which wanted to raze the *barrio* to make room for Joe Moore's magnificent industrial park.

Castillo was the first Mexican-American mayor in recent El Sol history. But he was actually the establishment's candidate; not even a local *barrio* "homeboy."

Born in San Diego forty-four years earlier, he'd been an engineer before he became a politician. He had originally come to El Sol as a soldier stationed at Fort Ricks. Although he was honest, Castillo had proved to be a weak leader, often foolish. He was no longer popular with even the Mexican-American voters, some of whom called him *"el más gringo."* Roughly translated it meant "the biggest gringo of them all." Aaron Anderson had been one of his original sponsors. And Aaron had told me that even Joe Moore was favoring Castillo's reelection.

El Sol had always been more of a skillet than a "melting pot." Contained by the same desert rim, blasted by the same fierce sun, the many groups who comprised El Sol's population had never "melted" together.

Mexicans stayed in the *barrio* along the river: the largest and poorest group. The Anglo "natives" had always controlled the political machinery through their banks. The Army, with vast Fort Ricks, had tended to ignore the city while exploiting it. Finally, there was the latest group, the new Anglo immigrants from the rest of the country. Attracted by the climate, the expanding industry, the low cost of living, these middle-class "pioneers" were neither poor nor powerful. They had a very dim idea of who ran what in El Sol. Yet they were fast replacing the Mexicans as the biggest bloc of voters in the city.

Leo Mulcahy was their self-appointed leader. He now rose to refute Mayor Castillo on Proposition 8. Who said it would be "inhuman" to relocate people out of their old neighborhoods and into beautiful modern communities? "A year ago," Mulcahy said, "you same people who are complaining about being kicked out of your wonderful *barrio* here were calling it a filthy ghetto, unfit for human beings. The fact is, some of you folks don't know *what* you want."

A young man rose behind us and shouted, "It's a

ghetto, man. But it's ours. You can't take it away from us."

"That's very touching," Mulcahy said. "But this is the United States of America. We're a democracy on this side of the river, sonny. The voters will decide next Tuesday. A majority will win, one way or the other. Who's got a real question?"

Mulcahy was too crude to be a true conservative. He was running on ambition and a gut feeling that "something stinks" downtown in City Hall. It was the politics of Vague Paranoia. He would be far less easy to control if elected than a pragmatist like Mayor Castillo. The Establishment was embarrassed by Mulcahy's crudeness. His "image" was too close to ridiculous, even for Joe Moore apparently. Yet all the polls were showing Mulcahy with a solid lead over Castillo.

"Please explain to us why factories take priority over people?" asked a middle-aged woman in a nurse's uniform. "Why can't they relocate the industrial park to the desert? And leave us here by the river where we've always lived."

"The entire point of locating the park beside the border is to take advantage of the Twin Factories Agreement between the United States and Mexico," Mulcahy said smugly. "Haven't you understood that elementary arithmetic yet?"

In "Twin Factories," the "twins" were by no means identical. American corporations could use cheap foreign labor in Mexico without paying any import duties on what they produced there. All the hard labor was done in Mexico. The automated work, and the packaging, took place north of the river.

I stood up, unable to stand Mulcahy's obnoxious hectoring of his audience any longer. "I would like to ask the mayor a question, if you don't mind."

Mulcahy looked disappointed, but he sat down. Mayor Castillo stood up. "Yes, Father?"

"You oppose Proposition 8. But you continue to support Proposition 3, which calls for a monstrous expansion of the city onto county-owned land. Don't you see that Proposition 8 and 3 are linked inextricably? Each is one side of the same coin. Joe Moore is not going to settle for one without the other."

"I beg your pardon, Father. Where did you ever hear me support Proposition 3? I have maintained my neutrality on that since day one. As yet, I have seen no sound evidence, Father, that Proposition 3 is going to be bad for our economy, our ecology, or even my own brothers and sisters in the Chicano community. If I had some evidence, I might oppose Proposition 3. Until then, I'll let the voters decide." He sat down.

Was the mayor waiting for Ralph Nader to drive into El Sol and present him with some "evidence" against Proposition 3? It was maddening to listen to a fatuous politician referring to people he undoubtedly despised as his "brothers and sisters," too.

Shortly after 1:15 P.M., Mulcahy announced that he had to leave to attend another meeting. Mayor Castillo, happy to have the excuse, said he also had pressing business back at City Hall.

I walked out onto the steps at the front of the mission. A black Cadillac limousine was waiting to collect the mayor. Mulcahy pushed his way past Mexicans who were trying to ask him questions, smiling grimly, and walked briskly with his aide toward a maroon Mercury Monarch. Meanwhile, they had surrounded Castillo.

The young people had him pinned against the side of his limo. These people rarely, if ever, got a chance to question their "brother" the mayor on the issues. Finally, smiling broadly, he pushed one woman and ducked under someone else's arm, snatched open the limo door, and jumped inside. He continued to wave back at the crowd as he spoke to his Chicano chauffeur. The black limo lurched forward, then took off in a smooth flow of speed. Some of the crowd shouted curses at it in Spanish.

"Hello," Father Ortega said, squeezing my arm. "I am glad you came. You are the only committee member who could make it."

"I wanted to come."

"Your question was well put."

"What did you think of his answer?"

"Strange," Father Ortega said. "I didn't hear any answer, did you?"

I laughed. Something had been bothering me ever since I had spoken to Jamie that morning. It was his remark about Dr. Munty. Now, against my better instinct, I found it impossible to keep my mouth shut. "Tell me, Father, do you know Dr. Munty well?"

"No, not well."

"What do you think of him? In the strictest confidence, of course."

He shut his eyes as if I had actually caused him pain with my question. "I do not like gossip," he said. "On the other hand, I cannot swear to what I tell you because I never saw it with my own eyes. And because of other reasons."

I nodded. He was talking of the confessional, of a silence that was sancrosanct. "I understand, Father Ortega."

"I believe Dr. Munty's respect for Mexican blood is not the same as his respect for Anglo blood."

I waited, but he was not willing to say more. Not sure what else to say, I thanked him for his candor and left the coolness of the old Mission behind me.

14

NANCY'S BROWN Rabbit was parked in my spot in the
rectory driveway. I had not seen it for many months.

Covered with oily grime, it had a jagged hole where
the right taillight had been. Missing from the car were
all the chrome trim, three hubcaps, and the rear window
wiper. A sticker on the bumper read: "Honk For Jesus!"
Was that someone's idea of a joke?

I took a deep breath before unlocking the door. My
heart was beating very fast. Would he be with her? I had
run the movie of beating Flipper's brains out through my
imagination so often those past months; suddenly I was
sure it was about to happen. Would I be on my way to
prison in a matter of hours? Prison images flashed through
my mind. I felt a jolt of horror, and instant remorse. Just
as I came face to face with Nancy.

She looked good. Sitting on the couch with her bare
feet on the coffee table, smoking a True, watching what
appeared to be *Wall Street Week* on the TV, with her
fingers curled around a glass of white wine, she looked
very good. Better than I had seen her look in years; perhaps ever. She had gained an extra ten pounds. Her face
was tanned and her hair was very blond. Her breasts
looked larger than I remembered under a T-shirt that
read:

I

DUG

GRAND CANYON

She wore a pair of light green panties with lace trim. I
had never seen either the T-shirt or the panties before.
It looked like she had taken a shower and her hair was
still damp. She looked so tan, it was as if she had been
lying on a beach since the afternoon she had left. Was
the hippie in the house? I thought I smelled marijuana.

"Hello, Fernando."

"Is he with you?"

"Is who with me?"

"You know his name. Your friend."

"You mean Flipper? Of course not. I haven't seen him
in months. How are you, Fernando?"

"I'm fine. When did you get here?"

"A couple of hours ago. I drove across from Palm
Springs, straight through. Were you down at the
church?"

I shook my head. I had been wandering around one of
the shopping malls most of the afternoon since I left the
Mission. Not wanting to go home or to the office, I had
spent several hours browsing in B. Dalton's, in a gourmet
shop, and in a wine store. In the end, the only thing I
had bought was a new bottle of Jim Beam. But that was
not who I needed at this point. This was an emergency.

"I'm going to make myself a drink," I told her, and
walked out of the room. I felt dizzy, nauseated. It was
about 5:45 P.M. The Beefeater gin was at the back of the
cupboard under the wall oven. I filled a twelve-ounce
glass with ice cubes and found an old lemon, rotten and
brown, with just enough salvageable peel to make a twist,
dropped it on the ice, and poured gin to the brim. I
stirred with my finger and drank about a quarter of it

[122]

straight down. "Do you want a drink?" I called out to her.

"I bought some wine, Fernando. It's in the fridge."

She was saying my name a lot. It struck me as practice, perhaps to keep her from slipping back to the names of recent lovers. I brought the bottle out to the living room. It was a cheap Frascati and I let her pour for herself.

Nancy was a New York City girl. Her father had been a wealthy, romantic failure, a Princeton man from Virginia originally. Nancy's mother had been one of his rich deb conquests back in the 1930's. She had been his prettiest conquest—he didn't need money—and he eventually married her in 1940. His name was Tyree and he had died in a plane crash in the Dutch Antilles in 1961.

Her mother had never remarried, had been drunk ever since. So Nancy and I had our dead parents in common. But self-pity and anger at a parent were probably not the best emotional foundations on which to build a marriage.

Nancy had always detested her mother, and envied men. "I could never be a feminist," she had told me the first time we saw a particular female novelist on the Dick Cavett show. "She looks like she uses her jaw to break rocks with." How she had changed her tune!

She needed to breathe, she'd told me ten months ago. El Sol was killing her quickly. It seemed to me that too many people blamed their unhappiness on cities or deserts or nuclear plants or the Democrats. But I couldn't say to them, "You're complaining? Just look at the starving people in Cambodia. In Africa. In Latin America." I couldn't say that, not even in the pulpit, because I complained about cities and the Democrats too. "Think of the poor starving people in India," our mothers had once admonished us when we refused to eat their food. How smug we were as children in the Fifties! How desolate as adults this spring of 1980. . . .

As a child, Nancy had loved to read war novels: *Battle Cry*, *The Naked and the Dead*, *All Quiet on the Western Front*, *Mr. Roberts*. Her mother watched her reading and rereading these books and decided something was wrong with her daughter's hormones. She had sent her to Park Avenue specialists, then a Fifth Avenue psychiatrist. An aggressive little tomboy at the Spence School, Nancy had dreamed of growing up to be the first woman to win the Medal of Honor in battle. Later, she had dreamed of being the biggest slut in town. Or at least the sophomore class at Sarah Lawrence. The last thing she ever wanted, she claimed, was to be a minister's wife. There was a time when we had many laughs over what we were becoming.

And then we were it.

"I took a shower," she said, noticing my eyes on her bare legs. "Is there somebody crashing here?"

"No. Why?"

"I saw the sleeping bag on the floor in your study."

"I sleep there."

"On the floor? You used to do that at Brown, didn't you?"

"Of course. You knew that." I reached over and shut off the TV.

"Yes. Well . . ." She pretended to get involved with the label on the Frascati bottle.

"So what's up?" I said finally.

"Not too much."

"I see. You look okay."

"Thanks."

"I'm curious. . . ."

"Yes, Fernando?"

"How long are you back for?"

"I'm not sure."

"Why did you come back?"

She shook her head, smiling weakly.

"Do you have any plans?"

"Not really."

"No?"

"I hoped we could talk. It's been a long time since we talked, you know?"

Did I know? I tilted my head back and poured gin down my throat until I almost gagged. "Yes," I said when I could talk again. "What in particular did you think we could talk about?"

"I don't know exactly."

"You don't?"

"All these months . . . I sort of forgot . . . the reality of what I remembered. I mean, I wondered if I remembered things the way they actually were. You, for example."

"Thanks for the postcard."

"Did I send you a postcard?" She suddenly looked a little frightened.

"The picture of the motel in Blythe? Right after you left?"

"Oh, that's right."

"I knew it was you, though you didn't sign it."

"I think I must have been stoned."

"Sure," I said. I poured gin down my throat.

"Well, what's been happening here?"

"You mean in this house? Not much, as you can see. It hasn't changed a bit, has it?"

"I mean in your life?" She had tuned a little nearer the frequency I was using. It was starting to bother her. "I know you're mad at me. I can understand if you are."

"Do I seem mad?"

"You seem pretty hostile, yes."

"Maybe you're misinterpreting? Maybe you just expected me to me mad?"

"Maybe," she said, almost a whimper.

[125]

"Aaron Anderson was murdered last week."

"He was the one who came to Denver, wasn't he?"

"Yes."

"It's so difficult for me to remember those days."

"Somebody tried to kill me the other night. They messed around with the Fairmont so I couldn't turn it off."

"I saw you drive up in that Mustang," she said. "I've changed a lot, Fernando."

"Liberated?" I said it with as straight a voice as I could.

She accepted it. "Yes, you could say that."

"Were you in California the whole time?"

"Oh no. I only just got back from Greece two weeks ago. I was in Crete."

"Greece?" I said. "Crete? Tremendous."

"You don't sound very happy about it, actually," she said, giving me a new look. Her confidence was returning.

"Why should I be very happy about it?"

"Perhaps because it was good for me. Because I grew. I feel so much stronger now, I can't tell you."

"They killed Johnny Attlee too. It was awful."

"Who's doing all this killing here?"

I shook my head. "Nobody knows. There's a tough election going on."

"Are you involved in that?" she asked.

"Yes, kind of."

"Good."

I stared at her. "You've got a great tan."

"I feel like such a stranger with you." She laughed. "It's so weird."

"I wouldn't mind fucking you, actually," I said. The gin was coming on very fast.

"Fernando?" She leaned across the cushion and stared at me. "Do you want me to leave or something?" But what about the green panties? The lace trim on her

[126]

thighs? She knew what got to me; she had been my wife for seven years.

"I'm not sure," I said. "Maybe I turned into a chauvinist pig while you were gone."

"Well, I've come back now. Maybe you could turn back into Fernando?"

"That may be impossible."

"Really?"

"By the way, I told everyone your mother was dying. You've been in New York nursing her, if anybody asks. If you stick around, you'll have to decide how she made out."

"What do you mean?"

"Did she recover or die? Your mother calls about every two weeks. We had some very drunken phone calls last winter. Lately, I've avoided fights with her."

"I really feel bad about not writing to my mother."

"Why didn't you, then?"

"I couldn't, that's all."

"Oh."

"My mother was part of what I had to work out."

"I see."

"Did you see *Kramer vs. Kramer*?" she asked.

"Yes."

"What did you think of it?"

"I didn't like it."

"Why?"

"I hated what they did to the kid at the end. He was all ready to go back with his mother. Then she ditched him a second time."

"But that was beautiful," Nancy protested. "He be-longed with Dustin Hoffman. And the mother wasn't really sure—"

The doorbell rang.

"Who the hell is that?"

Nancy looked from me to the door, and back. "Were you expecting someone?"

"Nobody. I don't get visitors here. I'm not ready for this." I was on the verge of shouting, "Can't they give me a break?"

Nancy was on her feet, heading in the opposite direction. "I'll go in the bedroom. Tell me when they're gone. Please calm down, okay?"

"Yeah."

I opened the door. A swarthy man with a receding hairline and exaggerated sideburns, dressed in a seersucker suit, stuck his wallet in my face.

"Father O'Neal?"

"Huh?" I was trying to focus on the badge pinned to the leather flap. "Yes?"

"I'm Roger Pasetti of the FBI. I have a few questions I'd like to ask you. It won't take more than five minutes of your time."

"Uh . . . yes, okay."

"Thank you."

"You're welcome."

I shut the door and motioned toward the easy chair. He disregarded me and chose to sit on the couch in the place Nancy had just vacated.

"Can I get you a drink or something?"

He shook his head. "No, thank you." He reached into his jacket and took out a small black notebook. Flipping this open while his other hand searched for his pen, he suddenly looked me in the eye and asked, "How did you get involved with Jamie Hillal, Father?"

"I beg your pardon?"

"Jamie Hillal. You know who he is, don't you?"

"Of course I do."

"You're good friends?"

"I've only known him for about six weeks."

"How do you know him?"

"We're both on a committee that is working to defeat Propositions 3 and 8 next Tuesday."

"Would this be," he began to read, "Committee to Save El Sol?" He smirked.

"Yes." I stopped myself from saying that I knew it was a silly name.

"How did you come to join that committee, Father?"

"I was asked to join by Aaron Anderson. Mr. Anderson was a deacon at my church. What is this about?"

Pasetti shook his head. "Just a couple of questions. Is Father Jose Ortega also a member of your committee?"

"Yes. I must ask why you are asking me these questions."

"For a number of reasons, all pertaining to an investigation being conducted by the Bureau. One reason directly concerns Anderson's murder. Did you know Anderson well?"

"Fairly well."

"You conducted his funeral, did you not?"

"Yes."

"There was a Mexican woman at the funeral who created some confusion, wasn't there?"

"Yes."

"Had you known Aaron Anderson conducted affairs with young foreign women?"

"No. But . . ."

"But?" the FBI agent asked.

"But there was no reason for me to know."

"Did Aaron Anderson ever mention blackmail to you?"

"No."

"He never mentioned anyone who might be trying to blackmail him?"

"I said no."

"Did he mention his gambling debts to you?"

"No."

"Did he mention a man named Montoya to you?"

"No . . . I don't think so. I have heard that name recently." Was it Jamie who had mentioned a Montoya? "Who is Montoya?"

Pasetti stared at me as if, mentally, he was slapping my face. "Montoya is a leading figure in El Sol's criminal underworld. He runs a poker game on the fourth floor of the Hotel Central downtown. It was a high-stakes game. Aaron Anderson was a regular player. I repeat, did he mention Raul Montoya to you?"

"No, he didn't."

He frowned. "Did he mention his stepson was in federal prison for smuggling narcotics?"

"No."

"Let's change the names here," Pasetti said. "Jamie Hillal. Did you know he earns his living by defending narcotics smugglers?"

"I knew he was a criminal lawyer, Mr. . . ."

"Pasetti. Special Agent in Charge of the FBI field office in El Sol County. What about Father Jose Ortega? Did you know Ortega was under federal indictment for smuggling illegal aliens across the Border?"

"Yes. I read about that a few months ago. Wasn't that a mistake or something?"

"No, Father, no mistake. Ortega faces a prison term if convicted. This is some committee you're involved with, isn't it?"

"I don't understand what you're attempting to prove here."

"You work with Hillal and Ortega on this committee, don't you?"

"Yes."

"Don't you think it odd that Aaron Anderson would appoint men like Hillal and Ortega to his committee—shortly before he himself was murdered?"

"Odd? Why?"

"You don't think Anderson was acting like a desperate man the last weeks before he died?"

"Absolutely not."

"Funny," Pasetti said. "His wife thinks he was. Those are her exact words: 'a desperate man.' "

"Well, she knew him better than I did."

"Did she, Father?"

"What do you mean?"

"His wife told us that you and Anderson were almost constant companions?"

"That's absurd."

"No? She seemed to think it was true."

"Aaron and Elwood Munty were best friends. But I certainly wasn't. I've been in this city for only eleven months."

"How often did you see Anderson during the weeks you worked with him on the committee?"

"Every couple of days. Sometimes he might stop by the church. Sometimes not for a week. He called on the phone a lot."

"Did you see him the day he was murdered? Last Wednesday?"

"No."

"Where were you last Wednesday evening, Father?"

"Why . . . Wait a second. I was here at home last Wednesday. If you want to continue this kind of questioning, I insist on calling my lawyer."

"Jamie Hillal?" He smirked.

"Yes."

"What were you doing at the Sandman Motel last night, Father? Was that church business or were you just taking a brief holiday in scenic South El Sol?"

"If you know all the answers . . ."

"If I were you, Father, I'd consider finding a new lawyer." He stood up and slipped the notebook inside

[131]

his jacket. "Thank you for your time. Please don't get up. I can find my way out."

"I'll be happy to show you out." I stood up. "I can't believe this."

"That makes two of us, Father. And a lot of other people, before it is finished."

"What are you talking about?"

"When the time comes, you will be one of the first to know, Father."

He opened the door before I could reach it. Stepped outside, turned, and said, "You are married, Father?"

"Yes."

"But your wife has been away?"

"Yes."

"You are not alone right now, are you?"

"My wife returned this afternoon, as a matter of fact."

His eyes flashed for a second, as if this was the first piece of unexpected news he had received since he started asking me questions.

"Are you trying to threaten me or something?" I asked.

"I asked you a few questions, Father. If you tell anyone I threatened you, it will be a total fabrication. I will have to call you on it. One more thing . . ."

"What is it?"

"Do you smoke marijuana regularly? Or does that butt in the ashtray belong to your wife?"

"You're nuts, Pasetti."

"Well, my advice to you is to empty your ashtrays in future. Good night, O'Neal."

He walked down the path toward a white Plymouth parked at the curb. The sun was still hanging high over the western mesa. Pasetti was about my age, I guessed, and roughly my size. I would have no more wanted to fight him than fight a half-starved Doberman.

I turned and went back into the living room, to find

Nancy standing with the ashtray already in her hand. "Can I have it?" I said.

"God, I heard. What the hell was the FBI doing here?"

"Can I?"

She passed it to me. The tidbit of burnt paper and ash lay in plain sight. She must have smoked it after her shower. I didn't know why I had missed seeing it. But I had. Pasetti had not.

"It's not my fault," she said.

"No."

"How was I going to know he was coming over here? What the hell is going on with you, Fernando?"

I ignored her question and looked at my watch. It read 7:12 P.M. I was already late for my meeting with Jamie. "I've got to go."

"What? You're leaving me here?"

"I have a meeting. I'll be back."

She sat down on the couch. "Here we go again," she said. "I had forgotten what it was like to be married to a meeting."

I just stared at her. After a few moments my anger subsided enough to allow me to speak. "Can I ask you something?"

"Yes."

"Did you leave because of what the doctor said?"

"You mean because I couldn't have a baby? No, not really."

"Did you leave because you wanted to screw that hippie? Or screw a lot of guys? Or just not screw me anymore?"

"All three, in certain ways, I guess."

I nodded. "Thanks for being so fucking honest."

"At least for a while. . . ."

"What do you mean?"

"Go to your meeting," she said. Tears perked in the corners of her eyes. "Please. This is very hard for me."

[133]

I picked up the ashtray and left the room. In the kitchen, I poured its contents down the disposal and ground them to sluice before shutting off the machine. Back in the living room, I paused with the front door open. "Do me a favor?"

"Yes?"

"I don't want any dope in this house. If you won't get rid of it, then please leave."

"You're serious, aren't you?"

I slammed the door for the first time in ten months.

15

ALL THE way downtown on the Interstate, I told myself reassuring lies. Nancy was back. I kept telling myself I could handle her, no problem. But Aaron's murder had hit me harder than I knew. I wasn't good at losing people. Too much practice.

Starting with my mother, who had died of leukemia when I was seven. My father had adored her. But he adored all women. Perhaps that was why he waited only two months to remarry. I had lost him, by choice, the day he informed me I was going to be getting a new mother. From that day on, I had vowed to hate his guts.

Lily was my first girlfriend. Her father was principal of the local high school, and her backyard adjoined ours. I had lost her my senior year of high school. She had a terrible case of TB and her parents had sold their house and moved somewhere out West. I often wondered if Lily might have recovered, married, and was now living somewhere right in El Sol. In any case, during college I didn't lose many people. Several lovers ditched me, I ditched several others. It all worked out. Imperfectly.

I had lost myself somewhere during my last year at Brown. It had to do with Vietnam, with my anger, with the Rockefeller grant that allowed children of the clergy to try a year at the seminary of their choice, tuition-free.

Nancy was a senior at Sarah Lawrence and I had met her at a party on Claremont Avenue, my first fall at

[135]

Union Seminary. We soon found an apartment, where we lived together for three years. Seven years after our marriage, I had lost Nancy to the hippie. If I was bad at losing people, was I any better at finding them again?

The lights were on in the upper windows on the second floor of the Hillal building. As I turned into the parking lot, I saw Jamie's red Porsche parked in front of the entrance. He was behind the wheel. The passenger door was open. I guessed he was late too.

I honked a greeting and drove straight back into the lot. After locking the door, I walked back around the corner of the building. Jamie looked like he was bending down to adjust his car radio. Or so I thought at first. Walking up to his side of the Porsche, I saw the blood all over him.

Christ, I begged, let this be a bad dream.

A bullet had slashed open the side of his face to the jawbone. There were more wounds in his upper body. His blue-and-white-striped shirt and cream-colored jacket were soaked black with blood. He was actually slumped with the gearshift supporting his right side. Whoever had shot him, I thought, had stood where I was standing at that moment.

A siren whined in the distance. Suddenly I realized how long I had been hearing that siren, and understood it was coming for us. If I had been on time, would I look like Jamie did now? Would I be dead?

I had thought he was dead until he moaned. His left eye opened. The eyeball made a jerky upward movement before the eyelid shut again. The more I saw, the worse it looked inside the car. At least he wasn't dead.

The first police cruiser came screaming to a halt at the curb in front of the building. Both doors flew open. The cops jumped out holding their guns, the one nearest me dropping to his knee and leveling his .38 at my chest. The driver used the roof of the cruiser to balance his gun arm. It made him look odd, as if he was exhausted or drunk, instead of deadly. A second siren, and then the new cruiser rounded the corner and lunged across the street in our direction.

The cops were shouting at me. I raised my arms and opened my hands wide. The latest siren died with an ugly gasp.

Within the next minute, a third car arrived on the scene. This was unmarked.

For the second time in less than forty-eight hours I was bent over an automobile and searched. It was not as bad as being raped, but it was not that much better, either. Some cops ran into the building, and others ran back into the parking lot. A detective in a khaki shirt and jeans, with orange cowboy boots, was giving orders. He reached in and checked Jamie's pulse and asked if an ambulance was coming.

"I heard them call one," one cop said.

The detective turned to me, taking my wallet from one of the uniformed officers. Flipping it open, he read my name off my driver's license. "Okay, Father O'Neal, relax. Did you call this into headquarters?"

I shook my head.

"He was like this when you arrived?"

"I haven't touched a thing."

"You see anybody leave when you pulled up?"

"No."

A cop came out of the Hillal building. Walking just behind him, hands in the pockets of baggy gray trousers, was Dr. Elwood Munty.

The detective recognized him. "Was that you called this in, Elwood?"

"It sure as hell was. Where is that ambulance?"

As if it had been waiting for him to ask, the ambulance turned onto Clay six blocks away and we all turned to watch its spinning red flashers.

[137]

"What happened here, Elwood?"

"Don't really know. Hillal gave me a call earlier today. Asked me to come over at seven o'clock. When I got here, there was one secretary holding the fort. She let me in and took me upstairs to this tomb of a waiting room. But she left to go off on a date, she said. Said Hillal was expected any minute. Next thing I heard was the gunshots. Sounded like four of them. I didn't think about it for a minute. Then I decided to have a look. Well, the doors were all locked except one. Even the elevator was locked. I was like a prisoner. But I did go into this one office and I looked down and saw the car here. The door was open like you see, on the passenger side. I couldn't see much, but then I saw his arm move down here, and there was blood on his hand. I put two and two together and called you boys. How is he?"

"You want to look at him?"

"I better," Munty said. He moved around the car and picked up Jamie's wrist through the window and took his pulse. Then he peeled open one of his eyes. "Bad news, I'm afraid. Thank heaven the ambulance is here."

A big white box with orange and red markings, the ambulance had disgorged a chromed stretcher which was being pushed up the drive by two orderlies in white cotton fatigues. The detective backed me off to the side as they began to lift Jamie out of the car. "Father, what church are you from?"

"Holy Innocents."

"And what were you doing here?"

"Jamie had asked me to meet him at seven o'clock. I was late. When I pulled up, he was sitting there in the car. I didn't see anyone. A few seconds later the first police car arrived."

The detective nodded. "Are you the Father O'Neal who took them on that wild chase a couple of nights ago?"

"Yes, I'm afraid so."

He cocked one eyebrow but decided not to say anything. He turned and looked around. "Whoever shot him probably drove away quick or ran over there." He motioned at the next lot, where a block of apartments came up to the parking lot's edge. There were several entrances into this apartment block where someone could have disappeared.

"What kind of meeting was this?" he asked Munty.

"We're members of a group fighting Joe Moore's two Propositions on Tuesday's ballot," Munty said. "That was what he wanted to talk about."

"You mean the drinking in the parks?"

"No, no. Two other propositions."

I stared at Munty. He finally acknowledged my presence. "Hello there, Fernando."

"Elwood."

An orderly came running over. He asked the detective if anyone would be going with Hillal in the ambulance.

"Elwood, are you going to the hospital with him?"

Munty scratched his chin. "No."

"You know who his doctor is?"

"No idea," Munty said. He looked at me. "Father, can I grab a lift with you? The old woman dropped me off. I was going to call her, but—"

"I thought I'd ride in the ambulance with Jamie," I said.

"You better hurry, Father," the detective said. They were about to shut the doors on the back. I shouted for them to wait and began to run across the pavement. I heard the detective telling Munty that he would be happy to drop him off.

I sat inside the ambulance on a small black folding seat and watched Jamie Hillal's face. It was covered with a clear plastic oxygen mask. It seemed to be growing paler by the moment. We sped downtown with the siren screaming outside, down to the County Hospital. The orderlies were very busy and I was pushed out of the way after a few minutes. An injection was given right through Jamie's blood-soaked shirt into his chest. There was plasma dripping into him and leather straps tied around his legs to keep him secure on the stretcher. I saw one orderly shake his head. The other looked at me and repeated the gesture.

"He's dead?"

They both nodded. "His pulse was gone when we pulled him out of his car. He was shot bad." He picked up a telephone and spoke into it. I gathered it was connected to the driver's compartment. Suddenly we were taking the corners on four wheels again. The siren persisted in shrieking, however.

I kept thinking about Munty. Had Jamie really asked him to come tonight?

What about Doll? Jamie had said she was "on ice" and that he would bring her to his office this evening—with the briefcase. It did occur to me that Doll might have shot Jamie. She was clearly as dangerous a woman to be around as Jamie had warned me. But it was hard to believe she could have shot both Aaron and Jamie.

I was standing in the bright tiled madness of the emergency room. There were stretchers being pushed into elevators; patients were moaning behind green sheets that hung from the ceiling as partitions separating the tables. I was looking for any familiar face, if only one of the orderlies who had been in the back of the ambulance. Jamie's body was covered and lying on a stretcher pushed up against the wall just inside the unloading zone.

I went over and stood beside it. Someone tapped me on the shoulder. It was an El Sol policeman. "Father, we've got a Mexican in here's crying for a priest. Can you give him the last rites or something?"

"I'm not a Roman priest, I'm Episcopalian."

"I don't think he'll notice much."

I nodded and followed the young officer back into the maze of green-cotton partitions. I saw one tall Black man standing next to a table clutching his side, blood seeping through his fingers. "What's going on here tonight?" I asked.

"We had more trouble in the plaza. Some GI's and the Mexicans. It's a war, is what it is."

He led me to the right cubicle. The Mexican stared up at me with glazed brown eyes: an enormous white bandage on his upper chest and entire throat, tubes going into his mouth, bottles floating over his outstretched veins like miniature satellites on plastic ropes. His eyes stared at me, and I had no idea if he saw me. They were fixed.

"Is he alive?" I asked the nurse.

"Barely."

I did not have a copy of *The Book of Common Prayer* with me. Nor had I given the Episcopal version of the last rites to anyone ever before. (In *The Book* it is called "Ministration at the Time of Death" and it says, "When possible, it is desirable that members of the family and friends come together to join in the Litany.") Improvising, I made the sign of the cross and bowed my head to pray the Lord's Prayer. Then I made the sign on the dying man. "Amen." His eyes never changed, and I stood for several minutes staring into them before the nurse nudged me and said, "I think it's okay now, Father."

Outside in the aisle full of nurses and orderlies scrambling from one tentlike cubicle to the other, I suddenly understood my responsibility. But once I had found the nearest telephone booth, I could find no listing for any Hillal in the book. I called Information and they confirmed that Robert Hillal's number was unlisted. I identified myself as a priest and the situation as a matter of the gravest urgency. Finally a telephone supervisor came on and agreed to give me the phone number.

After I talked to the maid, Robert Hillal came on the

phone himself. He sounded much younger than a man in his mid-eighties. I introduced myself and told him everything that I knew about his son's murder.

"Thank you for calling me. The police had not informed me of anything. Of course. Will you . . . you please excuse me?"

I could tell he was about to crack. "Of course."

"Perhaps you could call me tomorrow? Jamie had spoken of you . . ." He hung up quickly.

Who was killing us? I heard Jamie's voice in my memory saying, "Show them the blood on his hands." He was talking about Joe Moore's hands.

I went out past the counter where a harassed secretary sat behind a typewriter holding several reporters and a TV crew at bay. I passed through the rows of plastic bucket chairs, full of haggard men and women wanting Emergency attention, and walked out into the alley leading to the street. The Channel 3 remote truck was parked illegally at the mouth of the alley.

I was near the plaza. It was growing dark now. After dark, this was no-man's-land for an Anglo. I walked quickly toward the Sheraton, looking for a taxi. I found one waiting outside the hotel. I told him to drive me back to Hillal's office.

All the lights were on behind the black-tinted glass of the Hillal building. There was an orange van in the lot with "Evidence Search Squad" printed on the side in black letters. There were at least five unmarked cars parked around the lot in haphazard fashion, as if abandoned in a hurry. As if their drivers cared little for white lines on black asphalt.

Police. I got a twinge of strong paranoia. I had not felt so spooked since the late 1960's marching against the war in New York City. We had run for the United Nations Building, the part of the crowd I was with, after coming out of Central Park onto Sixth Avenue. The police had been waiting for us. They had ambushed us in a dead-end street, billy sticks flailing, stabbing, hitting. But I had nothing against cops in 1980. Or did I?

Inside the eerie foyer, an El Sol cop was sitting at the desk where I had seen the Black security guard last Tuesday morning. The cop looked up at me as if I might be the killer returning to the scene of the crime. He was opening his mouth to say something when the steel door flew open behind him. A tall man with an elegant mustache, he wore a green Lacoste shirt and brown corduroy jeans. It took me a second to remember him. He was the one who had broken up the fight between Jamie and Joe Moore after the burial.

He nodded at the cop and stared at me. I said, "I'm Father O'Neal. I just got back from the hospital. Jamie Hillal is dead."

"We know. You were one of the people who found him?"

"Yes."

He nodded at the steel door. "Were you going somewhere?"

"I was just going to tell them about Jamie."

"I wouldn't bother. They're busy fighting a civil war in there."

"What?"

"The FBI has arrived. A little matter of jurisdiction. Pasetti wants everybody out except himself."

Somehow the mention of Pasetti's name registered hard enough in my face to make this man laugh. "You know Pasetti?" he said.

"I've met him."

He looked at the cop, who was trying hard to pretend he wasn't listening to us. "Let's go outside, Father."

Once we were in the parking lot, the man took out his wallet and extracted something. He handed it to me: a business card listing him as Paul Havas, a "Special Agent" with the Department of Justice's Drug Enforcement Agency.

"You were with Jamie on Anderson's committee, weren't you?"

"Yes," I said.

"I liked your eulogy of Anderson. By the way, Jamie and I were pals. I know we were supposed to be enemies. He was a dirty Arab. I'm a lazy Greek. I arrest them and he springs them. Who found the body first—Munty?"

"Yes. He says he saw it from up there."

"He made the call?"

"That's right."

"Why were you two meeting Jamie tonight? Did it concern the committee?"

"We've been trying to get some evidence that will prove Proposition 3 is a threat to the city's water supply. Jamie thought he might have some for us tonight."

"What kind of evidence?"

"The Pointer Report."

Havas shook his head. "Never heard of it. You know what Pasetti wants?"

"What?"

"He wants to go through every file and piece of paper up in Jamie's office. He has a bench warrant that will allow him to do it. They're supposedly looking for the tapes the Garzas made of that FBI man down in San Antonio. Tell me, was this Pointer Report something worth killing a man for?"

"No. But now that Jamie's been shot, like Aaron, it doesn't seem so strange anymore."

"Like Aaron?" he asked.

"They were both shot."

"Yes, both shot in their cars."

"I hadn't thought of it like that."

He stuck out his hand and I shook it. He started for the white Cutlass Supreme that was parked near my rented Mustang. I waited for him to say good-bye, but the DEA agent was lost in his thoughts. He drove away without another word.

A few seconds later, I drove out of the parking lot too. The tall buildings towering above the rest of downtown looked like upended ice trays glowing against the indigo dusk. Over Gomez, the sun had burnt down to a dull yellow band on the hills. I was going to find that briefcase.

16

Up on the Interstate, I turned on the radio. All day I had been driving around the city listening to the radio without ever getting any news. This time I got news. Vernon Jordan had been shot in the back early that morning in Indiana. The Black leader was in critical condition but expected to live. Was it 1968 again? It seemed that way. As if, at that moment, there was a murder wave skimming across the West: Aaron, Jamie, Vernon Jordan. Was it the water? Or the ash?

The parking lot in front of the Rainbow was almost full. I left the Mustang around the side. The tattooed bouncer with the Fu Manchu mustache and the blue snakes in his skin took another two dollars off me. I went straight to the bar and tried to get Tiger's attention. She was busy filling plastic steins with Coors, slopping them on the girls' trays. They were frightened of her. Finally she came down the bar and asked what I wanted.

"Is Doll in the back?"

"No. She not here tonight. Her night off."

I walked straight out and got back into the Mustang. As I drove, I remembered standing next to Jamie's red Porsche, watching his eyelid shut, watching him bleed. I had been present his dying moment in the speeding ambulance. But I had been able to do nothing. It bothered me terribly.

So often I had wondered if, had I been a Roman Catholic priest, instead of a Protestant one, would I have done this or that *differently*. Not just the different words and rituals, for the difference was slight, and the effect, like my improvised last rites, equally tenuous. But I wondered if, as a Roman instead of a Protestant, my soul would feel different. It felt so empty now.

Something else was bothering me as I drove away from the Rainbow and headed for Doll's apartment. I still couldn't recall the details of last Wednesday evening. I had told Pasetti I had been at home the night Aaron was shot. Drinking, of course. But, thanks to the drinking, I couldn't remember those hours. The blank in my memory was starting to burn a hole in my guts. What was Pasetti's reason for coming to ask me those questions? What did he know that I didn't?

After fifteen minutes, the parking lot at the Sandman Motel welcomed me once again. There was the apartment complex at the back: two cramped rows of cinderblock "studios," all the doors spaced one room apart. Loud rock music filled the parking lot as I locked the car. This place gave me the creeps.

There were fourteen units but no sign of a manager's apartment. I couldn't find any mailboxes. So I crossed back to the Sandman's territory and walked around to the motel office. It was a young man behind the desk tonight. He nodded and began looking for a key to a vacant room. I quickly told him I wasn't a customer.

"I know her," he said in answer to my question about Doll.

"She lives in which apartment?"

"You want apartment nine, sir."

I took out my wallet and extracted two dollar bills. It felt strange tipping someone for information, unreal as the movies. But he accepted the money as easily as real life.

The loud rock music was, in fact, coming from Apartment 9. It stopped a few moments after I knocked on the door.

"Who is it?" A male voice.

"Is Doll there, please?"

I heard a bolt slide back. The door opened and blue light spilled out into the parking lot. A tall blond boy, about seventeen years old, with reddish circles under his blue eyes and wearing jeans but nothing else, not even socks, smiled at me. He took a drunken swig out of a bottle of Bud, hiccuped, and shifted his weight clumsily from foot to foot. "He's in the shower. My name is Jim."

"My name is Fernando. I'm looking for a girl named Doll?"

He raised his eyebrows. He was very skinny, his ribs visible, his stomach full of beer so that it protruded like a toddler's after his bedtime bottle. He could have been a basketball player, but his voice sounded too effeminate. "I'm afraid you've got the wrong apartment, Fernando."

"They told me nine at the office." I heard the shower turned off in the bathroom. "Who does live here, by the way?"

"Ray does."

"Ray . . . ?"

"Montoya."

"Of course."

"Do you want to come in, Fernando?"

"Sure. Thanks, Jim."

He smiled, and hiccuped again. "Would you like a beer or something?"

"No thanks."

The bathroom door was unlocked. "Jimmy, you okay?" Montoya called. "You get rid of your hiccups, baby?"

"Ray, there's a guy here. He's looking for a girl named . . ." The boy turned to me. "What did you say her name was, Fernando?"

[148]

"Doll."

"Her name is Doll."

There was no reply from the bathroom. Montoya came around the corner with a white towel around his waist. There was a chromed .32 automatic in his hand. He was a dark, very muscular man, handsome, with his wet hair combed straight back. He held the towel up with his left hand while his right moved the gun from my face to my heart to my belly as he examined me. "What you want?"

"I'm looking for Doll."

"You go eat shit. Who are you?"

"Fernando O'Neal. All I want is—"

"You're the priest, right?"

"Yes."

He laughed. "What's the matter? The whore has you by the *cojones*? Too bad. She went back to Mexico."

"When?"

"Couple days ago. So long, priest."

"Not true," I said. "I was with her last night. Where is she?"

He shook his gun at my face. "Priest, don't tell me bullshit. She left today. Few hours ago. Look around. See? She went to Mexico."

I could see he was stoned on more than Bud. And he was clearly anxious to get back to his little party. I backed out of the door. "Where in Mexico?"

"Juarez. Shut the door, Jimmy."

"Sure, Ray." The kid smiled at me again, a stuffed animal's smile. He shut the door. I stood there trying to think of what to do next. Suddenly the drapes were pulled aside in the window. Montoya pressed himself against the glass. He tapped it with his gun. He had dropped the towel and he was naked, the steam from the bathroom giving him a weird ghostly look in the blue interior.

I turned and walked away as fast as I could. When I

got back to the Mustang, I found a note under my windshield wiper.

> No parking here if no guest!
> the manager

I folded the note and put it in my pocket. It made sense. More sense than anything I could remember having made for hours.

I drove back to the Interstate and headed for Cottonwood. It was one of those very bright clear nights in the desert. I could almost feel each star as it throbbed its light across the years. The stars felt as near as the tall mantislike lights outside the malls or the constellation of lights that was the *barrio*. I remembered one of the lines from "Ministration at the Time of Death"—the only one I had ever memorized. It had once struck me as a rather unfortunate translation into modern American: "That it may please you to grant him a place of refreshment and everlasting blessedness . . ." A place of refreshment? It made heaven sound like a hamburger stand. Was that where Aaron had gone, and Jamie? Or was that El Sol? This "oasis" I was crossing in my rented Mustang on the raised concrete slab of highway.

The lights were off when I pulled into the rectory driveway. I locked the garage and entered through the kitchen. The bottle of Beefeater gin was where I had left it on the Formica counter. I poured myself a glass of Jim Beam instead.

For an hour I sat in the living room and listened to FM stereo through earphones. I heard Blondie and Billy Joel and "Love Stinks" and Stevie Wonder. There was no doubt in my mind that I would never see Doll again. Why the hell had Nancy come back? I shut off the receiver and took the glass of bourbon down the hall to my study. The bedroom was dark, the door ajar. I ignored the bedroom. After undressing and shutting off the light, I lay down on the study floor and pulled the sleeping bag over me. I felt something, and turned toward the hallway.

Nancy stood framed in the door, wearing nothing at all. Her pretty breasts were just visible in the soft illumination from the streetlights. I lifted my glass and swallowed as the ice cubes knocked against my lip.

"Get out."

"The phone has been going crazy with reporters," she said. "And I can't just get out."

"Why can't you?"

"I don't want to. Are you drunk?"

"Yes."

"Why can't we talk, Fernando?"

"There's too much to say," I said. "And you don't want to start, do you?" I was telling myself not to lose my temper.

"I don't mind," she said. "You know, I was thinking. My father died when I was eleven. Your mother died when you were seven. That's probably why we're together."

"Are we?"

"Even when I was in Greece, I thought about you almost constantly."

"What does that mean?"

"It means I thought about you."

I swallowed more bourbon as she approached me. If only she was Doll, I told myself. I raised myself and found my arm encircling my wife's knees. I kissed the soft cushion inside her upper thigh. Nancy cried out at my cold lips on her warm skin.

Friday

17

THE SUN woke me early, streaming through the bedroom blinds. Nancy was curled in my arms, her hip against my crotch, holding my right arm. There was no wedding band on her left hand. I wondered what she had done with it.

I stood up and found my undershorts on the rug in a corner of the room. Her suitcase lay open, an unpacked chaos of sweaters and underwear, hair dryers and tampons at the foot of the bed. I stepped over it, went and took a piss, then stepped under the shower. Alternating blasts of hot and cold washed me.

She was still asleep after the shower, her face relaxed, slightly puffy. She had learned some new tricks while she had been away. Would I be able to keep from asking her the number of men she had fucked? Who had taught her the trick she had used so expertly a few hours earlier? Whose trick would she use next time? Nancy had always been a good lover. Now she was inspired, a technician. Should I send her lovers thank-you notes? Or should I kick her out? Before I incurred a new debt to some unknown man somewhere in California, or Crete. Forgiveness was no easy trick, it seemed.

I hadn't slept long enough; the bourbon had given me a rotten hangover.

I made a can of frozen limeade, a cup of coffee, and an English muffin. The boy had thrown the newspaper onto the driveway. I had to cross the front yard in my shorts to retrieve it. I wasn't ready to stare at my own face on the front page of the *Post-Examiner*. But there it was, under the banner headline "DRUG LAWYER SHOT DEAD." Obviously the *Post-Examiner* was no friend of Jamie Hillal.

My photograph was small, one of three faces arranged in a vertical row down the side of the half-page photo of the bloodstained Porsche with its door open. My face was wedged between Jamie's, on top, and Roger Pasetti's, below. It was the same photograph that had run in the paper next to the announcement of my appointment at Holy Innocents back in April 1979.

I sat in the kitchen reading three news stories over and over. Least interesting was the story about the facts of the murder. Except for listing me as the person who had discovered the body (instead of Munty), it was an accurate account. Far more intriguing was the article on Jamie Hillal's career. There I learned, among other things, that Hillal had been divorced once; that he had won a national prize as a debater as an undergraduate at the state university; that he had edited the law review in graduate school; that he had been indicted twice by federal grand juries but never convicted.

The most interesting article, by far, was the one under the headline "FBI GIVES EL SOL ULTIMATUM." Roger Pasetti had, thanks to a U.S. judge's order, taken full control of Jamie's office. In an interview on the doorstep, he had told the reporter that Jamie's murder was part of a "huge conspiracy." He linked "underworld figures" with some of the city's "leading citizens." The FBI had been investigating "white-collar investment" in crime, including narcotics and vice, for fifteen months, Pasetti said. Hillal was one of the focal points of the investigation. Apparently Hillal had extensive files—including the Garza tapes—

that Pasetti was now going to examine. Against the wishes of the Hillal family, the reporter noted. But Pasetti claimed the search was necessary to find Jamie's killer.

"What we have in this city are businessmen, doctors, lawyers, leaders from every part of the community, who have been corrupted. Some of these men have been black-mailed into giving money to the underworld. Others have invested for fabulous profits. Still others have become involved for a variety of personal motives."

Pasetti was giving people three weeks to turn state's evidence. Or else he was going to start the federal-indictment process rolling and let the chips fall where they might.

It was an astonishing ultimatum. What exactly was the nature of this "conspiracy" that had corrupted the El Sol establishment? Who were these "underworld" criminals? Did "leaders from every part of the community" mean priests too? If I was going to be indicted for receiving "fabulous profits," where was my money? Pasetti's charges were absurdly general, yet the newspaper was billing them as the last word in tough talk.

The telephone rang at 7:20 A.M. It was a reporter named Sarah Nelson from Channel 10. She wanted to meet me as soon as possible. Could she come out to the house with a crew? I told her no. I would be working all day at the church. She could call my secretary after 8:30 about an appointment.

"Come on, Reverend, you have to be joking? An appointment is not what I need. I want your account of finding Hillal's body. What were you doing at his office last night? Was it this Committee to stop Joe Moore?"

I hung up on her. Nancy stood in the doorway, blinking, dressed in her old silk Japanese robe. "Who was that?"

"A reporter from Channel 10."

"Oh, Sarah Nelson. She's nice."

"How do you know?"

"I talked to her at least six times last night. The nasty one is called Barlow or Beerlow. He's from the newspaper. He called four times. And there was a detective who called twice."

"You didn't tell me this last night."

"Yes, I sort of did." She turned from the stove to take the milk out of the fridge for her coffee. "You were drunk, you said."

"I sat listening to music for about an hour with the earphones. I wonder if anyone called then."

She nodded. "It did ring once after you came home. Sarah Nelson again. I lied for you. Actually, I figured you were drunk and it could wait until this morning—"

The phone rang. I looked at Nancy and she shrugged, but picked it off the wall and said, "Hello? Oh, hi. Sure, I know."

For several minutes she stood there saying "sure" or "no, that's his decision" or "I'll try, okay?" until she finally hung up.

"Who was that?"

"Sarah. She's very upset about her job. She needs it. Her car is about to fall apart. One of her kids needs remedial-reading classes. She needs this story to help her keep her job. She would really like an exclusive with you. So far nobody else has got you. I'm supposed to explain to you how important it is that you talk to her."

"I can't believe this. How self-centered is this bitch?"

"Self-centered, maybe," Nancy said, sitting down at the table with her coffee. "But why 'bitch'?"

"I've got a hangover."

"No reason to start getting sexist."

"How self-centered is this *woman*, okay?"

"That's fine. Now, tell me, what's this all about? Who

is Jamie Hillal? Did you get hurt or what? And where were you all night? Sarah told me Hillal was shot before eight. You didn't get home until close to one."

"Midnight."

"Midnight or one, what's the difference? Were you out drinking or something?"

"This is unbelievable. You go away for almost a year. Then you come back, and less than twenty-four hours later, you're nagging me like a shrew housewife. I don't have to tell you where I was last night."

"Well, I think you're drinking too much. I saw the bottles out in the garage. And who was stuck answering the telephone here all night?"

"Nobody asked you to answer the telephone."

"Maybe not, but I did. And I deserve a few answers." She brushed her blond hair back out of her eyes. Light green eyes, they had been the first thing I had ever noticed about her. "We are still married, you know. We aren't divorced."

"What?" I jumped to my feet. I was about to slam my fist on the counter—she was asking for marriage as usual after her ten-month fling?—when the phone rang.

"You're out of your fucking mind." I picked up the phone. "Hello?"

"Father O'Neal? This is Barbara Anderson. I was just reading about you in my newspaper."

"Yes, Barbara. How are you?"

"Fine. But I was reminded by your picture that you were supposed to get back to me this week. I think I have been more than patient. Have you seen this Mexican girl again?"

"As a matter of fact, I was just about to call you. I tried to locate the girl last . . . yesterday. I was unable to find her. Someone told me that she has gone back to Mexico."

"Who told you that?"

"A man who lived in her apartment building. Actually, I'm still looking for her."

"You told her about the three hundred I was willing to pay for the briefcase?"

"Yes."

"And she just went back to Mexico without bothering to collect three hundred dollars? I find that hard to believe."

"I know."

"What do you think happened?"

"I have no idea. I am going to be talking to some people this afternoon who might be able to help."

"You mean the police? Was this girl involved with the Hillal thing?"

"Not exactly. Listen, I'm afraid I'll have to call you back, Barbara. It's frantic around here this morning. Reporters, everything. I'm sorry."

I hung up and turned to watch Nancy stride out of the kitchen. Someone had just rung the front doorbell.

The telephone rang again.

"Father O'Neal, this is David Snow."

"Professor, how are you?"

"Most unhappy and concerned with what I read in this morning's newspaper, Father. Were you on the scene of this murder last night?"

"No, I came just afterward."

"What do you think happened?"

"Well, Professor, I really don't know."

"Someone cut down the Arab. That much is apparent. But I think you and I must put our heads together very soon. Can we say this afternoon at—"

Nancy was standing in the doorway, looking urgent.

"Uh, I'm very sorry, Professor. I don't think I have the time this afternoon. Why don't I call you later, though?" I hung up. "Who is it?" I whispered to Nancy. Even as

[160]

I did so, the phone rang again. She started to speak, but I turned my back on her and angrily spoke into the receiver. "Yes, who is this?"

"Is this Fernando O'Neal?" demanded a familiar voice.

"Of course it is. Who are you?"

"Leo Mulcahy. Father, you undoubtedly know I'm a candidate in next Tuesday's election."

"Yes, of course."

"I've been reading the morning paper here. You found this dope lawyer's body, didn't you? That gives you quite a bit of prominence locally."

"What?"

"Everybody is going to see your picture in today's paper, that's what I mean. Now, you and I haven't met. But I would very much like to sit down and talk with you, Father. In the meantime, my campaign is getting a full-page ad together for the *Post-Examiner* starting Saturday. It's going to run through election morning. We want as many names of respected local leaders—I emphasize the word 'respected' in your case, Father—as possible. If you could authorize me to use your name, I would be—"

"Excuse me, Colonel Mulcahy, but I really don't know if I can endorse you as a political candidate."

"Father, we already have fourteen local ministers, priests, and rabbis for the ad. I know the Pope just said something about Roman Catholic priests running for office. As a Catholic myself, I agree with him. But nobody said an Episcopalian can't endorse a candidate for mayor if he—"

"It's not that. It's your policies I'm not sure I can endorse."

"My policies? Sure, I can fill you in on them. Number one on my agenda, once elected, is to clean up the corruption in this city. Under Castillo, El Sol has been turning into a cesspool, excuse the language, from top to bottom. We have got a criminal conspiracy in this town; narcotics, hookers, murders in the streets."

"What is your current stand on Propositions 3 and 8?"

"Yes on both. We're going to turn this city into the shining capital of the entire Southwest. Let's get the illegal Mexicans back on their own side of the Border and let big industry move in here. We'll have an international airport as big as O'Hare in less than ten years. You'll see the school system swell from maybe four hundred teachers to—"

"I'm sorry. I can't support you. I'm on the Committee to Save El Sol, and—"

"What? Wait a second. Were you at that meeting over in the Mission yesterday?"

"Yes."

"You and Anderson and Hillal and this wetback priest Ortega on that committee. Father, what's with you?"

"Nothing is 'with me,' Mulcahy. It's a question of wanting to stop two disastrous propositions."

"Do you know anything about progress, Father?"

"I know Ronald Reagan made a fortune talking about it on TV."

"You mean to say you don't believe in progress?"

"I'm a cleric, Mulcahy. There's no place in the Old or New Testament where God is defined as progress."

"What's your God's name, Karl Marx? There are too many preachers like you in this country, O'Neal. It's no wonder we're going atheist. You think the Bible gives you the right to preach communism and abortion from every street corner—"

I hung up on him. Nancy was back in the kitchen with a very worried look on her face.

"Who is it?"

"Detective Dorfman."

"Shit. Did you offer him coffee?"

"He said no."

I walked out to the living room, wishing I was wearing more than just my blue undershorts, and Dorfman stood up from the sofa. The small, balding detective wore a loud plaid jacket over double-knit trousers, and a pink shirt open at the collar. "I hope you don't mind my coming out so early, Father?" He was staring at the way I was dressed—or undressed, actually.

"That's fine. I think I should put some clothes on before we talk."

"No, don't bother. If your wife doesn't mind, I don't. I only have a couple of questions. It *is* hot this morning, isn't it?"

"Yes. Why don't we sit down?" I gestured toward the sofa and the chairs grouped around the coffee table and we took places facing one another.

"Do you own a gun, Father?"

"No." I gulped. "There are no guns in this house."

"You're sure?"

"I've never owned a gun in my life. I don't even know how to shoot a gun."

"Were you in the armed forces?"

"No. I was given an exemption because of my theological studies."

"You didn't think of becoming a chaplain or anything?"

"No. There's only a limited demand for chaplains in the armed services."

Dorfman nodded and crossed his legs. His tongue shot out and licked across the bottom of his neat mustache. "Tell me what happened last night when you discovered Hillal."

I told him the entire story.

"Are you sure you didn't arrive at the parking lot five or six minutes before you found the body?"

"Of course I'm sure."

"Maybe you just sat in the car for a few minutes to collect your thoughts. Or there was something you wrote down. Or even something on the radio."

"No. I parked and went straight to the front of the building. Just like I told you."

"We have a record of what time Dr. Munty called us. And we know what time the first police cruiser arrived on the scene. You say you arrived moments before the first police. But we have gotten a report that puts a red Mustang in that parking lot a good six minutes earlier. I'm trying to see how these facts fit together. With time, there's always a few discrepancies. All I want is to get a decent idea of how it happened."

"I've told you the truth. The best I can remember it."

He stared at me with no sympathy. "I'm sure you have."

"What was this report you just mentioned?"

"Just a report. By the way, you left County Hospital last night and took a taxi back to Hillal's office. Our officer there saw you talking to DEA agent Havas, right?"

"Yes."

"I was upstairs at that time. And you drove away again?"

"Right."

"But you weren't at home at eleven last night when I called here. Nor at eleven-thirty. I spoke to your wife. She wasn't sure when you might get home. Where did you go, Father?"

"I was looking for a friend."

"Yes. Where does your friend live?"

"She used to live . . . It doesn't matter, she's left town now. I found out last night that she has gone back to Mexico."

"She went back to Mexico, Father?" His eyes rolled slightly as he said "she" and "Mexico."

"Yes."

"Can you give me her name?"

"I'd rather not. I know what you're thinking . . ."

"What's that, Father?"

"You seem to think I killed Hillal. But that's total insanity."

"Father, I got a report on your car yesterday. It said that it took someone fifteen minutes to take off the Fairmont's steering wheel, mess with the lock, and put the thing back on again. And *he* was a pretty good mechanic."

"So?"

"So you told us the other night that you weren't in the Rainbow Club for very long."

"I was there for about an hour. I told you that."

"Have you ever worked on cars, Father? I'll bet you—"

"Never in my life."

"Who was your friend who went to Mexico?"

"Okay. Her name was Doll, her stage name. She danced out at the Rainbow."

"You mean you weren't just there out of curiosity the other evening, like you said?"

"No. I went there to talk to her. Okay?"

"Father, it's your life. I'm no judge. Not even a priest. Just a cop doing my job. But what the hell were you doing with someone who calls herself Doll and who dances at a topless club over on the East Side?"

"She was involved with one of my congregation. I was trying to help her."

"Wait a second here." Dorfman's eyes hardened into two black darts. "Was she Aaron Anderson's mistress?"

"Yes."

"We've been trying to trace that girl since Monday. You knew where she was? I could have you indicted on a felony charge for withholding evidence in a murder case."

"I know I made a mistake," I said. "But—"

"Let me ask you again," Dorfman interrupted. "Are

[165]

you sure you didn't faint or something after you pulled into the lot at Hillal's last night?"

I began to wonder myself. "No, whoever made that report got the times wrong," I told him. "I was only there for a minute before the first police car arrived."

"Father, if that's your story, unfortunately, it makes you a prime suspect in the murder of Jamie Hillal. I'm not going to charge you with anything at this point. But I am going to ask you not to leave the city."

"Tell me who made this report. Who saw me in the lot five minutes early, so they claim?"

He stood up and shook his head. "I cannot tell you anything. I have to get back downtown. Don't bother to show me out."

"What if I do want to go out of town for any reason?"

"You call me first."

I didn't know what to say, so I said nothing. After he had shut the door behind him, I turned to face Nancy. She had been eavesdropping from the kitchen. Her arms were clutching her rib cage in a way they did only when she was very nervous. Her skin was pale and I saw panic flicker in her green eyes.

"What's wrong?" I asked. "Is it getting to you too? They actually think I might have murdered this man. Yesterday the FBI accused me of killing Aaron, practically. It's insane. Maybe I'm dreaming."

"Why did you lie about the gun?"

"What do you mean?" I asked. "What gun?"

"The gun we found in Colorado. It was a thirty-something-or-other, you said. Up in the attic wrapped in that greasy rag."

Then I did remember finding it. "Yes, okay. I forgot about that gun. But it was never *ours*. We left it in Colorado."

"No we didn't."

"Sure we did."

"No."

"I never packed it."

"Well, I did," she said. "In one of those boxes full of yard stuff."

"Those are in the garage. But you never told me you packed it."

"I thought I did tell you," Nancy said. She shrugged and walked back into the kitchen.

I passed her on my way to the garage. Thirty minutes later, the boxes lay empty on the concrete floor. Nozzles, twine, various shears and trowels, dozens of seed packets, were strewn across the garage. But the gun was nowhere to be found.

She was sitting at the kitchen table, the newspaper open to Ann Landers' column, when I came back into the room. "Did you find it?" she asked.

"No."

"Maybe I didn't pack it. I don't know."

"What?" I was furious.

She looked up at me, then turned back to the page of printed advice. Minutes passed. The phone rang and I let it go on five, six, seven times. It stopped.

"What did you do with your wedding ring?" I asked her.

She didn't answer, nor look up. After a minute I saw her eyes were filling with tears again. Suddenly she stood up and cried, "Who is Doll, anyway?" She stormed out of the room, and a second later she slammed the bedroom door.

18

THE SUN was an orange coal burning the oxygen out of the sky. It stung my face through the open car window, and it was barely nine o'clock in the morning. Not knowing what else I could do, I had left Nancy sulking in the bedroom. Left for work.

I was driving on Desert Hills Avenue, about midway between the rectory and my office at Holy Innocents, when a tan Datsun pulled up on my left. It began blowing its horn wildly. I looked over and saw the driver staring at me through his closed passenger window. Unlike me, he had his air conditioning working this morning. He had reddish leathery skin on his face and unkempt silver hair, and a pair of clip-on drugstore sunglasses riding the bridge of his nose. Did I know him? He was waving at me to pull off the highway.

I shook my head in bafflement. He leaned over and started yanking down the glass window. We were both driving close to fifty miles an hour side by side down the highway in moderate traffic. As he worked down the window, his Datsun swerved over a foot in my direction and I quickly pulled the wheel of the Mustang out of his way.

"Father O'Neal, it's me."

"Professor Snow?"

He nodded vigorously. The sunglasses had completely fooled me. "Pull over, Father. I have to talk to you."

I looked down the road and saw McDonald's coming up on the right. I had already been blatantly rude to Snow once that morning. "Okay," I shouted at him in the next lane. "Just up here."

Snow went past McDonald's after I had turned off, then turned right into the lot in front of Food City and came back to park beside me. "I just missed you at your house. Your wife said she didn't know where you were bound for. But I guessed you would be heading in this general direction."

I nodded. "Sorry I had to hang up on you this morning. It's been a hell of a morning."

"Shall we go inside and talk?" He nodded at the brick franchise, its yellow arches shaped like the letter M, its exposed "beams" serving no function. There was a kiddie playground, empty. Inside there was nobody except the uniformed helpers at this hour of the morning.

"We could talk in my office," I suggested.

"We've stopped now. Why not talk here, if you don't mind?"

I shook my head and got out of the Mustang. Several minutes later, we were seated on uncomfortable molded chairs, facing each other over Formica and plastic coffeecups.

David Snow was extremely upset by the news of Jamie Hillal's death, which he had read in that morning's newspaper. His hands were shaking as he said, "I hope you don't think me a shameless slanderer, Father. I am not the kind of person to go around shouting boo in the dark. I was mistaken about the Arab, that is most evident now."

"Yes, it is."

"Hillal was quite correct."

"How do you mean?"

"About Joe Moore, I'm afraid. Let me ask you something. Did the police make you promise not to reveal the manner in which Attlee's body was found dead?"

I stared down into my coffee. Why did he still want to know about Attlee's body? "Yes, I did promise the police not to discuss it."

He nodded. "I thought so. You see, I know quite a few local police officers here in the city. After all, I go back a long time in El Sol. I know that Attlee's heart was partially removed from his body."

I brought my eyes up to meet his. His gaze was steady now, but full of anxious intensity.

"I see."

"I am appalled, Father. By the way, I believe my telephone is being bugged. Have you noticed any strange mechanical noises on yours in the past few days?"

I shook my head. "No. Why would they tap our phones?"

"I think this man Joe Moore has managed to call upon several powerful constituencies. Tribes, if you will. One, my informants tell me, is the Mafia. The other are local . . . call them primitives, I suppose. Tribesmen of Aztlan. Chicanos. Whatever."

"Mafia? Chicanos? What exactly do you mean, Professor?"

"Let me tell you the implications. First, none of us on Aaron Anderson's committee are safe. Our lives are in extreme danger. Did you read my Aztlan book?"

"Yes," I lied. Snow was leaving me no room for polite evasion this morning.

"Then you read my account of the Aztec human sacrifices. Of the victims bent over the stone and the priests who could pluck out hearts as easily as opening up a pomegranate. Do you remember my description of the Yopi rites? Yopi was the god of spring, also known as a god with three distinct personalities: Totec, Xipe, and Tlatlauhguitezcatl. Didn't it strike you how close this was to the Christian Trinity, Father?"

"Not exactly . . ."

"Of course not exactly. This is Aztlan, not Rome. Not the Holy Land of Asia Minor. But the parallel has struck many in the past."

"These human sacrifices are so alien to the Christian faith. Perhaps that's why it didn't—"

"Do you think so?" Snow asked. "What about the communion of flesh and blood? And Christ's death and resurrection? The doctrine of transubstantiation itself?"

"I'm not a Roman Catholic, Professor. I see what you're saying, but I still don't . . ."

He shook his head sadly. "No, you can't, I suppose, see it when you are so firmly a part of your own cultural tradition. A priest."

"Yes," I said. Yes what?

"The Aztecs, of course, believed in multiple creations. The world would be created, then destroyed, then reborn. Over and over. Quetzalcoatl went down to the underworld to recreate the final generation, called the Fifth Sun. The great sun god gathered all the bones of previous humanities and splashed his own blood on them, bringing them to new life. Thus did God's blood recreate mankind. God's sacrifice."

I listened to Snow's lecture on the Aztec religion with my eyes averted, watching two young counter girls stare out at the deserted parking lot with bored expressions, too bored to even gossip. I had to listen to Snow but wished I didn't. He was clearly upset, and these deaths had triggered something in his memory—the violent Aztec rituals—that had to be conveyed to someone. Someone like me, I guessed.

"Human sacrifices were the Aztecs' way of repaying and replenishing their gods. You see, like Christ, the Aztec gods had human blood in their veins. This blood carried the magic substance of life. Thus the importance of the human heart. Do you see why Attlee's death strikes me as religious rather than simply a mutilation?"

"Are you saying that people still practice these bloody rituals? Don't tell me, Snow, there are still Aztecs around here plucking out hearts like pomegranates or something?"

"But of course there are Aztecs. And Toltecs. And Zapotecs. And many other tribes. Mexico is full of the descendants of the ancient tribes, some almost pure-blooded. Now they have been reduced to the worst poverty, to the status of slaves. But still they must be respected—and feared."

I didn't know what to say to him. Had Moore ties to the Mafia, as Snow claimed? Had the Mafia employed "tribesmen of Aztlan"—local Mexicans, I guess that was what Snow meant—to kill Aaron, Johnny Attlee, and Jamie Hillal? Apparently that was Snow's belief, underneath all the references to Yopis and Tapotecs, the unfamiliar names of his life's scholarly pursuits.

"What do you think we should do?" I asked him gently.

"Father, I went looking for you this morning because I felt I had to warn you. El Sol is not your native ground. You are, forgive me, a relative orphan here. An outsider. Why don't you leave for a while? I think your life is in grave danger."

"Why exactly do you think that, Snow?"

"The pattern is clear. Those who have died already. Those who will have to die next, if this pattern persists."

"One attempt was already made on my life this week."

"Really? How?" he asked with great interest.

"My car was broken into and the brake lines were cut. It was quite a terrifying chase while it lasted."

"Chase?"

"Yes." I didn't elaborate for him, although he waited for me to continue. "What about you, Professor? Isn't your life in grave danger too?"

"Yes, yes, it is. And I treasure my life in this city. I

have never been so happy as in these past years, as in these most recent months, in fact. But where would I go? Like the young Aztecs who willingly allowed themselves to be roasted alive over the flames in honor of the goddess Chihuacoatl, I must accept my fate here. Can you understand?"

"No. You're advising me to leave, but you say you can't go, even though your life is also in danger. I don't understand that."

"Go away until the election is over. Then return after Moore has either lost or won."

"That's probably good advice," I said. "I wish I could take it. Unfortunately, I've got a parish here that expects me to perform my duties as their rector. And I don't know where I'd go anyway."

Snow removed his sunglasses and wiped his eyes with the side of his hand. He looked rather miserable. I hadn't understood how much he cared for me. His warning seemed motivated by genuine concern, perhaps a little eccentric, but heartfelt and not without a germ of truth.

"I'm sorry," Snow said. "I suppose you think I am just a crazy old man."

"Not at all. Thank you for your concern."

"You have impressed me a great deal, Father. I hope you will be very careful. El Sol needs men of your caliber in its ranks. Our tribe is growing, and despite men like Joe Moore, I think we will survive all this."

"I'm sure we will." I stood up and put out my hand. Snow took it and we shook, looking into each other's eyes. I had the feeling that something had passed between us, a chapter had closed, without my full understanding. I thought it had a lot to do with the difference in our ages—and the distance each of us felt in our minds between that blazing hot morning and the moment of our deaths. I was sure it was a long way off, while Snow might have been holding the moment right in his very palm. He was an old man.

"I must go," he said. "I wanted to stop by the post office before the line gets too long. A new shipment of books, you know. Why is it they never deliver these things when one is at home to receive them? I'm sick of these pink slips from the post office."

I laughed and held the door open for him. Outside we shook hands once more between our cars. He went around and climbed in his Datsun. I got behind the wheel of the rented Mustang and continued on down to the church then, pushing Snow's warning as far out of my consciousness as it would go. That wasn't all that far.

Maggie had been waiting for me at Holy Innocents, the front page of the *Post-Examiner* spread open before her. I looked from Maggie to my own image, minuscule and upside-down on the newsprint, and took the handful of telephone messages she offered me without a word.

There were calls from Sarah Nelson, from Fred Brandon of the *Post-Examiner*, and from Elwood Munty, who wanted to know if I would meet him at the Sheraton for lunch. There was also a call from Joe Moore. The message he had dictated said he was extremely disturbed by Jamie Hillal's murder. He understood that Hillal was going to be buried on Saturday afternoon. (Was that the Arab way, I wondered, to hold the burial within forty-eight hours?) Could I spare an hour after the funeral to talk to him?

I threw all the messages into the wastepaper basket. With my head supported on my open hands, I stared down at the varnished top of my desk and wondered how the hell I was ever going to write a sermon by next Sunday. What would I preach on? The telephone rang, and without thinking, I picked it up. It was Paul Havas, the DEA agent, wanting to know if I could meet him in forty-five minutes in front of the fountain inside Rio Oro

Mall. He had seen the newspaper this morning. How was I feeling?

I told him Dorfman had been at my house early. I was feeling so-so. Yes, I could meet him at the mall. We hung up and I immediately told Maggie I was leaving and got out of there as fast as I could. I didn't want to talk to Sarah Nelson, Fred Brandon, Elwood Munty. Or, God forbid, Joe Moore himself.

Rio Oro had been the premier mall in the city. A Z-shaped arrangement of department and national chain stores, five restaurants, a bowling alley, a cinema, and a discotheque, Rio Oro was now marooned in a sea of empty parking lot. Last year's mall was not a pretty sight: the covered arcade was almost devoid of shoppers, the air languid with Muzak and silence. Rio Oro had been eclipsed by the new Rambler Mall, three miles farther east on the Interstate.

Havas stood waiting for me in a light gray suit, a blue broadcloth shirt, polished wing tips, with a copy of *Forbes* magazine rolled under his arm.

"Are you going undercover to bust some Wall Street addicts?" I asked him.

"Listen, ten years ago this would have been *Ramparts*. Now it's *Forbes*. Times may change, but everybody's still got to have an image."

We went into Farmer John's Ice Cream Barnyard for coffee. It was Havas' choice. At that hour, the place was empty. We sat in a booth under a mural of dancing sheep and Little Bo Peep. Havas had said "coffee" but asked for tea from the waitress. He smiled apologetically. "Coffee is not good for my ulcer."

"They have good ice cream here."

"Ice cream makes me fat." He slapped his flat belly. "I'm already fat. My wife is a true Greek. She pours olive oil on everything she cooks, even my Wheaties."

"Really?"

[175]

"Almost. I don't eat Wheaties. You want me to straighten your head out?"

"It could use something."

"You've got to remember that Roger Pasetti is a lunatic."

"You think Pasetti killed Jamie?" I asked incredulously.

His face darkened. "No, all he did was bug his office. I wish I knew who killed Jamie. I intend to find out."

I nodded.

"Pasetti is a psychopathic liar."

"Oh?"

"Sure. A lot of agents are psychopathic liars. The same way beat cops get flat feet. As for his conspiracy, this ultimatum, that's bullshit."

"But he couldn't just make up a statement like that if there wasn't some truth in—"

"Don't be silly. He's up for career review next month. Roger's angling for a post down in Florida. He's got one daughter left at home and she's dating a Mexican boy. He wants out of here. Pasetti is trying to pull off a bluff, catch a couple of tax cheaters or something. Washington is hot for white-collar crime this year. And Roger has had a slow three years in El Sol."

"Are you sure?"

Havas laughed. "Listen, the mob earned roughly a hundred and fifty billion dollars last year. That's more than anybody except maybe the oil companies. Do they need white-collar investors to lend them money to buy drugs? Don't be crazy. Roger's got it all backwards. They need people willing to take the money off their hands. He is so stupid I can hardly believe it. Can you picture some big mob *barone* asking a little honky doctor here in El Sol to lend him ten thousand bucks so he can finance a run down to Colombia?"

Our waitress arrived with my coffee and Havas' orange pekoe. She made a big production of wiping the table, calling us "dearies" and asking us to promise that everything was perfect before she would leave us alone.

"Don't worry about Dorfman too much," Havas said when she was gone. "The mayor is pouring heat on him to catch this killer."

"Who do you think the killer is?"

Havas almost choked with amusement. He reached over and punched my shoulder. "You ought to be on TV. I haven't the faintest idea."

"I'm sorry."

His smile disappeared as suddenly as it had arrived. "Don't apologize. Listen, I'm just like you. Except my job has more security than yours. Working for the government is more secure than being a priest. But I'm no hero. Plenty of agents are action junkies. I hate to go undercover myself. Think about it. If someone I'm trying to hustle when I'm undercover sells me some bad dope, I'm really stuck. I have to shoot his knees or something because he burned me. That's how these punks work. If the dope was really bad, I have to shoot him in the head. So then I will look very convincing to the bosses, to the next dealer who replaces him. That's part of my job. Unfortunately some dealers don't always let you shoot them in the knees without a little argument."

"I can imagine."

If I was crazy, then Havas was insane. A lean giant with curly black hair cut straight above his heavy eyebrows, he was not what he appeared. He wanted to talk: he loved to hear himself talk. He told me about his wife. Her name was Anna. He had flown back to his grandparents' village on the island of Chios to find her. She had come with a dowry of twelve sheep, thirty-two olive trees, and seven acres.

"Basically I'm nothing but a peasant," he said. "I grew up in Queens. My uncle had a fish store there. Back in Greece, all my family were fishermen. It's in my blood.

You can't escape your blood, Fernando. How come you're half a spic anyway? And you've got two Catholic names but you're some kind of Episcopalian."

That was how he worked: interrogating by trade, by talking as much as he could, and then hitting you with a question here, there, in quick jabs. It was far more sophisticated than what either Dorfman or Pasetti had used on me. I told him about my parents. About growing up as the "half-spic" son of the local Connecticut priest/Don Juan. I realized that he considered himself a modern Odysseus, the crafty one. Havas wanted to be both a simple Greek peasant from the islands and the ultraslick James Bond from New York City. He knew when I didn't want to answer his questions. He asked me about Nancy several times. About Doll.

He kept coming back to Doll.

I told him about Aaron's fear that the water was running out under the desert. "He was goddamn right," Havas agreed. "Joe Moore is looking for fast bucks. Not the long haul. He'll be developing the Kalahari Desert when the water runs out here."

I told him there was a Pointer Report—and an appendix that had the truth about that water under the desert. I believed in this, I said, because Aaron had.

"Anderson was about as straight as they get down on this Border," Havas said, as if he were the best judge of such matters. "That's not exactly straight."

"I think Aaron had found a copy of that report with the appendix. I think he was shot for it. And I think Jamie was shot because of that report, too."

"Doll was bringing it to him in the briefcase last night, is that it?"

"Yes. Jamie knew her boss at the Rainbow. He knew this Montoya. I guess he was her pimp."

"Raul Montoya is a sick piece of work," Havas said.

"Is he big in drugs?"

"Big. Not the biggest."

"He's gay," I said.

"I know. Isn't that sweet? I hate Montoya."

"Is there any chance you can get your agency to look for Doll across the Border?"

"Difficult." He looked away for a while, out the window at the empty arcade, at the Zale's across the way, the Florsheim next door. "It's almost impossible. She may be dead. If she is, it would be easier than trying to pry her out of the back of some Gomez whorehouse."

"Montoya said she went down to Juarez."

"You believe Ray Montoya?"

"I guess not."

"There's another possibility, isn't there?" he asked.

"What?"

"You were actually late for your meeting last night. Maybe, before you arrived, Doll and Jamie were waiting upstairs. Maybe he had to leave. He left the briefcase up there."

"That would make Munty a liar."

"Yes. But there's another possibility, too. I've been thinking about that open passenger door on the right side of the Porsche. I keep seeing Doll jumping out of that door as someone blew slugs into Jamie's side of the car. I see her running. I don't see her suddenly coming back to pick up the briefcase in that situation."

"Assuming she was in the car when Jamie was shot."

"Yes."

"The briefcase wasn't in the Porsche, though."

"It might be in Hillal's office," Havas said. "Unfortunately the office is Pasetti's at the moment. He'll be messing around up there, knee-deep in paper, reams of Xerox copies, sending it all back to the Bureau, understanding nothing. He's liable to get the Government sued for a few million bucks this way. I hope so. The stupid prick doesn't deserve Florida."

"What about Aaron's ticket to Denver? I told you that I gave it to Jamie yesterday afternoon. Could you see if it was found on his body? If not, it might mean he left it with the other things. Upstairs in his office perhaps."

"I'm wondering how to get old Roger to invite me upstairs. Maybe it's worth calling Washington for some pressure. Tell me something," he said. "Are you in this for revenge or something?"

"It's not revenge."

"Well, for me it is. Jamie was a good friend. And you don't strike me as someone who is going to settle down in El Sol for the rest of your life. I don't mean to belittle your conscience. But this city was Aaron Anderson's whole life. And El Sol was Jamie's turf. What is this place to you?"

"Okay. There's something else besides my conscience involved, you're right."

He took a sip of tea. The grin was slow to reveal his teeth, but once it was there, it wouldn't leave. "Is she a good dancer, Fernando?"

"Yes."

"You don't love this Doll?" Havas asked. "Don't tell me that."

"I don't think so," I said. "I don't think I said that."

He nodded and called for the check.

19

LATER THAT afternoon I sat at my desk in Holy Innocents waiting for Havas to call me. I wanted him to have found Doll. Or, at the very least, found out if the police or FBI had Aaron's airplane ticket. But Havas never called.

Plenty of others did call.

Elwood Munty was downtown at the Sheraton and wanted me to come have a drink with him. I asked why. He said it wasn't a telephone-type conversation, but had I been visited by the police? When I said yes, he cursed. The police thought he had killed Jamie, he said. He insisted that I come down to the hotel immediately. He was sloppier drunk than usual. I would try to make it, I said, and hung up. I promised myself not to go within a mile of the Sheraton.

I thought Munty was too far gone to be dangerous. Still, I didn't like the fact that he had been inside Jamie's office when the shooting took place. If I wasn't familiar with Hillal's waiting room myself (it was windowless), I would never have believed Munty didn't see the murderer. But I thought an alcoholic Munty and the security-tight Hillal building added up to an improbable fact: his story was true.

Every reporter who called wanted answers to the same questions. I managed to dodge most of these and keep my cool. The police, I lied, had asked me not to give interviews. No, it was not true that I had been sitting next to Hillal when he was shot. Yes, I was on the committee fighting Moore's Propositions. No, I wasn't a Mexican national. Good-bye.

Lindy called to ask if I would see her. Fifteen minutes later, Barbara Anderson's half-sister sat on the gray chair opposite mine in the office. She had her long chalky hair tied up in a twist and she wore a sleeveless pink frock. About a dozen gold chains hung from her arched neck. I wondered why, in such heat, she would want to lug all that around. Especially when the rest of her appearance was designed for the desert. It wasn't vanity, I guessed. The gold made her feel more secure about herself—and she was quite nervous.

"How is your sister, Lindy?" I asked, not wanting to pressure her about what was bothering her.

"Oh, she's okay. I guess." She looked confused. Then she blurted, "The thing is, I want to get married."

"Congratulations." It was only weeks since she had returned to El Sol after her divorce from the Chicago dentist. "Who is the lucky man?"

She blushed. "That's the problem. I need your advice. Opinion, really."

"Of course."

"I love him, Fernando. But he's my half-nephew. Not only that, he's over ten years younger than I am."

"You want my opinion on what, exactly?"

"I'm thirty-seven years old. Roy's only twenty-five."

"I can't believe you're thirty-seven, Lindy." I could not believe she wanted to marry Roy. I was stunned.

"Don't flatter me . . ."

"It's true," I lied.

"But what is . . . the official church position?"

"On older women marrying younger men? I suppose our official position is that it's wonderful. You're divorced, and if you were Roman, you'd have a problem getting married in church. As an Episcopalian, there's no problem. No problem at all." I smiled, trying hard not to bite my tongue. I could talk such lies.

"I meant about an aunt marrying her half-nephew? I know first cousins aren't supposed to marry. But Barbara is only my half-sister."

I nodded with understanding. There was no point in searching my memory for the correct answer. I knew it wasn't there. "Lindy, don't worry," I said. In fact, Roy struck me as someone to worry about.

"You mean it's not considered incestuous?"

I shook my head. "Your mother was Roy's grand-mother, but that's not incestuous. In your case, the church would have no reservations about marriage."

Why was I telling her this? It was undoubtedly my duty to contact my bishop and ask for the Episcopal Church's position on a half-aunt marrying her half-nephew. But I couldn't stand Bishop Fred Pelpy. I had never once called Bishop Pelpy for his opinion on anything. I certainly wasn't going to start now. Especially since I truly liked this woman. Lindy was lost. But so was Roy, from what I gathered. Two lost souls . . .

See how they run.

That wasn't the way the nursery rhyme went. But it didn't matter. "I hope you two will be very happy."

"We are, Fernando, we're really happy. And now that you've said this is all right, I know . . ." She couldn't finish; she was overcome for the moment.

I handed her the Kleenex box. "When do you think you'll have the ceremony?"

"Soon," she said. "Roy wants it soon. I do too."

I nodded agreement. If it was incestuous, it was the incest of two people related by loneliness, not blood. One ex-con and one ex-wife. Two blank futures: two blind mice.

See how they run.

That was the rhyme. Almost.

"Roy was thinking of flying up to Reno to get married," she said after blowing her nose. "That way we could honeymoon in San Francisco. I've always wanted to ride a cable car. Don't you think that would be nice?"

I nodded. "It sounds like a great plan." And it got me off the hook of having to give them a church wedding. That was one hook. A few minutes later, having said good night to Maggie and walked Lindy out to her car, I climbed into the red Mustang. I drove off in the direction of a much larger hook.

Home is where the heart is. Occasionally.

Since I had left her in tears that morning, I was prepared to find Nancy in a rage when I arrived at the rectory. Or gone off again.

I found her in an apron in the kitchen, the Julia Child book open on the counter, measuring spoons and wooden chopping boards, paper towels and small piles of flour strewn everywhere, the entire room enveloped in a cloud of fantastic bouquet.

"It smells tremendous," I said. "What is it?"

"Veal Prince Orloff."

"Not that one?" I put my hands on her shoulders. She leaned back against me, arching her shoulders. "That's the one we used to laugh about. It's impossible."

"Just typical," she said. "It's about five recipes disguised as one."

"Where did you buy the veal?"

"Gonzales cut me a roast. There's white wine in the fridge."

"I'm going to have a bourbon." I was bending down to the cupboard as I spoke.

"I thought you would. But look in the freezer first, please."

"Okay." I straightened and crossed the room, opened the freezer door. "Don't tell me. A bottle of aquavit."

"Just like old times, remember?" Nancy said. "Would you pour me one?"

We had discovered aquavit in the pages of *The New Yorker* when we were first in St. Louis. Somehow, drinking it had seemed to light up those first dark nights of pastoral assistantship, far from New York City, far from sophistication as we thought we knew it.

"Yes, of course." I got down two shot glasses out of the cabinet. "Any more detectives come visiting? How about the press?"

"Sarah Nelson wanted to come for dinner. She was really desperate and there wasn't much I could do."

I put down the bottle of aquavit on the counter. "Nancy, don't tell me you invited her . . ."

"No. I didn't. There was nothing I could do except tell her, basically, to fuck off."

I lifted the bottle again. Nancy had not been so agreeable in years. "That's wonderful."

"By the way, I flushed my dope down the john. So don't worry about that anymore, okay?"

"Thank you." What was this? It was difficult to adjust to this new Nancy.

"Fernando?"

"Yes?"

"Can you explain to me what is going on? I was so uptight this afternoon, I just had to get out of this house. That's when I decided to cook this meal. You don't have to tell me right now. I know you're tired. But maybe after dinner?"

"Yes, of course I can tell you. At least I can tell you what I know. That's pretty limited."

"Could you kiss me?" she asked. She had turned sideways and was holding a wooden spoon.

I crossed the kitchen and we embraced. After a moment, I set the aquavit on the counter and she threw the spoon aside. Her breasts pressed against my body. The kiss grew, and so did my erection. Nancy's mouth tasted like raw carrots and wine. She broke the kiss. I thought she wanted to get back to the meal. Instead she went down on her knees on the linoleum. She looked up at me, and I smiled, embarrassed, as she brushed her cheek against the front of my trousers. I played with her hair, so blond, as the muscles in my legs began to shiver. She unzipped me slowly, teasing with the back of her fingers as she lowered the tab. Then she took out my cock and covered it with her mouth. I had to hold on to her head for balance as she began to caress me. Her technique was unlike anything she had ever demonstrated before. Just as I came, she threw her head back, stroked up and down with her fist, and let the semen fall on her lips and cheeks. That was one part I didn't fancy, unfortunately. The man who had taught her this trick had to be a fan of porno movies. In the XXX-rated films I had seen, orgasms always spurted in front of the camera. It bothered me to watch these filmed images of *coitus interruptus*: I found them far from erotic. But I guessed they were meant to prove there was no simulation. In my own kitchen, with my wife, the technique's effect was reversed. I felt pleasure dwindle beneath a rush of suspicion. Who was simulating here? And why?

Nevertheless, I embraced her when she rose. She reached behind me for a paper towel with which she cleaned her face. Then she hugged me again, ground herself against my crotch, and said, "You can pay me back later."

"With pleasure."

"I can't wait."

"Neither can I."

"Why don't you get out of here so I can get this meal on the table?"

"Aye, aye." I zipped up, picked up my aquavit, and left the kitchen. After turning on the TV, I sat down on the couch and put my feet on the coffee table. Next to my feet was a book. It was David Snow's *The Aztlan Empire*. I leafed through its 450-odd pages. In the center, there were about fifteen pages of illustrations: photographs of boring desert locations and, in contrast, some highly colorful drawings of the Aztec gods. These were almost like Cubist paintings.

"Where did you get Snow's book?" I called to Nancy.

"He gave it to me today. Wasn't that nice of him? Oh, I forgot to tell you. He stopped by here this morning."

"I know."

"He was looking for you. The poor man was very upset. These murders are too much for him. He's afraid for his life, I think."

"Did you look at his book yet?" I asked. "It's very interesting. About the Chicanos on the Border, and their ancestors."

"I want to read it."

"Poor Snow is kind of hard to take sometimes. He talks incessantly and he uses ten-dollar words where fifty-cent ones would do. But I think he's basically one of the more interesting people I've met in this city."

"Oh, definitely, Fernando."

I turned on the TV then. It was just time for Walter Cronkite with his report on Vernon Jordan. In the middle, I got a chance to watch Joe Moore's latest commercial. It was a montage of film: empty desert, bustling factories, a helicopter shot of dingy downtown El Sol, a spectacular helicopter shot of skyscrapers flashing gold as the sun rose over New York, then another shot of empty desert. "This is our future," said the anonymous voice. "Think about it." The camera lingered on the sheer emptiness as gradually the images of factories and skyscrapers emerged out of the picture like magic, superimposed over the brown flats and the distant line of barren hills. "Vote Yes on Proposition 8."

I was fairly high on aquavit by the time we sat down at the dinner table. The veal roast was stuffed with so much rich filling, it almost made me dizzy to eat it. Nancy claimed she couldn't taste a bite. (She always said she could not taste her own cooking.) She had bought a Wente Chardonnay and it was fairly good. It was hard to find excellent wine in El Sol.

I told her about the committee, about Jamie and Doll. She asked a lot of questions. I answered most of them truthfully, too drunk to lie very convincingly. As I talked, I felt Doll's image growing more distant. Until now, I had been holding her in my mind as a kind of protection against whatever Nancy might decide to do next. Even if she was almost a fantasy, Doll was strong enough to keep me from feeling as if I was at Nancy's mercy.

Midway through the dishes, I took Nancy down the hall and into the bedroom. The booze was roaring in my ears. I had a picture in my mind and wanted to make it come true. I wanted to open her legs, to pull open her sex until her clitoris left its hiding place, to lick her until she forced me to stop. I wanted to show Nancy a new technique: one husbands had been showing their wives for centuries. Without simulation. . . .

We were on the bed. The bedroom was dark except for the light from outside. I had Nancy's legs spread wide, her knees in the air. My head was bent low as she held open the folds of her vagina. "Hold it open," I had told her. She was whimpering with pleasure when I noticed the light change in the room. Something had passed between the window and the streetlights.

I did not move, but lifted my eyes, left toward the window. I saw a hideous orange face, and the glass exploded. Nancy screamed. There was a second shot. I pulled her off the bed by her leg, onto the floor. We crawled around until we were wedged between the mattresses and the closet door as the shots blasted along the fragile wallboard just above my outstretched legs.

It stopped. I heard running footsteps. I leaped up and crossed to the window. There was nothing to see but the opposite house across nine yards of Astroturf and white gravel. The light went on in my neighbor's bedroom.

By the time I got the front door open, I realized the footsteps had gone across the backyard, over to the next street. No point in following. I was naked, drunk, and had no weapon. Nancy suddenly ran into the living room and stared at me with her eyes panicked, wide open, frozen.

"Are you okay?"

She was shaking her head from side to side, her mouth trying to scream itself rid of the silence. Staring at me as if I was an orange mask. Her head kept going back and forth, side to side.

Nancy wasn't hit. I was. I saw a thin trail of blood across the rug leading from the hallway to where I stood on top of some red footprints. I touched my back, my ass, looking for it. Then my left hand discovered the wide abrasion across the back of my left thigh, sopping wet, just beginning to burn now.

Saturday

20

WE HAD no sleep Friday night. Soon after the police arrived, the reporters came and set up aluminum floodlights in the front yard. The house blazed with white light, phosphorescent, so that we all looked like photo negatives, like zombies. It seemed the entire neighborhood was outside in their bathrobes, along with the video cameras and the flashing red lights.

Dorfman took pity on Nancy and had the ambulance back into our garage. That way we avoided the cameras for the ride down to County Hospital. I sat and covered my face with my hands. This was a nightmare that was real. I was in a kind of shock.

The doctor was about forty-five years old, stout, with a brown goatee and circular plastic glasses, cherry-red glasses. He cleaned and bandaged my thigh, calling the wound a "graze." This brought back memories of cowboy movies I had watched when I was a kid. I asked him, "Could you call this a flesh wound?"

"Like in the movies?" He saw my point. "Sure, call it a flesh wound. Do you want some Valium, like your wife?"

"No, thanks. I drink too much. You don't have a shot of bourbon?" My headache was becoming monumental.

He shook his head. "Sorry. All we've got is some California brandy. I've got to save that."

Dorfman met with us in an empty office outside the

main area with those hanging green sheets. He already had the story. But he was angry. Angry that the bullets they had found embedded in our mattress were .22-caliber, not .32, like the bullets that killed Jamie, or .38's, like the ones that had killed Aaron. "If this is the same guy, he's real smart," Dorfman grumbled. "A different goddamn weapon every time."

It seemed to me Dorfman was furious, above all, that he had not foreseen this attempted murder somehow. He was a weird kind of perfectionist, this cop. We kept going over the orange mask in the window. Was it a mask or a face? A ski mask? A bloated face? One of those Halloween masks? Maybe pantyhose stretched over the head?

Every time I answered with the truth (It was too dark and too fast to see exactly), Dorfman got nastier. If you see something, you *see* it. Or don't you? He threatened to take me down to headquarters and have me hypnotized. I told him my lawyer would sue him and the city for millions. Amused, he said, "It's so convenient the way you don't see things, Father. You can't account for your whereabouts the night Anderson was shot. You appear at the scene seconds after Hillal's murder, but you see nothing. Now you and your old . . . your wife are shot at five times in your own bed. You can't give me a single bit of decent evidence."

"You've been talking to Pasetti or something," I said. "I was at home the night Aaron was shot, and that's the truth. I just finished telling you, for the sixtieth time, it was an orange mask."

"How did you manage to make this so damn frustrating?" Dorfman asked. "It's unbelievable."

"Are you accusing me of hiring someone to shoot at me in my own bedroom?"

Dorfman stared at me with surprise. "Sarcasm doesn't suit your situation, Father."

"Why not?"

"You're in a very tough spot."

"What spot is that?"

"I wish I knew."

"For once, I agree with you," I said.

A few minutes later, another detective came in with the news that the press had followed us and were now set up out in the waiting area of the emergency room. I was beginning to feel at home there, and that was not a good feeling.

"Do you feel like facing the cameras?" Dorfman asked.

I thought Nancy was going to faint. She sagged on her feet and reached out to take my arm for support. "Please. I can't do that. Please, Fernando?"

I looked at Dorfman and raised my eyebrows. He turned to the detective and said, "Pull a car around back. Tell the press we're taking the O'Neals into protective custody for the night. No interviews."

The detective nodded and left. "Thanks," I said.

"I could lock you both up over at headquarters. You want to go home? Or a motel maybe?"

"A motel sounds good," I said immediately.

"Any preferences?"

"Someplace with plenty of locks on the door. I don't think Nancy is ready for an encore."

"We'll have two men outside your room tonight. Compliments of the city budget."

"I paid my taxes." Suddenly I didn't think Dorfman really believed I was a suspect anymore. "You won't give our address out?"

He shook his head. "I want you both to get some sleep. Maybe your memory will improve in the morning. By the way, you haven't heard from your friend the dancer since we last spoke, have you?"

"No."

"Too bad."

We ended up checking into the Cactus Inn several miles north on the Interstate. Our room was on the second level; the window facing the walkway was covered with thick drapes. A uniformed cop brought a chair up from the pool area and sat down right outside the door. Nancy didn't undress but lay down on the sheet, a limp Valium doll. I lay beside her, gradually drifting into a trance where half-dreams kept jumping up on the edge of my consciousness. I felt more afraid than at any time since I was a little kid. When the bullets had stopped, and missed, then the fear took over in earnest.

Half-dreams are usually nightmares. It was like trying to sleep in a cheap shooting gallery that night. Bells kept clanging, gunshots exploded in my nerves, masks dropped in and out of sight, little orange candles flickered in bullet-scarred windows. A miserable few hours. I tried to talk to Nancy, but she could only shake her head. I wondered if she was going catatonic. I wondered if she had taken LSD with Flipper. She rolled over into fetal position after two hours flat on her back staring at the ceiling. I wondered if I was lucky to be alive.

Who was trying to kill me?

About seven o'clock, exhausted, I rose, opened the door, and asked the cop if he would mind getting me a copy of the morning newspaper. He took my dollar and came back ten minutes later with the paper and two containers of coffee. I said Nancy was still sleeping so he should drink hers. I thanked him.

I spread the paper on the floor and sat down on the rug. They had scooped out the center of the front page and inserted the briefest of stories, under the large headline "KILLER WOUNDS PRIEST" in red letters. There was a blurred photo of Nancy's profile in the back of the cruiser that took us from the hospital to the motel. It was an extra edition.

What did the El Sol *Post-Examiner* mean by "killer"?

He had missed me? The 250 words of hastily written text did not explain. Typical El Sol journalism. The newspaper was actually nothing more than a vehicle to carry coupons to the bargain-searchers. Or so it often seemed.

I sat and read the rest of the Saturday, May 31, edition. There was a long article on Jamie Hillal with the sub-head "Robin Hood or Rogue?" An editorial praised FBI Agent Roger Pasetti's "vow to clean up the bad apples at the top of the city barrel." But it cautioned people not to conclude El Sol was a "bin of corruption" like so many other American cities. As for national news that Saturday, the paper featured articles like "Lava Dome Rises in Mt. St. Helens" and "Gay Prom Couple in Mass.," as well as the news that the president was "concerned" over the big drop in the economic index for April.

Soon it would be time to head for home. How would Nancy handle that? I wanted her to sleep for as long as she could first. Someone knocked on the door. She stirred but did not wake. I thought it was the cop, and opened it.

"I'm so sorry about this," Joe Moore said.

21

HE WAS dressed for a game of golf. He wore pressed yellow cotton slacks, a knit shirt that read "Silverado" over the pocket, and white patent-leather loafers. Every single one of his rusty-blond hairs was in place, razor-cut, blown dry. But his overweight quarterback's face looked worried: there were dark crescents under his small blue eyes. The sight of him stunned me. "Sorry for what?" I asked.

"Disturbing you at this early hour."

"How did you find us here?"

"May I come inside?"

"No. My wife is asleep."

"I had to talk to you, Father."

"Fernando."

"Sorry. I had to talk to you today, Fernando. Hillal's funeral has been postponed, of course. So we couldn't meet there. The motel switchboard refused to put through my calls, on police orders. I thought I had better drive down here—"

"Jamie's funeral was postponed?"

"Yes. Dorfman wouldn't let the coroner return the body after all. Something about the gun or the size of the bullets, I'm not clear on that point yet."

As he spoke, I examined him even more closely. I knew Moore's age from the newspaper: thirty-four years old. He was a "boy genius" in the world of real estate. But there was an aura about him that seemed at least sixty years old. His body was soft, layered with those cushions of extra flesh you find only on certain American male bodies. It seems that different nationalities, and different classes, have their own unique ways of growing fat. No amount of golf would ever make Joe Moore trim again. The skin beneath his chin hung slack and red, like a much older man's. He needed hard exercise, but that was unlikely. He was too busy, of course. The oddest thing about him was the way his mouth stayed so tight, so guarded, when he wasn't speaking. It was the mouth of a man who used words the way a shark used teeth.

It didn't matter that Moore's voice could sound extremely humble or friendly: his words came out sharp as razors. All slanted back at his own gullet—for ripping.

"When will the funeral be now?"

"Nobody knows. It's up to Dorfman," he said. "You and your wife are lucky."

"I beg your pardon?"

"You could both be dead now," he said, adding, "Why don't we go for a ride?"

"A ride?"

"We have just got to talk. Do you know, I think people are trying to discredit me by shooting at you."

"What?"

"They must be crazy to do it," continued Moore.

"Are you crazy?" I demanded. "Those were real bullets they picked out of my mattress. Do you think the guy who shot them did it to *discredit* you?"

"I have so much to lose. I don't think you understand how much, Fernando."

"You must be out of your mind, Moore. You want me to feel sorry for you? Screw you."

He stared at me, working that tight mouth over his fixed jaw, wondering what approach to run at me next. "There's no need to curse, Father."

"What exactly do you want?" How had he managed to send away the police officer outside my door?

"I want to show you something fantastic. And I want to offer you some help."

"Why do I need your help?"

"You could use protection. I am willing to hire bodyguards to protect you and your wife."

"Bodyguards?"

"Please, Fernando? My car is just down there in the lot."

Surprisingly, I found myself considering his offer. Nancy was asleep. The motel room was making me very restless. Was Moore the key to these murders, as Jamie had believed? If so, was he crazy enough to try to have me shot one moment, and then come to call on me the next? What did he want to show me? I was more intrigued than suspicious—but I was exhausted and my judgment was certainly suspect. "Okay," I said. "But let's make it quick. My wife is very upset after last night."

"I can certainly understand. Are you ready right now?"

I nodded and shut the door. I followed him down the balcony to the outdoor stairs, down to the parking lot. I was taking a big risk.

The middle-aged Mexican chauffeur got out and held open the rear door of the Rolls-Royce Silver Cloud for us. Moore didn't have his chauffeur dress in a uniform, just jeans and a western-style shirt. It was equally pretentious, I thought, to pretend your chauffeur wasn't your servant. This servant never smiled.

The bronze-colored leather crackled under me as I sat down on the comfortable backseat. The car was very cold. The air conditioning was turned up full blast. There was a white telephone set into the side of the compartment, and in front of us was a walnut shelf and a bar holding polished silver flasks and a bottle of juice in a silver ice bucket. Moore asked if I wanted anything to drink.

"How about a vodka and orange juice? I have it squeezed fresh every morning."

"Why not?" I said. "This is quite a car."

"The finest automobile in the world." The way he said it, caressing each syllable as if he was reading an advertisement, reminded me of the last time I had seen Nancy's brother. He was a lawyer in Philadelphia and "into" French wines so heavily that you couldn't find a place to hang your coat in his apartment. Every closet was full of wine racks. Her brother "collected" wines, but I don't think he enjoyed drinking them. One night he actually lectured us on the correct way to swallow wine. Joe Moore's Rolls-Royce was like Nancy's brother's wines, on a far grander scale.

We took the Interstate north into the desert. On our way, we passed Cottonwood's exit, and on through newer and newer developments. The newer they were, the less I liked them. The drink tasted very good with the fresh orange juice, and the alcohol was reviving me for the moment.

Turning the desert into a garden spot was easy. First they came in with road-building equipment and laid down a network of asphalt lanes. Then they put up brand-new street signs on every corner. People could drive around and find their dream homes on real streets, undisturbed by the reality of how it was all going to actually look.

After the signs were up, with their great-sounding names—"Overlook Mountain Road" or "Eagle Drive"— the developer would construct two model homes: Type A and Type B. He'd hire a designer to fill them with beautiful furniture, and landscape the yards to the hilt. Once he'd taken orders for a third of the sites, he'd start bringing across crews of Mexican day laborers. They were good workers but they would be rushed into putting up a new house every ten days. A "custom" house because the buyer got to pay extra for his garbage compactor, his

[201]

wall-to-wall carpets, his gas-fired barbecue. He also chose the "style elements" of his house: New Mexico adobe, Texas ranch, California Tudor. Finally, he had his choice of fill on his front yard: white gravel, black volcanic stone, Bermuda grass, or Astroturf. By the time it was all over, the development was full of families in brand-new $59,989 homes. The neighborhood looked like it had been designed by a bunch of drunks with a building-supply catalog. Or a broken computer. Or five hundred average Americans and one unscrupulous land developer.

"I've had offers of four million just for my options out here," Moore said. "I've refused every offer."

"I thought the county owned this land." We were beyond the actual city limits now, beyond the last development. The desert ran as far as the eye could see: to the mountains, like a line of broken toys in the north, to the western mesa, to the horizon's edge in the east.

"The county and the Army, they own most of it. But I've got options to buy almost one hundred and fifty square miles. Can't buy if the county can't sell. That's what Proposition 3 is all about."

"You really want this land? What if there's not enough water in the ground to support half the people you want to bring down here?"

"There's no water shortage. I've drilled test wells. We hit water in at least five of them already. Sure I want this land. I'm not the only one who does. Ever hear of Harvest Incorporated? They're on the New York Exchange."

"No."

"They're a conglomerate out of Oklahoma City. Oil money that is being put into a lot of things like electronics, nursing homes, land. They offered me four million for my options. Do you know what my options cost me?"

"No."

"One hundred and seventy-five thousand dollars. And

that's against the purchase price. I could make over three-point-eight million by selling out to Harvest right now."

I knew from the sound of his voice that Moore would never sell out. He was trapped by his own particular vision of this wasteland. It wasn't profit anymore. That much was clear, and worth the ride. He was obsessed. His head went back on the leather and his eyes narrowed. He watched us approach the next exit. An exit that led nowhere as far as I could see.

"Harvest wants this land so badly," he said, " I think they've cooked up a strategy to get us both out of their way."

"Both?"

"You environmentalists who want to stop Proposition 3. And me. They killed Aaron and Jamie. And they tried to kill you."

"Have you told this to the police?"

"Yes, but they just laughed. I've got no evidence yet."

"Look, theories are fine. But it's a fact that everyone on the committee has received hate mail because of some of your TV commercials. Any nut could have decided to shoot us."

"Hate mail? I've received dozens of vicious letters since this started. Aaron's ads on TV aren't so sweet either. But these killings are really hurting me."

"Hardly as much as they hurt Aaron."

"He's not suffering now. Half of this city thinks I'm a cold-blooded murderer." For a second, as he said this, Joe Moore looked like a young boy again. He really was a good actor, I thought. "Worse, there are some nuts out there who love me because of it. I'm starting to get mail thanking me for what happened to Aaron. That I don't need. We have to work together. I want to show you why."

The exit road ran under the Interstate and then shot

[203]

to the northwest. We drove for fifteen minutes before I saw anything like a building. In the meantime, I finished my drink and refused Moore's offer of a second. At one point, I got a glimpse of my own face in the chauffeur's mirror. I needed a shave badly and my eyes looked like red slits. I had on my collar and clerical shirt, donned to greet the police a few hours before. The shirt stuck to my skin and the collar was chafing my neck. I needed a long hot shower and a decent breakfast.

It was a large garage. In the middle of nowhere, gray cinder blocks and six aluminum double doors formed an architectural paradox right out of Magritte. Just sky, brown desert flats, and a huge garage. Was this Joe Moore's dream for El Sol?

The door rose, but the Mexican chauffeur did not drive inside. He shut off the motor of the Rolls. I noticed a cooler on the garage roof, and two larger pieces of equipment which I couldn't identify.

"Come on, Fernando."

I opened the Rolls door and climbed out. It was like being smothered, stepping out into that heat, way over one hundred degrees. At least the humidity was zero. It could hit one-thirty-five in this desert and it would still feel better than New York City at ninety degrees. I felt light-headed, and immediately wished I had not had the drink.

I followed Moore and the chauffeur into the shade of the garage. It was air-conditioned, almost empty. Only what looked like two free-standing closets. I noticed the steel doors, sliding doors. These were not closets, they were elevators.

"What's down there?" I asked.

Joe Moore just walked over and hit a button. The door slid open to reveal a bright tan interior. There was no Muzak, but otherwise we could have been in any skyscraper, any corporate headquarters where the elevators ran on time.

"Wait for us, Benny," Moore told his chauffeur. "Come on, Fernando."

I shook my head in disbelief but entered. "I thought you only had options out here. Is this an Army base?"

He laughed. "There are some parcels of land that were homesteaded years ago. They are still private. I bought seventy acres two years ago from a man in Modesto whose grandparents tried to raise goats here back in 1901."

I couldn't tell if it was a long trip down or a slow elevator. "How deep are we going?"

"Only seventy feet," he said. "But deep enough to withstand anything but a direct hit with a one-megaton nuclear warhead."

"Great. Are you expecting nuclear warheads? Don't tell me Harvest has the Bomb?"

"You laugh," Moore said. The elevator came to a gradual stop. "But you won't laugh when the Russians attack us."

The doors slid open. As they did, I could hardly believe I wasn't dreaming. "When's that going to be?"

"Anytime. But clearly before the turn of the century."

I was looking at the ocean from atop a cliff. Below me, slightly to my right, was a spectacular house built into the crest of the land. It was a modern house, redwood and glass. I could look right through the living room onto a terrace, at the ocean beyond. There were pines and cypress trees and lush grass. Bright flowers arranged in neat beds framed the back patio next to the swimming pool. There was a separate smaller pool for the Jacuzzi. The air was cool, in the high sixties. It carried an unmistakable salt tang. There was no breeze. Set among the blue-and-white corners of the painted ceiling were banks of powerful lights that almost matched—but not quite—the quality of sunshine.

The elevator door shut behind us. I said nothing. For the next fifteen minutes I followed Moore around on a room-by-room tour of the house, then the guest house built in one corner, then the murals, and finally back to the swimming pool. The furnishings were lavish, as if everything had come straight off the floor of Macy's and Sears and Neiman-Marcus. The main house had a living room, a den, and an "entertainment center" with a giant built-in TV screen and stereo controls poking out of the surface of the custom coffee table. The master bedroom had a sunken tub (as if the pool and the Jacuzzi were not enough), a fireplace, and a large area that was really another living room. In the kitchen, there was both a regular wall oven and a microwave oven, and an indoor barbecue with a hood to suck the smoke up and out of the room, the house, the whole underground complex.

"Look at this," Moore said. He picked up a fat plastic spigot covered with buttons that was on the end of a chrome hose, built into a recess in his giant refrigerator door. With his other hand he opened a cupboard and brought down a wineglass. "You've got your cold orange juice," he said, pressing a button so that the spigot poured orange juice into the glass. "And now your vodka." Another button pressed: a stream of clear liquid shot into the orange. "Here, drink it." He handed the glass to me.

"No, thank you," I said, refusing to take it. There was a kind of madness in the air.

Outside I ran my hands over the wall, over the blue-and-white paint of the mural depicting the ocean that rose until it became a mural depicting the sky. It was a sky with a ninety-degree bend where it became the ceiling about thirty-five feet overhead. What made this place so staggering, initially, was the vast scale, the mindless realism. The fact that they had sculptured the floor to slope like genuine landscape was enough to throw me. But the clumsy murals soon gave themselves away. They were awful. They had worked best just after the elevator door opened.

"We've got three feet of steel-reinforced concrete on all four sides of us," Moore said. "Between the ceiling and the concrete roof is the machinery: water pumps, air conditioning, et cetera. That ceiling is one-hundred-percent soundproof, as you can hear."

"What's the salt in the air?"

He laughed. "Good, you noticed. Sea salt in the humidifier. That was my own idea."

"But where are we supposed to be?"

He frowned. "You mean you don't recognize where you are?" He waved at the walls. "This is Carmel, right near Pebble Beach. The most beautiful piece of coastline in the world."

"I've never been there."

"Well, now you have."

I nodded. Was he serious? Of course he was, as serious as every piece of redwood furniture, every can of diet 7-Up in the place. "My wife and I come here for weekends," he told me. "Maybe you and your wife could join us one weekend soon?"

"I don't know . . ." Perhaps I had made a terrible mistake about him. Was he just obsessed, or a murderer too? This place defied all my logic.

He ignored me. "When we swim, I adjust the lights for our tans. If we want to get romantic, around cocktail hour, I can have the fog roll off the Pacific." He nodded at the wall where the flat blue crests of the "Pacific" climbed up to the false horizon.

"Do you see it?" he asked finally. The tour was over. We were sitting on redwood recliners beside the pool.

The total area, he'd told me, was two and three-quarters acres. I was wondering where he'd put all the sand, rattle-snakes, and black widows.

"You tell me, Joe."

"An underground world. A perfect city. Under the natural desert. Never too hot or too cold. Forget about pollution. We won't allow gasoline-powered engines. Everything can be run on electricity from our solar generators on the surface."

"Transportation?"

"Electric-powered mass transit. Like golf carts."

"Everybody can have his own hole?"

"No, it will be one large excavation. The ceiling can be supported with pillars disguised as trees, towers, different things. Think of the opportunities for artists."

"Wonderful."

"Solar power. No more nuclear accidents."

"One big bomb shelter?" I said. The man had convinced me, for the moment, that he was not a murderer.

"Hardly a bomb shelter. A desert community for the next century. The twenty-first-century equivalent of the Gila cliff dwellings. Able to shelter millions of people. Talk about natural? There's a tradition behind this."

"Why haven't you . . . ah . . . publicized this place?"

"It's fantastic, I know. But you have to see it. I'm afraid people would think I was nuts."

"What did it cost you?" I didn't really care. I was more concerned with another question. Who was murdering Aaron's committee?

"Twelve million. A lot of cash. You see what I have to lose if Proposition 3 doesn't pass?"

"What about Proposition 8? You can't tell the people down in the *barrio* that you plan on moving them to a big hole in the ground."

He smiled, losing his patience. He was getting tired of

[208]

my lack of enthusiasm. The shark was growing restless. "All I ask is that you make a statement, Fernando."

"Yes, what kind of statement?"

"That you met with me. And we talked amicably. That you respect me and are sure I had nothing to do with these unfortunate killings. As for Propositions 3 and 8, you can just say that you respect my sincerity. You don't have to give me a full endorsement."

"Why?"

"Why?" he said. "What do you mean?"

"Why all this?" I waved my hand at the murals and the house and the swimming pool. "Can you give me one good reason why we should start to live like rabbits, like moles?"

"Control. We can control our own destiny."

"What about the water supply?"

"Look, I'll build a pipeline up to Colorado, all the way to Alaska if there's any problem. Water is easy."

"Why is this necessary?"

"I've explained to you about solar power. A nuclear confrontation with the Soviets, maybe even China, is certain in the next—"

I shook my head and raised my hand. "Okay. Why should I make a statement for you, Joe?"

He stared into my eyes. The seconds ticked past. The faint humming of the air conditioning rattled the plastic grass, despite his "soundproofing." I broke the stare and looked up. There, on one side, was the sun. Yellow and false as the waves in the painted ocean. As much like the star that was burning the sand seventy feet above our heads as Joe Moore was like Aaron Anderson.

"Say one hundred and fifty thousand dollars, with an option to buy five square miles. That alone is worth millions."

"Never."

He shrugged. "I thought once you saw all this, once we talked, you would want to help."

"Help you, Joe?"

"Yes."

"Can we go back to the world now, please?"

22

THE ROLLS-ROYCE dropped me back at the motel. The whole way back, I kept thinking the polls had to be close. Otherwise he would never have offered me money. Joe Moore didn't like risks, he wanted sure things. But I could think of twelve million risks he had already put on the line. He didn't want to lose. He even repeated his offer to provide Nancy and me with bodyguards. But I told him I wanted no part of his protection. And thanked him for the ride.

Nancy was awake, in the shower when I entered the motel room. I sat down and waited. It was Saturday morning, and in twenty-four hours I would have to preach a sermon. What was I going to preach on?

Nancy came out wrapped in a skimpy motel towel. She looked tired and nervous, but sexy. "Where were you?"

I told her. I tried to describe Joe Moore's sunken vision out in the desert. There was no way I could do it justice. She thought I was talking about a large bomb shelter or something; she hadn't seen those murals, the orange-juice spigot, the sun.

"I'm starved," she said.

"Let's drive over to the Chuck Wagon." This old restaurant was an El Sol institution that served cowboy breakfasts: all the eggs and flapjacks and bacon and home fries and ham you could eat for practically nothing.

Orange juice came in pitchers that never seemed to get empty. Hot biscuits. Warm honey.

But I had forgotten the Chuck Wagon finished serving breakfast at ten o'clock. We had to drive back to Desert Hills Avenue. We passed the Cashway, Seven-Eleven, Taco Bell, K Mart, Exxon, Hobo Joe's, The Sizzler, Pizza Hut, Motel Six, Quality Inn, Long John Silver's Sea Food Shoppe, Wendy's, Texaco, two drive-in banks, Cottonwood Lanes, and Colonel Sander's before we reached Sambo's. Nancy had said she wanted their waffles. I had scrambled eggs and bacon. We both drank iced tea and put three quarters into the jukebox unit. Who knows why?

"I'm afraid to go back to that house," Nancy said. "I don't think I can handle it."

"Do you really want to move into the motel?"

"Don't you hate this city yet?"

"No, I don't hate it."

"You actually like this stinking place?"

"Maybe I do."

"You like being a big fish in a small pond, that's why."

"It's the desert I like, not the city."

"How can you like the desert?"

I thought about this until I recalled something Moore had just said. "Control," I told Nancy.

"Control? What do you mean?"

"There is none in the desert."

"There's nothing in the desert. And this is Stupidville. Everything between New York and California is Stupidville."

"I don't want to fight with you. If you hate it here, you should leave. I still don't know why you came back."

She didn't answer, just sat there staring at her finger as it traced some spilled water on the brown Formica. I was sure she didn't know why she had come back either.

When I stood up to pay the check, she stood too. She followed me out into the heat. I sat down in the Mustang and reached over to unlock her door.

"I have to start looking for a new car," I said to her. "By the way, what happened to your Rabbit?"

"It was hit. I don't know what happened. I was in Greece at the time."

"You left it with someone in California?"

"No, I took it to Greece with me on the airplane. What do you think?"

"It was insured. We can get it fixed."

"Why bother? It runs. I don't care what it looks like. It's just a car."

"The police could stop you for the broken taillight."

"They already have," she said. "You know what you are in this city?"

"What?"

"You are what you buy. Not what you think or what you do. You are what you buy."

"That's the whole country, Nancy."

"To hell with this country."

"What?"

"We're doomed."

"Joe Moore thinks so. Do you want to live in the ground?"

"I want to live someplace. You know what?"

"What?"

"I need lots of action."

We drove the rest of the way to the rectory in silence. Was she ever going to tell me about Crete? I wondered. I was not going to ask any questions. I was not going to set myself up.

After we arrived home, Nancy went straight out onto the back patio and put up the umbrella. I went in and took my shower, shaved, changed into fresh clothes. I looked through the window and saw she was reading a paperback gothic. She'd already read this one before, back in Colorado. Rereading a gothic seemed like the outskirts of despair to me.

I went into my study and sat back in my desk chair. I had to think of a sermon topic: that was my job. Usually I would look in the back of the prayer book, finding that Sunday's readings, and then evolve a commentary that would have to do with the news, or my own mood, or a parish event.

I wanted to preach on a miracle, I decided. I didn't need to look in the prayer book because I suddenly knew which miracle: Jesus walking on the water. There were descriptions of this in Matthew, Mark, and John. It was Matthew's account I needed.

But that was as far as I got: the story of Jesus walking on the water. I couldn't evolve any commentary beyond the story itself at that moment. I couldn't even think of what it was. My mind was too full of Jamie all of a sudden. Finally I picked up the telephone and called his house. When I got his father on the line, I said that I had been thinking of Jamie and his family. Could I possibly come by?

Robert Hillal said he would be happy to see me.

It was a deceptively simple house, surrounded by a thick wall of cypress and evergreen trees near the third fairway of the golf course. I looked at the beautiful grounds of the Cottonwood Country Club with a new kind of respect. All this belonged to one man. The man I was about to meet.

A soft-eyed Mexican maid led me through a house furnished with a far-from-simple taste: Persian carpets, rare woods, floors of luminous white marble. A table had been set under a bright green awning on the terrace overlooking the green fairway and an artificial pond. Robert Hillal sat at a table where the fine china and crystal contrasted vividly with a blackened pot full of what looked like stew. This turned out to be something called "laham mishwee": roast lamb with a mildly spicy sauce. He said his wife had cooked it that morning.

"I don't know how she did it," he said. "She is stricken with this death of her son. Here, you must eat with me."

"I've already eaten, actually," I said.

"But it's just one o'clock. Time for lunch. Have you eaten lunch?"

I had to admit that I had not, realizing that it would be an insult to continue refusing his food. He stood up and began to fill my plate.

At eighty-three, Robert Hillal was thin, darkly tanned, with a full head of silky white hair above an angular face. A face dominated by a large ridged nose and two light brown eyes that shone like amber, shone with sadness. He was a curious mixture of foreigner and native. He looked foreign and his taste, judging from a quick glance around his house, was far more sophisticated than the average native of El Sol. On the other hand, his voice had no trace of foreign accent. He was soft-spoken, but his voice carried that unmistakable border twang. Still, the words he spoke were far from commonplace.

He watched me eat with a slight smile on his face. I thought it wasn't me he was watching but his son's likeness, projected by his grief onto my face in that familiar place at his table. Jamie and I had been the same age. Robert Hillal insisted on refilling my glass with lemonade before I had taken three sips.

"Jamie spoke highly of you," he began. "I rarely leave this house since my stroke four years ago. One leg is useless, almost paralyzed. If I make mistakes with my speech, please correct me. I would have gone crazy in this house, with nothing but women, if my son had not told me everything. Thanks to him, I still feel alive in the world. I miss new faces. You have a generous face."

[215]

"Thank you."

"Do you like our city?"

"I like it more each day. At the same time, I don't know how much longer I can take all this . . ."

"I understand," he said. "I have read the newspapers. You and your wife are fortunate to have escaped."

"Yes."

"My son and Aaron Anderson were not so fortunate. Aaron was not my friend. He was, in some respects, my rival. But we respected one another."

"Of course."

"We both loved this city. And we had found a common enemy these last months, unfortunately."

"Joe Moore?"

He nodded. "El Sol is a small refuge in the middle of a great emptiness. I see no hope for man if he has forgotten the most basic needs of survival. Look at other cities: Phoenix, Los Angeles. You wonder if man is determined to destroy every trace of God left on the earth. Here we can still breathe the air, at least. In many cities today, the air gives you cancer."

"It's like an epidemic."

"Not 'like' but *is* an epidemic. In Europe, during the time of the Black Death, one in three died of the plague. Today the cancer deaths in America are approaching this. At least we can breathe in El Sol. For how long, I don't know."

"Aaron once was talking about the water in El Sol. He called it 'God's hospitality.' "

"Yes. Let this Joe Moore try to teach twenty million people to live without water."

"Do you think Joe Moore is responsible for Jamie's death?"

Hillal raised his hand and stroked the side of his chin with his fingers. I saw that, although he had shaved, there were patches of white on his face where his razor had missed. His amber eyes studied my face as he thought of his answer. He decided to answer with a question. "Do you?"

"I don't know. Joe Moore came to see me this morning. He took me out to his buried house, out there in the desert. Do you know about that?"

Hillal nodded, his eyes betraying nothing.

"It is incredible. I didn't know what to say. He must be at least half-nuts to have put all that money into that place. On the other hand, who knows?"

"What did he want from you?"

"A statement. He wanted me to tell people I thought he was a swell guy and sincere and that he'd never hurt a fly. He offered me a bribe. A lot of money."

"Yes, I'm sure he did. You didn't accept?"

"No. But the fact is that I have this strange feeling he's not lying completely. There is clearly a conspiracy taking place in this city that is responsible for killing your son, killing Aaron and Johnny Attlee. I believe that. I just can't figure it out. It's not logical. Why Johnny Attlee, for instance? Why Jamie? And, as he says, why would Moore involve himself when he is obviously the main suspect in these killings? He was Aaron's and your son's biggest enemy, and everybody knew it."

"Do you know what the FBI is doing?"

"You mean in Jamie's office?"

"My office too. Pasetti has a judge's order that is allowing him to sift through every paper, every contract, every letter in my business, my son's law practice. That is another conspiracy."

"It's terrible," I agreed.

"My lawyers have already agreed with the American Civil Liberties Union lawyers to sue the government. And this fool, Pasetti. This stupid FBI fool has no idea what goes on in this city. What he says is pure fiction. And you know, I think, that Jamie's office was bugged?"

"Yes, I was there when they found it last Tuesday."

"The government did not like my son. He was too smart for these public attorneys. And there is so much confusion in this country about a man who will defend criminals, drug smugglers. My son was a brilliant lawyer. Yet he was under constant surveillance, as if *he* was the criminal. America has forgotten how to live by its own laws. We have forgotten how to survive."

"You think the Government might have had something to do with Jamie's death?"

"My wife believes this. She sees them going through his papers, my papers, and what does she think? She hardly speaks English, my wife. She thinks in Arabic. In Arabic, this conspiracy seems clear to her. But I no longer think in any language but English. Even so, it is my own kind of English."

"Joe Moore seems to think—or claims to think—there is a company called Harvest Incorporated up in Oklahoma City that is after El Sol's desert land. Moore says they want to buy his options but he won't sell. And he claims they are killing people here to try and frame him. At the same time, they're getting rid of environmentalists who would oppose their development plans. Have you heard of Harvest?"

"I've heard of it," he said. "So that is Joe Moore's conspiracy? Harvest Incorporated. They are a powerful group. No doubt they could pick up Joe Moore and swallow him in one gulp if they tried. Are they trying? I don't know."

"If only I could find this copy of the Pointer Report. Aaron was sure it would convince people to vote against Moore's Propositions, once they saw exactly how precarious our water supply was here."

"Yes, Jamie told me about this Pointer Report which Anderson believed in. I'm afraid I can't tell you anything about it."

"I think I know who has a copy."

"Who?"

"This girl who called herself Doll."

"The dancer at Mirabi's?"

"Yes," I said. "But she's disappeared."

"Do you know where?"

"Across the Border, I was told."

"I can ask friends of mine," Hillal said. "I have friends on the other side of the river. I will ask them if they know where she is. Doll is her name?"

"La Muñequita is what they call her in Spanish, I think."

He nodded his head as if he were telling himself he must call his friends as soon as I left. I wondered if these "friends" were his old partners back in the days when he was smuggling whiskey across the river. Then he said, "I miss my son."

"I'm sure you must."

He shook his head impatiently. "You don't understand. Every bone aches with missing him. He was my life. Literally, since my stroke. I have a confession. You are a priest and I have to confess something to you."

I started to protest, "But I'm not—"

"I have obeyed God all my life, as best I could. But I do not understand how God can let me, an eighty-three-year-old man, live but take my young son just as he begins his life. All I want is to die. That is my confession. Of course, I will wait until God gives me death. But I am impatient now. I want to see my son again."

"You will," I said. My voice sounded full of confidence. Where did it come from? "But not too soon, I hope. Now, I think I really must be going. I have a sermon to write."

"Yes, of course. Before you go, let me tell you something. If you look for this conspiracy very hard, and still can't find it, you must begin to wonder if you aren't part of it. The more any man looks at himself, the more he doubts himself. If you want to find the conspiracy, don't look for it. Look for a man."

"Or a woman," I said without thinking.

"Yes, or a woman. Do you know where to look?"

I shook my head. He was staring very hard into my eyes now. There were flecks of green in his brown eyes. "Where?"

"Look for an open door, a window, an exit. Look for a man who is fleeing. There are many ways to flee, of course. Many different escapes."

"I understand." I was lying. I wanted to understand but could not. Robert Hillal was speaking incomprehensible words. Perhaps it was his stroke. Somehow I doubted it.

I rose to my feet. "Mr. Hillal, I want to say again how sorry I am about Jamie. I think, had he lived, we would have become very good friends. Thank you for this talk. And for a delicious lunch."

He did not rise, nor did he put his hand out to shake mine. He stared off at the green grass of the club, then abruptly swung his eyes back to fix me with a troubled stare. "Do not thank me," he said. "It was good to see a new face."

It was four P.M. and I had been in my study for thirty minutes since arriving home. The paper with its thin blue lines crossing the yellow lay empty on my desk. I had the Bible open to Matthew's Chapter 14: the account of Jesus walking on the Sea of Galilee.

Nancy knocked on the study door. "Can we talk?" she asked. She had changed into a pair of baggy white shorts and a green T-shirt.

"Of course."

Seated out in the living room on the opposite end of

the sofa, she brushed her blond hair out of her eyes and said, "Do you understand what happened last night?"

"Yes."

"We were almost killed."

"Yes."

"And you were actually shot! Are you sure you understand?"

"Of course."

"Then why the hell don't you act like you do?" She sat bolt upright on the couch, her face red, furious. Her fists were clenched in front of her and I had the feeling she wanted to pummel me.

"What do you mean? Calm down. You say you need lots of action? Then why can't you handle this? Wasn't last night exciting—or was it *too* exciting?" I was angry also, angry at the way she was glaring at me, the way she was acting.

"You're going to get yourself killed, aren't you? Just to prove you don't need me. Is that fair?"

"Nancy, that's nonsense."

"Is it? Why don't we just go away to Europe? Pack and drive to the airport and fly out of here."

"You already tried that. Why did you come back if all you want to do is repeat the performance?"

That did it. She shouted, "It's no damn performance!" Then threw herself at me, trying to rip my arms with her nails, to knee my balls. I held her off, just. After a moment, I turned her around and threw her back on the sofa while I retreated to the center of the room. I stood there staring down at her. "You know why you came back?" I said.

"Why, you asshole?"

"You came back to see if I still loved you," I said. "And you found out that I do."

She shut her mouth and her eyes blinked. Her arms

[221]

came up and folded themselves anxiously around her middle. She said nothing.

"You can't stand me loving you. You know you're bad. You have no doubt that you're worthless. Why else would your father have gone off and died, leaving you with your mother? You hate yourself. So anybody who loves you, they must be hateful. I love you and you want to destroy me for it. Thanks a lot."

"I love you," she said very softly.

"No, you don't."

"How can you say that?" She was starting to cry. "I do. I love you so much."

"You're engulfed in Nancy and nothing else. You don't love me. I can't blame you. I'm trying to."

"If you love me, why didn't you make love to me this morning? Why weren't you there when I woke up? Or you could have made love to me when we got home."

"But you just went out and read that book on the patio . . ."

"You didn't come out and get me."

"Sex is not enough, Nancy. And how do I feel after you've gone off and screwed half the Cretans on Crete or whoever taught you to make love like a porno star."

"You bastard." She stood up. "You are a bastard. Why am I crying for you? Why do I—?"

The telephone rang. It put her off, and she cursed. "I'll get it," I said.

"Damn you. I'm going. Don't be surprised if I never come back."

"I won't be surprised." She headed for the door, then remembered her purse and had to backtrack to the bedroom. I lifted the receiver in the kitchen.

"O'Neal? This is Havas."

"Hello."

"I have some news. I think it will make you happy."

"Tell me."

[222]

Nancy slammed the front door shut behind her. I guessed she would head for the Interstate in her Rabbit, drive for an hour, realize the next city was still two hundred miles away, turn around, and come back. As it turned out, my guess was almost accurate. All I missed was the bar she stopped in on her way home, the three double Scotches she consumed there. Plus the "assholes" who bothered her.

"We've located Doll," said Havas. "I put out a request. We got the answer back, from up in Vegas, this afternoon."

"Doll was nuts about Las Vegas."

"She's working out of the Atlantis Hotel. It's a medium-sized place, a block off the Strip."

"She's dancing?"

"No, she's a whore."

23

ON THE airplane, the day's last flight to Las Vegas, I tried to work on the sermon. Against my will, I felt excited by the prospect of seeing Doll. My memory kept supplying the images as I fought to concentrate on Saint Matthew's words.

This miracle was one of the most popular sermon topics, of course, and I had heard priests get carried away by overdramatic gusts of their own windy rhetoric as they tried to rise to its occasion:

It is night in Galilee. The disciples are in a boat, having been sent away by Jesus after his miraculous transformation of the loaves and fishes into supper for the multitudes. A great wind is stirring up the surface of the lake. The disciples spot something walking among the waves. They are terrified. A ghost? But Jesus calls out to them. Peter answers, "If it is really you, Lord, bring me out on the water beside you." Jesus tells Peter to come ahead.

The disciple steps out of the boat. Then he loses his nerve and begins to sink into the waves. He calls for Jesus to save him, and Jesus takes him by the hand, saying, "O thou of little faith, wherefore didst thou doubt?" As soon as Jesus and Peter are in the boat, the storm subsides. All the disciples join in proclaiming Jesus: "Of a truth thou art the Son of God."

But my mind kept throwing up images of Doll's body, thick nipples, strong thighs, her concave belly as she danced on stage at the Rainbow. She was nothing like Nancy. She was, I thought, quite possibly lethal. Yet she made my cock hard just thinking about her. How was I going to write a sermon?

It was sunset in Las Vegas. The 727 came down out of a sky full of royal and murderous colors, crossed the high desert basin on its final approach, then we saw a line of flickering yellow rhinestones below. The Strip.

As soon as the hatch was opened, the crashing din of slot machines filled the airplane. Row after row of slots stood up outside the arrival gate. I walked through the machines to a moving sidewalk in the main hallway. The faces of my fellow tourists were unreal. Everyone in the Las Vegas airport looked as if he'd just been stunned by a flashbulb.

The taped voices of Vegas comics jabbered one-liners out of speakers in the ceiling tiles, each voice fading, to be replaced, a few yards along, by the next would-be Berle or Rickles. It was exotic in a harebrained way. Like spending fifteen years as a coin changer in a penny arcade, the moving sidewalk was an unimaginable experience.

I took the taxi straight to the Hotel Atlantis. It was a slightly smaller version of the enormous Miami Beach-style hotels I passed on the Strip.

My room was large, semiluxurious, with many mirrors. White carpets covered the lounge area and, up three steps, the same white carpet had been sewn into a comforter over the king-size bed. The bathroom was standard, but reached via a dressing room with enough theftproof hangers to accommodate a Saudi harem. Did some people come to stay for weeks, months?

The view was disappointing, discouraged by curtains. When parted, they gave an enigmatic look at the parking lot through a scalloped screen of concrete. I turned on the TV. It was tuned to closed-circuit: a medium-famous

TV comic welcomed me to the hotel and offered to instruct me in "gaming" as practiced in the Atlantis. The tape came to an end, then began all over again. Looped, I could imagine losers sitting in their rooms, drunk, watching this over and over again.

I went downstairs to the bar and ordered a shrimp cocktail and a Jack Daniel's. The shrimp tasted like they had been frozen for twenty years: tasteless, rubbery. The bourbon tasted just great.

Wandering through the casino, it struck me as a logical extension of the airport. It was too bad the moving sidewalk couldn't run straight from the airplanes down through all the Strip hotels, and on through the near-miss hotels just off the Strip. At the black-jack table, I won twenty-five dollars very quickly. A girl at one of the craps tables caught my eye, even though I could only see her back. I strolled over; it wasn't Doll. I put a bet down anyway, a bet on something called "Pass." I was surprised when the shooter rolled and nothing happened to my bet. It took ten minutes before I lost my dollar chip. In the meantime, the excitement at the table had grown to hysteria. Men had won tall piles of fifty- and hundred-dollar chips. My single dollar sat there on "Pass," passed by all the shouting, the luck, the action.

A waitress brought me a complimentary bourbon while I stood there. After I lost the dollar, I returned to check the bar. Havas had told me to watch the bar nearest the tables. That was where you would find the hookers.

"Always?" I had asked.

"No, not always. You have to be subtle. The casino security have their eye on you. They want you to have a good time, but not too good. If there's a big convention in town, chances are the hookers won't be in plain sight anyway."

"What do I do then?"

He had explained several different options, should the whores not be on display.

In the Trident Bar overlooking the casino, along with the bald-headed gamblers, dour cowboys, and Arizona couples drinking Coco Lobos, sat three whores. Two blonds, one brunette. The blonds sat together, wore party dresses of lime polyester, their knees locked primly, handbags on their laps. At first glance, they looked pretty. A closer look: you could see all the work done to grab your first look. Makcup and hair frosting, they were prom-girl hookers. I watched a short, rotund man in a blue serge suit and heavy old-fashioned shoes, about seventy years old, go poke his large Cuban cigar in their faces. He bantered with them. They laughed and shook their heads, sipped their soda waters, and waved ta-ta when he'd finished trying to bargain them down.

The brunette sat alone at the bar, her back to the casino, hoping she looked like a Mystery. Her hair was very thick, falling down to the center of her back like a fur cape. She had painted her lips scarlet red, the fashion the year before, along with her nails. She stared hard at me. Depressing. I turned away. Did I really want to ask her if she happened to know a Mexican whore with black hair and bright blue eyes who called herself Doll?

I took another slow tour of the tables, hoping I would find her at one of them. I lost back my twenty-five dollars at black jack, plus another thirty. I watched the craps table again. There was a square called "Field" where you could bet on every dice roll. It seemed to provide plenty of action. I cashed in three twenty-dollar bills for five-dollar chips, and, betting carefully, managed to lose only fifty dollars over the next twenty minutes.

It was getting late. Another drink at the bar. I decided I had to try Havas' advanced strategy for finding whores. Or the night might slip away and I would wake up in

Las Vegas without Doll. I didn't want to spend another night in the Atlantis.

"The pit boss in the baccarat section," Havas had said. "The one in the chair overlooking the action."

"I just walk up and ask him?"

"No, you have to play. But be careful. It's a twenty-dollar minimum bet most places. The odds are fifty-fifty. You can't make a mistake—the croupiers won't let you. But it looks intimidating."

I soon found myself crossing the satin-rope barrier into the baccarat pit. It was crowded, but a seat had just opened at one of the tables. Suddenly I was a player, one of a dozen intent faces watching a box of cards calculate the evening's luck.

I took two hundred-dollar bills out and threw them on the green baize. (The hotel had earlier cashed my personal check for five hundred dollars, just as Havas had predicted.) The two bills were swept up and ten twenty-dollar chips spread out in their place. I watched for five minutes before making my first bet. I lost. My next bet was a winning one. I lost the next.

All the time I was playing, I was acutely aware of a suntanned face, hawklike, staring down from the tall wooden chair beyond the end of the baccarat table.

It soon occurred to me that I might as well bet a large amount as a small one. I was going to lose anyway. I knew my limit. Why not take a chance on winning a real piece of their money while I was biding my time before approaching the pit boss?

One hour later, I had won $1,640. It seemed impossible. A joke beyond the frontiers of humor. While I had sat there, a German, with what I calculated as roughly $35,000 in $500 chips in front of him, had gotten up to leave. Ten minutes later he'd changed his mind and returned to the table. His seat, which had been filled, was immediately cleared for him. In fifteen minutes the German had to sign his first credit slip for $5,000. I started to rise from the table. My winnings were so puny compared to what was happening around that table. I pushed it all out onto "Player."

We won with a natural eight.

I felt like pouring champagne over myself, like someone who had just won at Le Mans in a turbo-charged Fairmont. My pockets were so heavy with that $3,280 in chips that I thought of asking for a wheelchair to take me to the cashier's window. Actually, I was terrified of making one more bet.

The pit boss bent down to present his left ear, never lifting his eyes off the table below. Did he know where I could find Doll?

"She regular here?"

"Yes."

"You're staying in the hotel?"

"Yes."

"Go ask Ron at the bell captain's desk. Say Angel sent you. Have a nice party. We'll see you later?"

"You sure will." Never, ever, I thought.

The bell captain's desk was located between the cashier's windows and a lighted advertisement for French perfume. Ron turned out to be a middle-aged thug in a green tunic sitting there with a can of Coke.

"I'm Ron. What do you want?"

"Angel sent me over."

"You a guest?"

"Yes. Room 516. Do you know a girl named Doll?"

He raised one eyebrow and picked some dead skin off the side of his nose. "Were you here the other night?"

"Yes."

"She's new, that's why I ask. Yeah, Doll's in the hotel tonight. What time you want to see her?"

"Soon."
"Ten minutes okay?"
"Yes."
"She's on her way up."

24

THE BARTENDER in the Trident Bar sold me a bottle of
Moët & Chandon for seventy-five dollars. Along with two
glasses, I carried it up to my room. I popped the cork
immediately, let the stream of froth pour into my glass,
then down my throat.

I waited with my legs stretched out on the imitation
velvet sofa, the radio playing some rock Muzak, trying to
imagine the room. A seraglio, somewhere in the hotel,
where the ladies awaited their assignments from Ron the
bell captain. Was it luxurious, soft-lit, full of low divans
and Ravel? Or, I suspected, if such a room existed, was
it more like an employees' canteen? I could see the folding
chairs and tables, the fluorescent lights, perhaps even a
time clock? The Atlantis was a paradigm of efficiency.
Sin on the assembly line: luxury out of a vending machine.
Las Vegas was the Id of the last quarter of the twentieth
century. Postindustrial lust.

A quick knock on the door, and I was on my feet. Who
was it?

"You asked for me?"

"Yes I did." I had to remove the chain lock. She wore
a jade-green dress, slit to her stocking tops.

Doll's mouth dropped open and her eyes suddenly went
far away. She tried to smile at me.

"Hello, Doll."

"You surprised me."

"Please come in."

"You asked for me, right?"

"Yes."

"Does Montoya know I'm here?" She looked terrified.

"No."

"That's good."

"A friend of mine, he works for the government, traced you here."

She nodded and finally stepped across the threshold into my room. I shut the door behind her. She walked over, more confident now, and stared down at the bottle of champagne. "For a priest, you know how to live."

"Thank you. I just struck it rich tonight."

"Very good. I have to tell you something. This hotel is something else. Serious, understand? I have to give my boss one hundred dollars for this visit. That means you've got to pay me two hundred."

"Ron is your boss?"

"Yes."

"Okay." I reached into my jacket pocket and took out my wad of hundred-dollar bills. I peeled off two of them and gave them to her. "How long do I get for that?"

"A few hours. There's no big hurry. We can relax."

"Good. I didn't come here to sleep with you. I came here to find out what happened to Jamie. And to get Aaron's briefcase."

She dropped the two bills, folded into a small rectangle, into her purse and set this on top of the TV. Then she smiled at me as if she hadn't heard a single word. Either she didn't want to or she was very stoned. Both, I thought. Reaching behind her, she pulled down her zipper in one smooth motion. The next moment she was standing there in a push-up bra that exposed her nipples, a black garter belt, and black stockings. She wore no panties and her pubic hair had been completely shaved. Stepping up

[232]

to me, she touched herself, running two fingers down between her legs.

"Feels so good. Do you like me?"

"I'm sorry." I shook my head. "Put your clothes on. Were you in the car when Jamie was shot?"

She tried to laugh. "Why do you talk like that? Don't be silly."

She walked carefully on her stiletto heels, a few steps this way, a few the other, displaying herself as if she was back on stage at the Rainbow. I looked at her eyes closely. Was it heroin? Angel dust?

She suddenly pushed me back onto the couch and sat down beside me. Laughing hysterically, she tried to kiss my lips. Her hand fumbled in my lap and she started to yank at my zipper. I reached down and took her hand.

"Doll, please listen to me. I don't want to fuck you. I want the briefcase. I want to talk."

How could I get Doll up to my room and not fuck her? I had spent the evening with my mind full of images of her body. I had bought the champagne with two glasses. But something had happened the moment I saw her standing out in the corridor.

She looked like a real whore now. Not a young Mexican girl with little choice but to live off her body. This wasn't a lousy topless club on the Border. Doll was now a slick Las Vegas party lady. It had happened so fast, I could not accept that it had to be this way.

"Talk? Silly. Too silly." She squirmed out of my hands and dropped her head onto my lap. She turned her face up and winked at me. "I can suck you, okay?"

I felt a burst of anger. She was treating me like a john, like that old man with the Cuban cigar and the old-fashioned shoes. I began to shake her by the shoulders. She shot her right hand out and tried to claw my eyes. I got her arms tied up in mine behind her. "Stop it."

[233]

"Motherfucker bastard I kill—"

"Do you want me to hit you?"

"*Hijo de puta!*"

"Please stop it!"

"Eat shit, *maricón* priest!"

I let go of her arms and said, "Look, please . . ." She slapped me across the right side of my face. It hurt and I hit her with my own right hand, the slap landing higher up her head, stunning her. The next thing I knew she had stopped fighting and was sitting on the rug, weeping. I fell down on my knees and put my arms around her from behind. I kept saying how sorry I was. Her weeping grew louder and she tried to shove me away violently. Finally I let go of her and rolled myself across the carpet and onto my back. I had ruined everything.

"Fernando?" Twenty minutes later, her weeping had gradually died to whimpers, the whimpers to sniffs.

"Yes?"

"Can I have a glass of champagne?"

"Of course." I rose and walked over to the bottle in its plastic ice bucket. I poured my old wine into the bucket and filled both glasses with fresh silver froth. "Here." She took it and sipped it all down in one long gulp. "More?"

"Yes, please."

I got her another glass. "I'm sorry I lost my temper."

"You have a right. I hit you first. And he was your friend, no?"

"Yes."

"They both were your friends. I love champagne. I haven't tasted this since Aaron . . ."

She looked like she was going to start weeping again. I didn't want that. "What happened with you and Jamie? Were you there?"

"You know I was. I was in the Porsche. I had called and told him I couldn't make it to his office by seven

[234]

o'clock, as he'd said. Not unless he picked me up. So he came to pick me up."

"You had Aaron's briefcase with you?"

"No, I lied to him. I didn't have the briefcase."

"But he'd asked you to bring it?"

"No, my boss, Mirabi, told me to bring it to Jamie."

"What happened then?"

"He came to the Denny's on Carlotta Road. He was angry about the briefcase. But he said he had to go back to his office to meet people anyway. So we pulled up in front of his building. Very fancy place, right? The next thing he said was, 'Hello, Doc.' I looked around, and there was this man beside the car. He had a gun and started to shoot. The bullets were hitting him and splashing blood all around the inside of the car. I had to get out and run. He didn't shoot me. I couldn't believe I was still alive. But he put all the bullets into Hillal. I knew I had to get out of the city fast. I had seen this man. He thought so. And I was the last one with Hillal. I don't even have my papers anymore. Montoya took them back."

"You saw his face?"

"No. He stood too close to the car on Hillal's side. I only saw his shirt and the top of his pants. Nothing else, except the gun."

"Well, what was his shirt like, at least?"

"Nothing. Just ordinary. White, I think."

"But you did hear Jamie call him 'Doc'?"

"Yes."

Unfortunately, I had heard Jamie call many people "Doc" since I had first met him. It was a habit of his that I found obnoxious.

"What kind of man was he? Old or young? Was he Anglo?"

"Yes, of course. Anglo. I think he was old."

"Was he a big man?"

"That car was very small. Everybody looks big when

you are sitting way down in such a car. Yes, he looked big to me."

I still couldn't help thinking that "Doc" and her impression of a big man had to mean something. Dr. Elwood Munty could have shot Jamie, then gone inside and called the police. For one thing, Elwood usually wore a white shirt. I had never believed Munty was a serious suspect. Perhaps because I had never considered Munty anything more than Aaron's alcoholic sidekick. Munty must have told Dorfman he'd seen my car parked outside Hillal's five minutes before the murder. I knew Aaron had helped Munty a hundred different ways. Perhaps Munty had resented so much help. Perhaps a sum of money had been offered to him by Harvest, or even Joe Moore. How much did it take to kill your best friend?

"You were lucky to get away."

"Yes. To tell the truth, I tried hard not to see the face. All I wanted was to get away. I was wearing that yellow dress Aaron gave me. You remember?"

"Yes."

"It was covered with blood. I had to throw it away. Too bad, I loved that dress. God, it seems so long ago. You saw me throw the salt?"

"I saw you," I said. "I still don't understand why."

"Neither do I. It was just something he did once."

"Aaron?"

"Yes, once when we were making love. He was drunk. He was a good man. He liked to make jokes all the time, you know."

"I know he did."

"This one time we were making love in the Sandman. And he was drunk. He called down and made them bring up some salt. I asked him why. He said it was because he liked to put lots of salt on what he ate. You know? He put it on me and he ate it off. He was very funny, Aaron.

[236]

I had to laugh all the time." She looked like she was on the verge of weeping again.

"I'll bet you laughed," I said. I was feeling horrified. For the first time, I saw a new view of Aaron. His "jokes" were meant to shock people. As vulgar as they were, I had always forgiven him for those jokes. But the jokes had never been at my expense.

Aaron had treated this girl like a piece of cheap dirt. I could see him saying that, see them in the room in the Sandman, and I wanted to shut off my mind. Who wanted to see that? Aaron was a vulgar, sadistic man. Perhaps that was one reason I had wanted to look up to him as my father—he was so unlike my real father. It was pitiful. Yet I had seen only the silver-haired, noble Western gentleman in Aaron. Never the drunken pig. The rich Anglo who could buy a little Mexican girl anytime he wanted and then pour salt on her like she was a piece of fried chicken.

I was glad he was dead.

"What did you do with his briefcase?" I was sitting next to her on the carpet, sipping champagne with one hand, stroking her hair back out of her weepy eyes with the other. "It's very important."

"It's in Mexico."

"Why in Mexico?"

"I can trust my friends to hide it good. The briefcase is my insurance. In case I ever go back to El Sol, you know?"

"You can sell it to me."

"What?"

"I'll pay you two thousand . . . No. I'll pay you three thousand dollars."

"Three thousand?" Her eyes widened into blue coves where the pupils could not believe what they saw. "Why?"

"If you promise to leave Las Vegas. Come back with me tonight, to El Sol. In the morning, we'll go get the briefcase and I'll give you the money. With three thousand dollars, you wouldn't have to work here . . . doing this, would you?"

"Are you joking? With three grand, why would I want to hook?"

"What would you do?"

"I don't know. Maybe I could start my own business or something. Maybe I could start a beauty salon."

"Maybe you could even travel. You could go to Europe."

"Europe? Hey, that's too incredible. Where did you get this money?"

"I won it downstairs."

"And you want to give it all to me?"

"I think Aaron would want that," I lied. "And I know that you want to find out who killed him, and Jamie. That same person has tried to kill me twice."

"Is that true? He tried to kill you?"

"And my wife."

"This is terrible. You are a good person, a true priest. I am sorry for . . ." She looked down at herself. "You could have done anything to me, but you didn't. I can give you one hundred back, but I have to give Ron his money."

"That's okay. Will you fly back with me tonight?"

She looked into my eyes. I don't know if she was trying to read my intentions in them, my honesty, or just imagining what she would do with three thousand dollars. "Yes, I will go with you tonight. To tell you the truth, Las Vegas is not what I thought it would be. Only one thing I ask you, please?"

"Anything."

"Don't let Montoya find me."

"I promise that won't happen."

As it happened, we had to wait until 2:35 A.M. for Continental Flight 029 that would stop over in El Sol on its way between Seattle and New Orleans. We hung around the airport and I drank coffee in the snack bar while Doll played the slot machines with money I gave her. I was happy to give it to her. It belonged there.

As soon as we were in the air, Doll fell asleep with her head on a pillow jammed against the bulkhead. I had my yellow pad out on the folding tray. The sermon came all at once, like a knife through butter, a hard stare through a sick man's joke.

As truly miraculous as Jesus' walk on the water was, the story impressed me most for what it said about Peter. And about myself. It was the man who had risked his life on the waves, who ultimately lost his nerve, but who survived.

What did Jesus risk? It was his miracle. But it was Peter's courage.

In those fifty minutes on the airplane, I finished the sermon. I didn't want it to be too dramatic or too boring. I wanted my parish to feel awe for both Jesus and Peter as they faced each other among those violent swells. I wanted them to feel awe for themselves, too: shoulder to shoulder, in the heat of Sunday-morning church, in El Sol. I was, I now realize, preaching to myself as I wrote that sermon: Don't lose your nerve, Fernando. We are twenty-seven thousand feet above the desert in the cold night sky and heading home. Look at what you have done already, and what you have seen. You won't sink.

Sunday

25

THE TERMINAL at the El Sol airport was brightly lit and fast asleep when we walked off the plane at 3:40 A.M. We were the only passengers in the baggage area. "Where will you take me?" she asked. We were standing there under the blank signboards, watching the unmoving conveyor belt.

"To my house. I have got to sleep for a couple of hours. I think it's the safest place, if you don't mind?"

"No, I don't mind."

Suddenly the belt jolted into movement, and a minute later, Doll's cheap pink-vinyl luggage came up out of the floor. We walked out to the parking lot and I put her bags in the trunk of the Mustang.

I had promised to protect her from Montoya. He would want revenge for being left, she said. Nor could I risk losing her again. The election was in two days. I needed that Pointer Report and I was sure it was in Aaron's briefcase. That was the only thing that made sense.

Nancy's Rabbit sat in the driveway of the rectory. Somehow I had been sure she would not take off for California that night. I parked the Mustang, took out Doll's luggage, and carried it into the house.

I told her to wait while I went back to the darkened bedroom. I called Nancy's name softly, stood beside the bed, and listened to her steady breathing. Then went over to the linen closet and found two sheets and a folded quilt.

"I'll make up this couch for you," I said back in the living room. "My wife's asleep. This won't be too comfortable, I'm afraid."

She tried to take the sheets out of my hands. "I didn't know your wife was back. Please, let me do this."

"I can do it. If I can't give you a real bed, the least I can do is make this up."

"Thank you. When did she come back?"

"Thursday."

"I'm happy for you," she said. Sadly, I thought. She sat down in one of the easy chairs and pulled off her shoes, crossed her legs. I pulled at the sheets, trying to smooth them neatly over the two awkward cushions. I couldn't help glancing at her from time to time. Her face had lost the hardness of Las Vegas in just a few hours.

Her surroundings seemed to be able to mold her, like iron around water, in a very short time. Yet she always survived to change again. The little Mexican girl I had never known, could only sense, had somehow become the star of the sleazy Rainbow Club. Then a fancy Vegas hooker, in just two days. Now, in a priest's living room, in the middle of the night, she was a beautiful young woman, lost, very sleepy.

"We'll go across the river in the morning?" she asked hopefully.

"I forgot to tell you," I said. "I have to conduct the worship services this morning. And there's something else that will take about an hour. After that we can go. Sunday is the one day I just can't avoid working."

"I understand."

We said good night. I left her to turn out the lights when she was ready. After shutting the bedroom door, I undressed and slipped under the sheet beside Nancy.

My foot grazed hers. She yanked her leg away, and rolled over to the far edge of the bed. "Who is that out there?"

"That's Doll."

"What? You brought that slut back here to my house?"

"This isn't your house, nor mine. It belongs to the church, fortunately. Yes, I brought her back. Didn't you see my note?"

"Why here?"

"She's going to give me Aaron's briefcase tomorrow."

"You fucked her, didn't you?"

"Don't be stupid."

"Then why did you bring her back?"

"She's afraid of her pimp. I don't want her to run away again."

"So how was Las Vegas, Father?"

"I don't know."

"You don't? What happened to you?" She whirled around. "What do you mean?"

"I haven't had any sleep in two nights now. Please—"

"Are you going to church tomorrow?"

"Of course."

"What about her?"

"I don't know," I said. I slept after that. A deep sleep with no dreams. And not nearly enough of it.

"Fernando, come on. Wake up." Nancy was shaking my shoulders and I was trying to bury my face in the darkness under a pillow. I felt like I had slept only three minutes. In fact, it was slightly over three hours. "Look at this, Fernando."

"What?"

"The paper. Look at the front page of the *Post-Examiner*." I sat up and looked at the newspaper Nancy was waving over the bed. I took it from her. "Here," she said, directing me to the lower-right-hand section of the front page. Doll's photograph stared back at me. It was obviously a theatrical shot taken by a very mediocre professional. The headline read, "POLICE SEEK TOPLESS SUSPECT." They'd had fun with that, no doubt.

Dorfman had told the reporter that Doll was the most important link between the Anderson and Hillal murders. She was a material witness in both, he said, and she had disappeared before the police could question her. As for her background, little was known except that she was a Mexican national who had danced in nightclubs on both sides of the Border. Her age was given as twenty-one, but I guessed that was a mistake. Dorfman said there were reports that she had crossed the Border. However, he was sending out a national police bulletin with her photo.

"Where is she?" I asked Nancy.

"We're having breakfast. You'd better get up. Don't you have an eight-o'clock service?"

"Yes."

"We have to protect this girl, Fernando. They could try to blame everything on her. She's a woman and she's Mexican and they could railroad her. Just like that."

"When did you get up?" I was trying to absorb this new Nancy.

"I couldn't sleep, so I went out and read. Then Doll woke up a little while ago. I made her some coffee and brought in the newspaper. We saw this and started talking. I like her a lot, Fernando. She's tough and she's been through it, hasn't she? Working as a prostitute is fairly heavy."

"Yes, it is."

"I feel like she's my sister. I don't want you to let her get arrested. She didn't kill those men, did she?"

"I don't know," I said.

"What do you think?"

"I don't think she did."

"I'm glad."

"Can you look after her this morning? I have to go out to Cogswell Park for this damn picnic after the service."

"What picnic?"

"The annual Youth Fellowship picnic. I can't avoid it."

"Sure I'll keep her company. Then what?"

"I'm going to take her across to Gomez."

"You'd better get dressed. And you'd better shave, too." She turned and started for the door.

"What did you do last night, Nancy?"

"Oh, I went for a long drive. Then I got drunk at some hillbilly bar. These assholes tried to talk me into going back to their trailer. I wasn't in the mood, so I split and came home. I read your note and went to bed. By the way, what about your sermon?"

"I wrote it on the plane back from Vegas."

"You've been busy. You look terrible, by the way. How do you feel?"

"Okay."

She nodded and walked out of the room. Nancy had entered a new phase. I was familiar with it: the Efficient Nancy. It could last for a few days, up to a month. During this period, Nancy would be very active, independent, and not overly friendly. It was the Efficient Nancy that had gotten her through college. Unfortunately, the Efficient Nancy was usually followed by Nancy at her most irresponsible. Wild Nancy. It was Wild Nancy who had run off with Flipper. But I didn't have to worry yet, not while Efficient Nancy was in control.

At the breakfast table, Doll seemed to have withdrawn into herself since I had last seen her. "Are you feeling all right?" I asked. "Is there anyone you want to call? Anything you want?"

She shook her head and smiled, almost painfully.

[247]

"I have to run. I've got to open up the church this morning, since Johnny won't . . ." I didn't finish, just said good-bye to them and walked out.

When I arrived at Holy Innocents, I found the parking lot already filling and the doors wide open. George Lang, our choirmaster, had unlocked them early that morning.

Both the eight o'clock and ten-thirty services went smoothly, although several people later asked me if I was feeling myself. They said I looked very tired. They had all read in the newspaper about the shooting at the rectory. No doubt they had been gossiping about nothing else. Only one woman, old Mrs. Weeman, asked how Nancy's "poor mother" was getting along with her "illness" back in New York. Other ladies looked rather shocked. Nancy was back in town, but she wasn't in church!

For months, June 1 had been marked on my calendar with the word "picnic." As soon as the crowd had left after the main service, I would have to lock up the church and climb in my car and drive over to the park.

I had preached only once, as usual. At the ten-thirty service. (The eight-o'clock was especially designed for active people and those who hated sermons.) Standing on the steps after this service, I received four comments. Two people said, "Good sermon, Father." Old Mrs. Weeman said, "I couldn't hear your sermon, Father. Was the public-address system working today?" I assured her it was (I hated the PA) and said I would send her a copy in the mail. Finally, there was one man who liked it. Walter Mudge was a local city fireman, one of the least wealthy members of the parish. He said, "I think that was the best sermon you ever gave, Father."

I was thrilled. If I had to choose someone to like my sermon on Jesus' walk across the water, it might very well have been Walter Mudge.

By the time I got to the park, about one hundred teenagers and their friends were busy grilling hot dogs and hamburgers on the three-legged barbecues they'd brought from home. There were vast mounds of potato salad and coleslaw turning sour in the heat on one of the picnic tables. And countless garbage cans full of sodas buried in ice. I would have given one week's salary for a beer.

The truth was that I felt uncomfortable with these kids, although I tried to look relaxed. As a teenager myself, much to my father's chagrin, I had refused to join his Youth Fellowship or to participate in any activities connected with his church. Back in Connecticut, I had detested the "squares" who would waste their Sundays hanging around with my father. I wouldn't have been caught dead at a picnic like that one in Cogswell Park when I was sixteen.

As soon as the hamburgers were ready, I made a show of filling my plate. I ate as quickly as possible, fending off questions from a small group of teens who seemed to think I was their high-school teacher or something. They pretended to adore me. I suspected they thought I would write them glowing recommendations for their first-choice colleges. They kept trying to grab my notice with questions like, "Why do *you* think Jesus cursed the fig tree, Father?"

It was time to go. But the softball game, inevitable at such picnics, had just begun. And I had been chosen by one of the teams.

By the third inning, I had struck out twice, while my team was ahead 9–0. I was playing right field, very close to the road. Suddenly someone started honking behind me. The game stopped as everyone turned to stare at Nancy's Rabbit. Torn between embarrassment and jubilation, I told them it was an emergency and I really had to go. I raced in and got my jacket from under one of the benches, then jogged back across the outfield with their curious young eyes trailing me all the way.

"Good-bye, Father O'Neal," called my group of fans. I waved back at them without turning. Nancy opened the door for me and I jumped inside.

"I can't believe you are playing baseball while Doll and I have been waiting all this time."

"I did it for Jesus," I said. "And my job."

"Well, she's very uptight."

"Where is she?"

"At home."

"I hope so. Have you two thought up any good ways to get her across the Border?"

"What do you mean?"

"You saw the photograph. The police are looking for her all over the country. Don't you think they'll be watching down at the bridge?"

"You're probably right," Nancy admitted. "Anyway, we had a great talk this morning."

"I'm very glad."

"Why? We didn't talk about you."

26

WHEN YOU cross the Morales Bridge into Mexico, they
don't stop you on the United States side. They watch
you and they wave you through the three narrow, but
empty, covered booths. They may take pictures of you
and your vehicle in secret, but you can't be sure. You
drive across the lower level of the metal bridge, and
before you know it, you have been stared at by a Mexican
official in a somewhat shabby brown uniform with a high
collar and a Sam Brown belt, then waved on your way.
It is one of the easiest borders to cross anywhere in the
world. Much easier than, say, the border into Canada at
Niagara Falls.

Taking Doll across in the trunk of the Mustang that
Sunday afternoon was one of the hardest things I ever
had to do. It wasn't me against the officials. It was me
against myself. If caught, the worst thing that could
happen to me was that I would go to jail. In the United
States, they could put me in jail for hiding a fugitive, for
obstructing justice. In Mexico, I wasn't sure what they
could charge me with, although I knew they might put
me in jail for anything at all. For making them laugh,
perhaps. Bringing the wetback the wrong way across the
river.

I drove five blocks from the bridge through the narrow
streets of the old part of Gomez. Then turned into a side
alley and parked. I jumped out and ran around and opened

the trunk. Doll lay curled on the blankets we had arranged there, her knees up, her skirt bunched around her waist. The pink-vinyl luggage had made it a much tighter fit than it would have been if I hadn't insisted the bags be hidden. "Get out before anybody sees us," I told her. She seemed to agree, as she was soon standing beside me, trying to smooth the many wrinkles in her thin blue sleeveless dress. "Was it very bumpy?" I asked.

"No, not too bad. It was the heat and the dark I didn't like too much. But I knew it would be like that. Anyway, I have known people who drove two thousand miles up to Chicago from El Sol in the trunk of a car. Four of them in the same trunk. This was nothing."

"Okay, now you tell me how to get to your friend's house."

"Are you nervous?" she asked. "Don't be nervous. This is my country now. Everything is okay."

We drove past the old market, skirted the nightclub district, through block after block of small adobe buildings, shabby *bodegas, cantinas*, garages. The slums here were not much worse than those in El Sol's *barrio*, except they felt much worse because of the people. The people were wretchedly poor, dressed in clean but threadbare clothes, their ears sticking out from heads where the dark skin was stretched very tight over the skull. The eyes were swollen large, impossible to read. Survival was the ability to see sharp. The eyes raked over the red Mustang's exterior and across our faces inside. What were we looking for? They knew who we were.

"You turn right up here for Vista del Sol," she said. Her voice sounded excited, happy. "Do you know Vista del Sol?"

"No."

"You'll see."

I turned right, then left where she told me a few minutes later. We were on a road that headed for the chamois-colored mountains west of the city, climbing. From the flats, where the hovels were packed together and I had to crawl, at one point, at five miles an hour through a crowd of children and mangy yellow dogs, we began to climb a dusty slope. The hovels became houses. Then they became less and less frequent. In a few minutes we were passing large homes built onto terraces on the side of the mountain.

Some of these homes were detectable only because of their walls. You knew they must be there behind those twelve-foot-high walls: ugly new concrete, topped with rusty wire and, no doubt, glass shards, running for yard after yard beside the road. Other homes had no walls at all: modern ranch-style constructions with palm trees in their yards and double garages that sheltered the outrageously-taxed imported Camaros and Thunderbirds of Gomez' wealthy citizens.

Vista del Sol was hardly as wealthy and polished as Cottonwood. The road, for example, had suddenly gone from asphalt to dirt without warning. These homes, which represented millions on the Mexican side of the river— what would they represent if they stood in El Sol? Just another upper-middle-class ranch house with three bedrooms and air conditioning.

But the view was unique up here. This was the highest spot for hundreds of miles, or so it seemed when you looked out across both cities at the desert and the tiny edge of saw-toothed mountains to the north. You felt very high up in Vista del Sol, and I was surprised. Those chamois-colored mountains didn't look so high from the El Sol side of the river.

"When you see this next road to your right," Doll said. "Right around this curve."

It ran up a steep incline immediately after we had rounded the corner, as she'd said, and I had to throw the transmission from drive into low gear. We climbed slowly up the dirt track. In my mirror I could see the huge cloud of dust we were throwing up behind. The road entered a kind of canyon dug out of the side of the mountain by, I guessed, the sea. A sea that no longer existed. The vegetation changed as we entered this canyon. The yucca and scraggly piñon pines were joined by ferns, bracken, stretches of panicgrass, a few orchids peeking out of the brown stone. There must be a spring here, I thought.

The road clung to one wall of the canyon, then rose up a steep incline and doubled back. Suddenly we were running out on a ledge much higher up the mountain than before. The city of Gomez was spread out far below us and you could see the river like a crooked brown scar. El Sol looked so orderly and defined compared to the way Gomez was strewn about.

"Is this still Vista del Sol?" I asked.

"It doesn't really have a name. Look, here is the house."

It was perched there on the side of the mountain like one of those monasteries in Asia Minor that seemed to dare the eagles to reach its gates. But instead of overlooking the scene of Noah's shipwreck, this place overlooked the desert sister cities. It was much older than the houses we had passed lower down. It was entirely adobe, thick walls and deep windows, almost part of the mountain itself, so that it must have been impossible to see unless you were almost on top of it.

"Leave your car here," she told me. I parked it right there on the dirt track where it still looked wide enough to get it turned around. Then got out and followed her up to the house. The walls were quite tall; it was difficult to see the large scale of the place until you could actually measure yourself in the space of the doorway.

Doll pushed open one of the wooden doors and I followed her into the darkness. She called out someone's name. I had seen no cars outside. Ahead was a thin line of white light. She crossed toward this, and suddenly another door opened in front of us and I saw the patio beyond and the room I was standing in. It was a big empty foyer, with a staircase leading up the right wall. But Doll had already gone outside.

The patio was enclosed on three sides by the covered portico of the house, off which various doors opened, like the door through which I had just stepped. On the fourth side, the patio was open to the view. It was magnificent.

There was a fountain. It filled a third of the patio, a circular fountain with a raised pedestal, fluted, in the center, gushing with white water. The fountain was almost three feet deep. The water danced in flickering blue wavelets and it was hard to stop from throwing myself right in. It was at least 110 degrees in the sun in that patio.

"Inez?" she called again, her voice resounding off the three walls.

There was a high creak as a door opened into the patio. "Sí, María. Vengo," said a voice. Then I saw the old woman come out of the shadows of the portico. She was dressed in a brown long-sleeved cotton dress and black slippers, her hair white and hanging in a braid down her back, her face puckered and covered with age spots. She looked like a witch. I saw Doll was happy to see her, for she almost skipped around the fountain to embrace her.

I waited while they spoke in low voices, which, although I understood Spanish, I had no chance of understanding. Doll turned and said, "You wait?"

"Yes, sure."

They walked back out of the patio toward the direction from which Inez had come. I went and sat on the edge of the fountain and stared out at the view. After about five minutes, I had to move back to the shaded portico.

I heard the door creak and then footsteps on the stone floor. Doll walked down the portico, turned the corner, and came up to me. In her hand was Aaron's old-fashioned leather briefcase, which I had seen him carry the very first time I met him in the Brown Palace in Denver. "Here," she said, holding it out and then placing it at my feet.

"One second." I dug in my pants pocket and came out with the wad of hundred-dollar bills. "I counted them this morning. But you ought to count them too. There should be thirty."

She took the money and closed her fist around it, then put her fist in the small of her back. "Open it," she said. "This is what you wanted all this time."

I nodded and went down on one knee to unclasp the brass buckle. I stretched open the top and began to pick out the contents one by one, working from the pocket on the left. There were three inner pockets. My instinct was to empty it all over the floor and find what I wanted. Doll moved back a few steps. "Is this Inez's house?" I asked her as I pulled out copies of *Newsweek* and *Penthouse*.

"No."

"Does she work here?"

"Yes, she looks after this for many years now."

"Who are the owners?"

"They are Mexicans. But they choose to live on the other side of the river."

"They must be very rich." There were a number of annual corporate reports from various companies, including Lockheed, Arvin, and General Dynamics.

"Yes, very rich."

"What do they do?"

"He owns the cemetery in Gomez. Also a construction company."

"He owns the cemetery?" I said. "I guess that's one

way to get rich." There were several envelopes full of Aaron's personal notes. And a copy of the May 21 edition of the Denver *Post*.

"Yes, one way."

"Did you come all the way up here this week when you got that ticket?"

"Yes."

"How?" I had found a plastic bottle of Bufferin and a strip of Gelusil tablets in the third compartment.

"Taxi."

"You can get a taxi all the way up here?"

"Of course. Why not?"

"It's such a long way. Do the owners come back here frequently?"

"Never. The man grew up in this house. He hates it."

"Doll, the report is not in this briefcase."

"No?"

"I'm afraid not."

"But there are other important papers?"

"No, nothing important. Oh, maybe some of Aaron's notes are valuable. I don't know. But the Pointer Report is certainly not here. Nor is there anything that looks like a will."

"I know."

"What do you mean?"

"I know there is no will. I looked for that. But I did not know what this Pointer Report you wanted was, and so I could not look for it."

"You didn't take anything out of here?"

"Only the ticket."

"When Aaron left you that Wednesday evening, left this briefcase with you, did he take anything else with him? An envelope or a folder of any kind? Maybe just some papers?"

"Yes, I think there was something."

I stood up and turned to stare out at that brown-and-gray tableland with its scar of brown water. "I should have asked you that before. Not that it would have made any difference. I would still have wanted this."

"Do you want the money back?"

I laughed. "Of course not. A deal's a deal. It is so hot, I can't believe it. I feel like burying myself in that fountain."

"You can. Why don't you?"

I laughed. "That would hardly be very polite."

"It doesn't matter. I have gone in *la fuente*, and so has Inez. Why not go in? It is big as a lake."

"Maybe I will. I have no bathing suit, though. I guess I could just go in my shorts."

"Yes, why don't you?"

"I think I will."

I felt somewhat nervous about stripping off my clothes there in the patio. But once I was in the water, all that left me. It felt cold initially, wonderfully refreshing. Probably it was at least eighty degrees, but so much cooler than the air. You could almost swim. I kept putting my head under and staying down as long as possible, completely submerged in the coolness. One of these times I heard something and pushed my head out of the water to see Doll a few feet away. She was up to her neck, and I immediately wondered what she was wearing. Or was she naked?

"It feels so good, no?"

"Yes," I agreed.

"Are you very unhappy?"

"I suppose I am. It's just that I don't know what to do next."

"You'll think of it."

"I hope so. Do you swim here often? It's funny to be swimming in a fountain. I presume there must be a spring around here somewhere. Back in that canyon, I guess. I tasted the water. It's good and sweet."

"Yes, it's good. I don't swim here often, no. But I swam here when I was a girl."

"Did you grow up here?" We were bobbing in the water, our legs stretched out under the surface in front of us. I was no longer wondering. I knew for sure that Doll was naked.

"Yes, after I was eight years old."

"Who is Inez? Your aunt?"

"No, she is a friend of my family's. She comes from the same town, San Ignacio, in Sinaloa, where I was born. My mother had eleven children and my father did not earn much money. When I was eight, Inez came back to my town for a visit. She liked me, and so she arranged to take me here to Gomez."

"She adopted you?"

"Yes, sort of. You see, she could live here free. And she had good jobs in those days across the river. She cleaned two stores. We worked at night. In the daytime, we stayed here. That's when I would swim."

"So you lived here and worked with Inez cleaning stores at night in El Sol? How did you get down this mountain?"

"We had donkeys. It was not hard."

"It sounds very hard. And how would you get across the river?"

"We would just walk across. In those days, ten years ago, it was nothing to walk across the river. Later, of course, I had my papers, which Montoya bought for me."

"Where did you meet Montoya?"

"He bought me a whiskey at the bar in the Club Brazil."

"Were you dancing there?"

"No, I was working there. You know."

"How old were you?"

"Sixteen. This was two years ago."

"So he turned you into a dancer?"

"Yes, he got me the job at the Rainbow. But I had

danced before in Gomez. Montoya is a *maricón*, you know?"

"I know. Did he take part of your salary at the Rainbow?"

"No, never. Montoya only wanted me to dance there so I would make money for myself. I paid for my own apartment, my own food and clothes. For Montoya I only worked with special clients. He never asked these men for money, and neither did I. I think they paid him back with favors."

"Was Aaron one of these clients?"

"Yes. Then he gave Montoya money to 'free' me. That's what Aaron called it. So I was only for Aaron, and Montoya was not allowed to bother me. Of course, Montoya bothered me lots of times. He would bring one of his special clients to me even when he was not supposed to."

"Would you tell Aaron?"

"No. Montoya would kill me."

"Did you . . . ?" I couldn't finish my question.

She had kissed me. I put my arms around her under the water and our legs entangled. She held the back of my head with one hand, probing my mouth with her tongue, as her other hand slid down my chest. Then she pulled away.

"I am sorry about the papers. I wanted them to be important."

"It doesn't matter."

"I like your wife," she said. "But I don't think she will ever make you happy."

"Why?"

"I can't say. It's just how I feel." She came closer and we kissed again. This time I reached down and clasped her breast, feeling the nipple in the center of my palm, kissing her lips, her eyes, her nose.

"We can't do it here. Inez won't like it."

"Where?"

"Come on. I'll show you."

It was a door that led off the portico. Inside the room was dark until she opened the shutters, and then light poured in in a thick column, the dust we'd stirred up rising like smoke in the light, the walls covered with whitewash and a single cross of woven straw. There was a *matrimonio*, or double bed, with brass bedsteads and the mattress folded double. The only other piece of furniture was a tall cupboard of cedar with iron fittings. "Wait here," she told me. While she was gone, I unfolded the mattress on the single layer of rusty wire.

When she returned, she had a pillow under one arm and white linen in her hand. She told me to stand back while she fitted the sheet over the old mattress, tucking it very smooth and tight. Then she put the single pillow into the linen case and dropped it on the bed. She turned to embrace me.

"Did you sleep here?" I asked her.

"Yes, many nights. It was once the man's room, the one who owns the house. He grew up here."

"And so did you."

"Yes."

I wanted to go very slow and make love to Doll better than I had ever made love to anyone. We covered each other with kisses. She had a body that just took my breath away. And she was ready to serve me in any way. But I didn't know how to accept this from her. In ten years, since the second month I had known Nancy, I had been faithful to only one woman. Now I was inside Doll as she held her legs back by the knees and stared into my eyes. I couldn't meet that stare.

I made love to her in long slow surges, and then in short hard knocks. I took my cock out and ran it across her folds, across her clitoris, down between the cheeks of her ass. Then plunged inside her again. I wanted to go for as long as possible to make her come.

"Fernando," she said, grabbing me by the face and making me look her in the eyes. "Why don't you make love to me?"

"I am. What's wrong?"

"Why don't you please yourself?"

"I am. I want to please you."

"That's easy. I can do that whenever I want, with one finger. Go ahead, please yourself. Hurt me if you want."

"I don't want to hurt you."

"Then come all at once. Do you want to come in my ass?"

"No, I've never done that."

"Why not? It's very good. What do you want?"

"I just want . . ."

"Be a man."

"Fuck you," I said. "I want to fuck you." I was angry. Not at Doll, not at her. Angry at Nancy. At myself. I buried my face in the sheet but thrust savagely into her.

"Yes. That's good," she whispered. "Harder."

I fucked her harder. I was used to fucking with a semierection so that I could go for as long as possible. It took Nancy ages to come, even when she caressed her clitoris as I fucked her, or when I did. In fact, I was so used to making love that way that every time I began to get a full erection, I would stop or withdraw. I was always afraid of coming too soon. I almost never did. On the several occasions that I had reached orgasm early, and Nancy had not, she had been furious. Once she had even thrown a crying tantrum of sorts. I felt utterly worthless. A man had to make his wife come every time. And I had almost always proved that I was a man with Nancy.

Now I was very hard, on the verge of coming, and Doll was whispering in my ear. "Let it go. Harder. Let yourself go. Fuck me. Oh, Fernando."

I reached orgasm soon afterward, and as I did, I thought: She never made me happy. I began to cry. I meant Nancy had never made me happy. Doll suddenly had begun to grind and twist herself around my cock as I came. She had her hands pulling the cheeks of my ass apart and she was biting my neck, making a great deal of noise. I did not think she was coming, just urging me on, heightening it for me. When I turned to look into her eyes, I saw that she was gone too.

In the minutes that followed, as we rested before making love a second time, I thought of Aaron. The night before, Doll had, unwittingly, destroyed his image in my mind. He was no longer a father substitute, no longer noble Aaron the Western knight in shining armor after that. But now Doll, unwittingly again, had destroyed another illusion in my mind about Aaron. He wasn't any more of a monster than I was, really. What he had found in Doll, at least he had recognized it, and accepted it. Now I had too. I didn't feel proud of myself, that wasn't how I felt after making love to this Mexican girl. All I felt was like a man. As Aaron must have felt. We had to accept that. I was sorry Aaron was dead, not glad. Just as I was rid of some poison, perhaps an overdose of self-consciousness, rid of it thanks to Doll. I felt so sorry for her, but I could not pity her. For she had given me back the confidence to know that I too was just a man.

I left the room off the patio about eight o'clock that evening. Doll said she wanted to stay and talk to Inez. She told me how much she had once hated Inez, and how much she now loved the old woman. I told Doll that I loved her, and why. I don't know how much she understood of what I told her during those hours as the column of sunlight gradually left the bed, crossed back over the floor, and was gone. It wasn't dark, but the sun had passed to another section of the adobe house. We both agreed we would not see each other again for a long time, the way people agree that it has been a very wet summer.

I picked up Aaron's briefcase before I left, looked back at that fountain, and then went out and drove down the mountain.

Monday:
Election Eve

27

THAT NIGHT when I returned from Gomez, I found
Nancy sitting in the dark out behind the rectory. She
had pulled one of the aluminum-and-plastic recliners
onto the white gravel. I greeted her and she made a
sound, not a word. She was looking up at the stars.

I went inside and poured myself a bourbon. The light
was on inside the wall oven and there was a tuna casserole
warming on one of the racks. Tuna casserole was one of
Efficient Nancy's favorite suppers. But when, a few minutes later, Nancy came inside and opened the refrigerator
door to replenish her glass with white wine, it was obvious she had been crying. This was a third phase, which I
knew well, which I liked far better than either Efficient
Nancy or Wild Nancy. This was Sad Nancy. It was
closer than either of the others to how she really saw
herself, although Sad Nancy was, from my point of view,
still only a phase. The woman I had married was none
of these three, and all of them: the real Nancy was probably no more "real" than my love. I had loved her, even
if I could never worship her. As I set the table, she sat
down slowly in one of the chairs, her glass of wine in her
right hand, her face resting on the palm of her left as she
stared sorrowfully out the kitchen window at the neighbor's TV across the backyards. I felt that same love again.

The anger was gone. But it had left an empty space
in my emotions that no amount of nostalgic love could

fill. We were exactly who we had always been. There was no new love. This time Nancy knew better than to ask me any questions, and I knew better than to volunteer any answers.

The tuna casserole was, in fact, not bad. Especially with a glass of wine. After a while Nancy said, "You know what I said about those guys in the bar last night?"

"The assholes?"

"Yes. And I told you I wasn't in the mood? Well, I'm sorry I said that to you. I would never have gone back to their trailer, no matter what mood I was in. I only said that because I was angry that you had brought her here."

"I know."

A little while later I asked her about Greece. She told me the whole story about the guy she had met in San Francisco, the young guy, and how they had flown to London and then down to Athens in February, and finally taken the boat out to Crete, where they had lived in the caves on the South Coast. I had been hearing about those caves for years, and was surprised you could still do that. Yes, she said, but she had gotten fed up with living in a cave after two months. Nancy was thirty years old. When she left Crete, the young guy decided to stay on for the summer. I could tell she missed him, but not all that much.

We washed the dishes together. Then went into the bedroom, undressed with our backs to each other, and lay down together. We did not make love that night, but we slept in each other's arms like two children sharing the same bunk in a steamship as it crossed the dark moonless sea toward the island of their birth. Falling asleep that night felt like going home.

The phone rang early the next morning. I rolled over and grabbed the receiver, my eyes still shut, almost knocking the phone on the floor in the process.

"Hello?"

"This is David Snow. Can you talk freely, Father?"

"Yes."

"I am having trouble with my telephone. You understand?"

"Yes."

"Have you read this morning's paper, Father?"

"No."

"They are starting to burn down the city. This bloodshed seems to escalate minute by minute. All these inputs are overpowering. I have never seen so much bad material, as you called it, in this city before."

"I'd better go look at the newspaper . . ."

"I'm worried about us, Father."

"Has anything happened to you, Snow? You sound very shook-up."

"I'm not going to live much longer, Father. But before I die, I want to see this all ended. Aaron and Jamie were right, but they had to pay for being right. We have got to be very careful now. I don't want to say anything else on the phone. Can we meet?"

"It is the last day before the election, Professor. I am going to be very busy with . . . with several things. You know what I mean, Professor?"

"The report?"

"Yes."

"You have it?"

"No, but I'm going to give it one last try."

"I wish you wouldn't talk so clearly . . . the phone, remember?"

"Sorry. Would you mind if we met later in the week?"

I really didn't have the time to listen to Snow's rambling verbiage that Monday.

"Well . . . very well. But you will remember what I told you?"

[269]

"Yes, of course I will. And thanks for calling."

"Good-bye, Father."

I could hardly go back to sleep after that. I had to put on my shoes and go outside to find the newspaper. Nancy had rolled over and put the pillow on top of her head during my conversation with Snow. I saw no reason to wake her.

The headline of the *Post-Examiner* screamed "RIOT BURNS DOWNTOWN," but the third paragraph made it clear that the only property destroyed was several abandoned automobiles—all in the *barrio*. Two policemen had been taken to the hospital with undisclosed injuries, along with twenty-eight others. Two civilians were in critical condition with gunshot wounds.

It sounded like the police had overreacted to some stone-throwing and the whole thing had gotten out of hand. There had been rallies in the *barrio* all Sunday urging people to get out and vote against Proposition 8. And, I thought, who was that law banning alcohol in the parks really aimed at, if not the *barrio* kids?

But I was far more surprised when I turned to the bottom half of the front page and found "MULCAHY BLASTS LIBERALS, VOWS TOUGH CITY CLEANUP."

I felt my stomach knot with a premonition. Sure enough, where the story was continued on page 3, I found a paragraph I had been anticipating ever since Pasetti's visit to the rectory:

> "What are we to believe of do-gooders who have a knack for getting murdered? How good can they be? Of priests who are indicted felons, or who use narcotics in their own homes? Of a committee of liberals intent on keeping El Sol for their own private playground, for all forms of corruption and crime?" asked Mulcahy of his Kiwanis audience. "I'll tell you what to believe," he continued. "You can believe it's time for a change. Time

to stop putting up with liberal incompetence and corruption, time to launch our own New Frontier—one of freedom and self-control."

Father Ortega was the only indicted felon among the priests of El Sol, so far as I knew. Which left little doubt which priest on the committee "used narcotics," if you were to believe Mulcahy's second sentence.

I made myself a cup of coffee and drank it at the kitchen table. Perhaps I ought to sue him, I thought. At the very least, I wanted to deny it. But nobody had asked me any questions yet. My denial would certainly look a little fishy. I could have used another four hours of sleep; instead I went in and put on a fresh collar and a clean suit. I had a feeling it was going to be one of those days that lasted for ages.

I climbed into the red Mustang, laid Aaron's briefcase with its disappointing contents beside me on the naugahyde seat, and drove away from the rectory and my sleeping wife. I had thought of telephoning first, but vetoed the idea. I wanted to surprise her.

The Anderson driveway was not empty, not by any means. Joe Moore's Silver Cloud sat squarely in the middle of the asphalt, taking up as much room as possible. The Mexican chauffeur stared at me impassively in his door mirror as I parked and climbed out of my car. I wondered what he was doing there. Still, I wasn't really surprised.

Mimi, Aaron's old cook, opened the door a few moments after I rang. Without a word, she beckoned me inside. I followed her past the Indian art down into the living room with its lovely view of the mountains behind Gomez. I thought of Doll up there in the room beside the fountain courtyard. Then I was stepping through the door onto the terrace. Facing each other across the glass-topped table in the dazzling morning sunshine, Barbara

Anderson and Joe Moore looked rather shocked to see me. But Moore's initial surprise quickly turned into a bogus grin. While Barbara, seeing the briefcase in my hand, began to frown.

"Isn't this a hell of a coincidence to run into you here this morning, Father," Moore said. "I was just telling Barbara here how much respect I had for you."

"Hello, Joe. Hello, Barbara," I said.

"He was just telling me you ought to be forced to resign from your job because of drugs or something, Father," she said. She turned to him. "Come on, Mr. Moore. Are you afraid to tell him to his face?"

Joe Moore squirmed visibly in his seat. "I'm afraid you've misunderstood me, Barbara. Father, I was simply commenting on these wild statements of the FBI in the paper today."

"Which you must have loved," I said to him.

"I see you've finally brought it," she said, glancing from the briefcase to Moore.

"It's okay," I assured her.

"What did she get from you? I warn you, I won't pay anything over three hundred dollars."

"May I sit down?"

"Please go ahead." She reached out her hand to take the briefcase, but I ignored her. To compensate, she suddenly called for Mimi to bring more coffee and a new cup. A second later, Mimi appeared with both on a tray.

"What are you two talking about?" Moore asked innocently.

"Aaron's briefcase," I said.

"Yes," Barbara said. "Aaron left it with one of his sluts the evening he was shot. You saw the picture of that girl in the paper yesterday?"

"I saw it. She was at the funeral. The one whose head you nearly knocked off, right?" Moore said.

[272]

Barbara shrugged and looked vaguely embarrassed, as she thought she should look. "Fernando had promised me he would get it back."

"How kind of you, Fernando," Moore said.

"Thanks, both of you. I had to fly up to Las Vegas to get it. And cross the river."

"All the way to Las Vegas? I'm glad you took this so seriously, Fernando," she said.

"I'm not."

"Why not?" Moore asked.

"I thought it contained a copy of the Pointer Report." I stared into his eyes.

"The what?" she asked.

"Didn't Aaron even mention that to you?" I asked. "Why don't you explain, Joe?"

Moore nodded and took a sip of coffee from the Wedgwood cup. "Your husband believed that a report by an Army engineer named Pointer stated that the water resources under El Sol County were rather limited. Although copies of Pointer's report are easy to obtain, no copy I have ever seen includes any such fact. But Aaron believed in an appendix that, for some reason, was extremely elusive. Perhaps because it didn't exist."

"I see." She turned to me and asked, "Well, did the briefcase have this Pointer appendix or not?"

"I'm afraid not."

Moore looked relieved. He actually yawned. "You did check it out thoroughly?"

"I sure did, Joe."

"Was there anything else of any interest in the briefcase?" Barbara asked nervously.

"No."

"I see," she said, and let out a false sigh. "Short of another will, I couldn't think of what might be in it. Some of his love letters, I guessed. Or some incriminating diary or photographs. But I wasn't going to pay out more than three hundred dollars to save that bastard's reputation. Not after the way he treated me."

Moore looked pained by her remarks. He pushed his chair back and feigned a smile. "That was a memorable cup of coffee, Barbara. Congratulate your cook for me. And thank you so much for the chat."

"You're not leaving us?"

"Yes, I have to get down to my office."

"How do you feel about tomorrow's election?" I asked before he could rise.

"I feel quite good about it. The Propositions seem to be going to pass. I think my TV commercials have been effective. And, without Aaron, your committee's efforts have been kind of stalled this past week. Perhaps Jamie Hillal could have helped you. But alas . . ." He grinned in my face.

"Your grief becomes you, Joe. By the way, did you know that Aaron flew up to Denver and back the day he was killed?"

"No," he said. "I had no idea."

"Are you sure Aaron did?" Barbara asked, a perplexed expression on her face.

"I'm very sure. Can you think of any reason why Aaron would have flown up to Denver?" I wanted to see how both of them would react to this. But Moore seemed only mildly interested, while Barbara seemed to be thinking of something that disturbed her.

"Only Diane. And I'm sure Aaron would have just called her on the phone, not flown up there."

"Diane?"

"His first wife. Aaron was still friendly with her. They rarely saw each other, only talked occasionally on the telephone, the usual Christmas cards. This has nothing to do with anything."

"I really must be going," Moore said. He stood, and

I shook his hand. He gave Barbara a peck on the cheek. I was sure they were better friends than Barbara wanted me to know. "Be well, you two," Moore said.

"Good-bye, Mr. Moore," she said.

When he had left, and I had heard the front door shut inside the house, I took the liberty of asking her quite bluntly, "What did he want here?"

"Just a friendly visit. Except he did say that he'd like to see you lose your job at the church. You know, I think Joe Moore really admired Aaron."

"Aaron hated his guts. Tell me, what does this Diane do up in Denver? Aaron never mentioned her to me."

"He wouldn't. He still loved her. Diane was the one to reject Aaron, not like his second wife, whom he drove out of the house. Diane left him for a wonderful, handsome, dashing soldier. General Leon Cook. I suppose Leon was way before your time?"

"Yes."

"Leon was commandant at Fort Ricks back in the late Fifties and the Kennedy Sixties. He later went to the Pentagon after Johnson took over the White House. He and LBJ were old Texas buddies. Now he and Diane are retired. They live just outside Denver near their children."

"And you say he still loved her?"

"I know he did. More than any woman before or since. You see, ironically, Diane was Elwood Munty's girlfriend all through high school. They were engaged. Then Aaron decided to steal her for himself. Later, Leon Cook just stole her right away from under Aaron's nose. There was nothing he could do. It served Aaron right to lose her to a better man."

"Yet Aaron was on friendly terms with them?"

"He had to be. He never wanted to lose her entirely. And he certainly didn't threaten the general."

"Do you have her telephone number?"

[275]

"Just a second. It's in the address book. I'll go get it. And I'll get a check. I suppose you'll want your three hundred dollars for this briefcase."

"Here," I said, and handed it to her. "This belongs to you."

"You sure you don't need the money?" She smiled wickedly. "I know narcotics are more and more expensive these days."

"I may have to sue Mulcahy before this is finished," I said.

"Really? That will keep your name in the headlines for weeks, my dear young man. Don't tell me your wife doesn't smoke even a teensy-weensy bit of pot?"

"Who have you been talking to?"

"When are you going to learn?" She laughed, then stood up and smoothed the wrinkles out of her cotton skirt. "El Sol is a very small city. And the people here have very big mouths."

"What else do they say?"

"About you and your wife?"

"Yes."

"Oh, Fernando, don't worry. It will all work itself out. By the way, you'll be pleased to hear that, thanks to you, Lindy and Roy are in San Francisco today. They flew up to Reno and were married yesterday afternoon."

"How do you feel about that?"

She shrugged. "I suppose, in a slightly perverse way, it is all very flattering."

28

I HAD driven a mile down the road from the Andersons' to the Shamrock gas station, where I called Denver on the pay telephone, charging it to the rectory number.

Diane Cook had a young, almost playful-sounding voice, and I imagined for an instant how she looked and why Aaron had loved her so much. According to Barbara, this woman had broken Aaron's heart. If so, I now knew why he had been so kind to me after I told him of Nancy's departure with the hippie.

At the mention of Aaron's name, a pensive tone entered Diane Cook's voice. She explained that, yes, Aaron had come to see them unexpectedly on May 21. But it was better I discuss that with the general. Could I hold the line?

Leon Cook did not sound like an Army general. His voice was too understated; he was too willing to let me interrupt with impatient questions. He said they had been shocked when the news of Aaron's murder had reached them in Denver. He knew little of what Aaron was trying to prove by searching for this old "memo," as he called it. Did I think Aaron's death had been related? The general said he would give me exactly what he had given Aaron: a name and a telephone number of someone at Fort Ricks who could probably help—if anyone could.

I thanked him and said I was sorry to have disturbed

them. Nonsense, said the general. Would I promise to give them a call the next time I was in Denver? They'd have me out to their home and perhaps I could explain what this was all about. We said good-bye.

I had written the number down on a part of my checkbook. For some reason, it looked familiar. But I did not know why I should be familiar with the Fort Ricks telephone number of Major John Burter. There was nothing I could do except dial it.

A few rings later, I had a secretary on the line. "Archives. Major Burter is on the other line. May I help you?"

I said I would wait for the major. Soon a rather high-pitched voice said, "This is Burter speaking. What can I do for you?"

"My name is Father O'Neal. I'm a local clergyman here in the city. I got your name from General Cook up in Denver?"

"Yes?"

"I wonder if I could come by and see you this morning?"

"Is this about that Pointer Report again?"

"Yes, as a matter of fact."

"What do you want? Another copy?"

"Yes, that's just what I would like."

"We're in Building Forty-two on Sherman Road, beyond the Company Three mess hall. Are you familiar with the base?"

"No, but I'll find you."

"Just ask anyone for Archives."

"I'm leaving right now. Will you still be there in thirty minutes, Major?"

"Yes," he said. "You won't stand me up like the last fellow, will you?"

"No, of course not. I just want to ask you a couple questions."

[278]

"General Cook is a friend of mine. I'll answer any questions you've got."

From the Shamrock station in Cottonwood, I headed for the Interstate. It was almost the length of the city: the drive out to Fort Ricks. The sun flamed out of the cloudless blue sky. The heat was slamming off the road in waves. I had no idea if the Pointer Report he was talking about contained the appendix Aaron had remembered. I tried not to get my hopes up. In less than twenty-four hours the polls would open. Without evidence, it was likely Joe Moore would win this fight. Who knew what the future would hold for the city after that? I couldn't imagine what would happen to the Mexican-Americans and the other poor people—the working-class Anglos, the cowboys, the factory people, all the Border folk. Where would they go when the water was gone? Surely no place of their own.

At the Fort Ricks gate, I asked the MP for directions. He was very polite and very young. About twenty, I guessed. I was thirty-two years old. Somehow I couldn't get over the feeling that I had been twenty years old just a few months ago—when actually it was twelve years ago. I was too old for the Army, even for another Vietnam. Yet once upon a time I had changed my whole life to avoid being drafted.

I passed the big PX commissary and the NCO club. The base (it was never called the "fort," although it was Fort Ricks) looked surprisingly old and tacky. Except for several new concrete helicopter hangars and the nearby radar domes, most of the buildings looked like World War II vintage. Surely the little two-family bungalows where married enlisted men lived, sharing the carport and the scraggly front yard full of sand and juniper bushes, hadn't changed since 1945.

A little farther along, I passed a set of company barracks, mustard-brown boxcars without wheels. I drove by one platoon in their olive fatigues lined up on the gravel, taking their sergeant's angry tirade with stoic grimaces. Like all Army outposts in the Southwest, this had originally been a cavalry fort. I passed a sign reading "To the Polo Field" and thought, suddenly, of swashbuckling American bullies like Patton who had now been replaced by a breed of computer programmers and personnel managers.

A small sign reading "Ft. Ricks Archives," too small to read from the road, was nailed above the entrance to the wooden building. The number 42 was painted yellow and huge on the street out front. I parked and walked up to enter the small room full of card catalogs and a short-haired female sergeant who, I guessed, was Puerto Rican. I had an urge to ask her, but didn't. I knew how those questions felt.

"My name is Father O'Neal . . . ?"

"Yes, Father. The major is expecting you. Just go right through that door."

"Thanks, Sergeant."

It was a plain wood door. On the other side, I entered a tightly packed world of shelves and filing cabinets that filled the barracks from the floor to the eaves. It was like the stacks in a small university library, like standing inside a prison full of papers.

Off to my left was a tiny office completely filled by an old wooden schoolteacher's desk. A man with a gray crew cut was working at his desk. A corncob pipe jutted out of one side of his mouth, à la Douglas MacArthur, but his officer's uniform looked faded from years of laundering. Nor was it spectacularly pressed.

"Colonel Burter?"

"Father O'Neal. Come in and sit. I've got your copy of Pointer's report. You wanted the other part too, I assume."

"The other part?"

"The one labeled 'Memo Attached February 15, 1961' is what I'm referring to. That was what Mr. Anderson was particularly interested in."

"Yes, that's just what I want."

He held a buff-colored folder out to me. I opened it to find a photocopy of a typed report under the insignia of the U.S. Corps of Army Engineers. I turned to the back and found, under a separate clip, the "Memo Attached February 15, 1961." A palpitation made my heart jump to my throat. I shut the folder for the moment.

"This is it. Thank you so much, Major. You don't know—"

"Please feel free to ask any questions. Just fire away," Burter said.

"This is quite a place you have here."

"Well, Fort Ricks has been standing for over a hundred years. Somebody has to get stuck with all the paperwork. People don't think of the Army as a creative institution, but it sure creates a lot of paper. There's a fair pile of it." He nodded at the two levels of solidly jammed shelves.

"You said Aaron Anderson came to see you?"

"A week ago last Wednesday. He called from Denver first. Said he was getting to town about four-thirty. I told him Archives closed at five sharp. He managed to talk me into staying around ten minutes in case he was late. I was happy to stay. It was General Cook who transferred me over here to Archives in the first place, back in 1959. I'll be sorry to retire in three years."

I nodded understandingly. "But on the phone you said someone had stood you up? Was that Anderson?"

"No, Anderson came right on time. But I had another call last Thursday afternoon. Just like yours, except he didn't mention General Cook. He asked if I had something called the Pointer Report, and when I said yes, could he come over and get a copy. I said that was okay. But he never showed up."

"Who was he?"

"He said he was a member of the bar here in El Sol."

"Jamie Hillal?"

"That sounds about right."

"But he never came?"

"No, sir. I did wonder why. The copy I made for him is that one in your hand. By the way, we're supposed to charge seven cents a page for photocopies. But seeing as you're a friend of General Cook's . . ."

"Thank you. You don't read the newspaper, do you, Major?"

"On the contrary, I read the *Christian Science Monitor* every morning."

"I see."

"This local *Post-Examiner* is for the birds."

I laughed. His attitude was typical of most officers at Fork Ricks, as well as quite accurate. They had a base newspaper for their local news.

I opened the folder again and turned to the "Memo" at the back. It was eleven pages long.

"Have you ever read this?" I asked.

"Sure have. I remember reading it way back nineteen years ago when Pointer gave a copy to the Archives. He gave copies to a lot of people then. But I guess most of them got lost. Then I reread it last week."

"Was Pointer a good officer?"

"I don't know if he was a good officer. A nice guy. And a good engineer, I would guess. He was from South Dakota or Nebraska or someplace."

"He's dead, isn't he?"

"Yes, that's what I heard. He had a mind of his own, as I recall. They told him to make a precise list of all the wells pumping water in El Sol County. The reasons why the Army would be interested in that information are obvious."

"Yes."

"Along the way, he took it into his head to try to map the aquifer."

"The what?"

"The Gomez-El Sol Aquifer. The underground lake that holds all our water down there. He found it was too big to begin to draw a map, however. Too irregularly shaped. That's a job for more than one man anyway. But he had started taking these measurements. He discovered that the water level in certain wells was dropping at a high rate. As much as half an inch every few days. And that was back in 1961."

"Did you talk about this with Mr. Anderson?"

"Sure did. A nice man, that Anderson. He owns a bank, he said. Told me to come over and see him next time I bought a new car."

I nodded. Why tell him Aaron was dead? It would mean answering a lot of his questions, with answers that I had yet to find for myself.

"Does the 'Memo' estimate how long the aquifer will continue to supply us with water?"

"No. But Major Pointer said the aquifer couldn't be more than five hundred feet deep. Plus we know the water turns saline down there after a certain depth. He wasn't sure how fast the fresh water got replenished. Nor where the water came from in the first place. But Pointer recommended they keep an eye on just how fast we were emptying it. Oh, yes, there was something in there, a rhetorical question, about what would ten years of steady growth in El Sol mean for the aquifer? Something like that."

"And that was twenty years ago?"

"Nineteen years."

[283]

"Half an inch every twenty-four hours sounds awfully fast."

"I suppose that has to do with how much and how fast you pump."

"Has anyone done any updating of these figures?"

"I wouldn't know for sure," Major Burter said. "Certainly the Army hasn't sent me any more reports along the lines of Pointer's."

"Major, I want to thank you again. You don't know how much this means to me."

"You're welcome, Father. But this is just my job. I'm glad to have been able to help you."

"Major, do you know a man named Joe Moore?"

He thought for a moment. "Would he be in real estate around here?"

"Yes."

"I don't know him personally. But I believe a young lady who worked for him called me about a year ago. Then I think she came down here one day and made a whole bunch of copies of various documents."

"Could the Pointer Report have been one of them?"

"Sure. It's not a classified document."

"Is there any way you could check for me?"

He smiled. "Would you wait for a few minutes? It so happens that I keep the call slips on file here. I don't know exactly why. Just can't throw anything away, I guess." He rose and slid out between the desk and the wall.

Ten minutes later he was back with a little white scrap of paper. It showed that a Pat Curran of Moore's office had indeed examined a copy of the Pointer Report and the attached "Memo." Chances were she had photocopied it. I just wanted to know that for the record. I wasn't surprised in the slightest.

"Major, did you ever meet a Dr. Elwood Munty?"

He thought about that name for a minute. "No, it doesn't ring a bell."

"May I use your telephone out in the other room?"

"Go right ahead. Just ask Sergeant Vieras."

Once again I thanked him and rose to leave. I kept hoping that Havas had not decided to take Monday off to go fishing like his beloved Greek ancestors.

29

HE PREFERRED not to meet at his office. Was I familiar with an establishment called Freddy's Palapas Store? When I said no, Havas gave me detailed directions. It was located on a busy street about a mile west of the *barrio* in the Station.

The DEA agent sat in his parked car (a white Cutlass Supreme with dual tailpipes snaking down behind wide blackwall Goodyears) sucking on a yellow Popsicle. I parked next to his unmarked car. He rolled down the window and said, "Go get yourself a *palapa*."

"Is that what you call a Popsicle?"

"No Popsicle, Fernando. A *palapa*. This is not a Connecticut specialty, you know? Ask for mango."

I walked across the dirt lot and entered the concrete shack. A small crowd of Mexican children pushed and shoved in front of the counter. The man handing out the *palapas* looked like a Gypsy with a thin pencil mustache and a gold medallion hanging on a piece of rawhide outside his T-shirt. He ignored the kids when I entered and asked me what kind I wanted. I told him mango and he dug in the old freezer chest for it. We exchanged a *palapa* for twenty-five cents, and I walked out. I took one lick of pure frozen mango. It was spectacular.

Sliding into the Cutlass beside Havas, I said, "This is terrible."

"I know. I'm addicted. Mango. Banana. Pineapple. All *palapas*."

"Speaking of addiction, what do you think of priests who use narcotics in their own homes?"

"It's better than having them boozing in our public parks all night. Seriously, you shouldn't read the newspaper. It kills brain cells in this city."

"Should I sue Mulcahy?"

"If you know a nice lawyer you want to support for a year or two. But why bother? Let me tell you something. Mr. Mulcahy has got plenty of problems in his own home. I'm talking about this seventeen-year-old daughter of his. A bright girl, but she hates her old man. Did I say 'but'? Unfortunately, she's dating this low-life Mexican kid in her high school. He got her involved in this stolen-car racket the cops have been running. They have the kids steal the cars, while the cops are fencing them across the Border."

"My rental car was stolen last week."

"It's probably in Guadalajara by now. Don't the cops still have your Ford impounded too? They've really ripped you off this week, Father."

"How can you say the cops are running this?"

"How? Easy. It's true. Pasetti just found out a couple of days ago. I've known for months, of course. Somebody came to Roger after his big 'ultimatum' and pointed out that the boys down in Auto Theft at police headquarters are running the hottest car ring for six states."

"But how do you know?"

"I know, believe me. I had breakfast with Pasetti this morning, by the way. The moron wanted me and some of my agents to help him bust the entire El Sol Police Department this afternoon. I told him to go fuck himself. Pasetti is very happy now. He's finally got something that will look like a corruption bust when he sends Washington his report this month."

"And his daughter?"

"She was arrested two months ago. She and her boy-friend were caught stealing a new Corvette out at the Rambler Mall. The arresting cop wasn't hip. But she was let go without even a phone call to her old man. When this cop found out later, he sent a complaint directly to the chief. Nothing was ever done. So he went to Pasetti this week with his story. Now Pasetti believes the mayor is up to his elbows in stolen cars. Which is not true. But Pasetti went over to see Mulcahy this morning. He likes Mulcahy, of course. He's going to spare his daughter any bad publicity so long as Mulcahy cooperates."

"Listen, as interesting as this is, it's nothing. I think I know who killed Aaron and Jamie."

Havas had been chewing his wood *palapa* stick as if it were a cigar. He stopped, slowly removed the stick, and pointed it at me. "Who was that?"

Elwood Munty, I told him. I told him what Doll had said about Jamie calling his killer "Doc." I had done a lot of thinking about Dorfman's claim. Someone had reported my car was parked in Hillal's lot five minutes before the shooting. Who could that someone be? "It must have been Munty. He had to tell the cops that to take the suspicion off himself."

"I thought Munty and Anderson were supposed to be best friends."

"I'm not so sure. Aaron's first wife had been engaged to Munty back in high school. But Aaron stole her away. And I know Aaron never lost an opportunity to talk about what a lousy doctor Munty was."

"They sound like Greek best friends," Havas said. "They hated each other's guts."

"Another possible motive is money. Joe Moore could have offered a fortune to someone willing to kill Aaron. Moore has millions invested in this scheme he's got buried out in the desert. Munty may have needed money."

"What has Moore got buried?"

"That's right. I haven't seen you since I had my tour of Moore's hole in the ground. Excuse me, I mean his perfect city for the twenty-first century."

"You'd better explain."

I explained. Then I got out of the car, went over to the Mustang, and opened the locked trunk. I had hidden the Pointer Report back there. It was worth hiding if it was worth killing for. I brought it back and gave it to Havas.

He thumbed through it quickly. I told him it was the first piece of real evidence that could be used to support Aaron's contention that there was a severe danger of the water running out in El Sol.

"You know, I keep thinking about this lithium in the water here," Havas said. "I keep thinking maybe that explains why every punk I run into in this town lately is looking to shoot somebody. Then I keep reminding myself that we've just had the hottest May in living memory. And now, two days into June, we've broken two more heat records."

I shook my head. "I don't know about the lithium. All I do know is that, back in 1961, Major Pointer found the aquifer diminishing at a frightening rate. We still have water, but how long can it last?"

"Especially if Moore gets his way."

"Mayor Castillo said he was waiting for evidence that Proposition 3 would be harmful. *This* is the evidence."

"Mayor Castillo is going to be finished as a candidate by the time Pasetti has cracked open this car-theft scandal. Castillo won't have a chance tomorrow. Mulcahy is going to ride the FBI bust for all the 'corruption' headlines he can get."

"Do you believe Castillo was involved in the stolen cars?"

"No. I think Chief Almada was probably cut in for

some of the profits. But not Castillo. Castillo didn't appoint Almada, remember. They're rivals with their own political organizations."

"But if we could turn Munty over to the cops, and the mayor could take credit for that, it would top any headlines Mulcahy and the FBI could get for these stolen cars. What's the number-one story in town? It's who killed Aaron and Jamie."

Havas shook his head. "You're talking like a PR man, and what we're dealing with here is murder. Slow down. What do you want me to do?"

"Can you arrest Elwood Munty?"

He laughed bitterly. "On what grounds? Besides, I don't have a warrant."

"The thing is, I admit, I am not entirely sure about Munty."

"So?"

"So I thought maybe you could get him to confess. I trust you."

"You don't trust the El Sol police, is that it?"

"Dorfman is a nasty bastard. I saw the way the cops treated Elwood Munty too. Like he was a 'good ole boy' or something. I don't think they would take my word for it."

"They'd take mine?"

"Don't they have to take yours?"

"Not necessarily. The problem is that all I have to go on at this point," he said, "is your word."

"You don't believe me?"

He stared down at the folder with the Pointer Report on the seat between us. Then out the window at the line of kids waiting to buy *palapas*. "You know, Pasetti asked me this morning if I would bust you? He wants me to raid your fucking house."

"What did you say?"

"I told him to get his transfer to Palm Beach without

my help. I told him to go ream himself, of course. He swears there was a joint in your ashtray, though. Do you smoke, Fernando?"

"Not for years."

"So what's he talking about?"

"My wife does. But I told her to get rid of it and she did. If you want to raid my house, go ahead. You won't find anything."

He smiled, then shook his head. "There is no way I can go and arrest Munty. On the other hand, I see what you want. There is nothing to stop me from making a friendly call on the doctor."

I waited for him to continue. When he didn't, I asked, "What are you thinking?"

"Let's get this over with right now," Havas said. "Before somebody else dies."

"You mean you want me to come with you?"

"You're the one who has fingered Munty. It's your word against his. I think you ought to come."

"Are you ready in case he starts shooting?"

Havas pulled his lightweight jacket back at the hip to show me his snub-nosed .38 Smith & Wesson tucked into his waistband holster. "Am I ready?"

"I guess."

"I told you I was no hero." He laughed. "You didn't think I was stupid, though, did you?"

He turned the key and started his Oldsmobile while I shook my head.

"You know the way? Where does Munty live?"

"Cottonwood. But maybe we should try his office first. Or the Sheraton bar, where he hangs out."

"That's not a bad idea," Havas said.

Nor was it a very good idea. After an hour, and stops at both the Sheraton and Munty's clinic, there was no sign of the doctor. We decided to try his house.

That was a very bad idea.

30

"THAT HIS Caddy in the driveway?" Havas asked as we approached the long pink ranch house. I nodded. There was a wide lawn of emerald turf and a few magnificent old cottonwoods clustered around the place. These people had a good life out here in the middle of the desert.

Havas pulled into the driveway next to the Seville. We both jumped out and walked around to the front door. It was open, about two inches ajar. I was very nervous but Havas winked at me and rang the bell. There was no answer.

"Maybe they're out back at the pool," I said. He rang again. It was after three P.M., blistering hot. The only sounds were the cicadas and the parched call of a dove somewhere in the cottonwoods overhead. You could hear children's voices coming from a backyard on a nearby street. Havas rang a third time.

I was trying to imagine what words would be best to accuse Munty of murder with. Suddenly I saw Havas had left me standing on the doorstep. I followed him inside.

The interior was furnished in an old-fashioned manner: dark walnut furniture, china knickknacks, overstuffed chairs with lace doilies, and a beige carpet that felt like sponge underfoot. The pictures on the wall were mostly blown-up photos. There was a dining room off to the left, a large living room on the right leading into the pine-paneled den. In the living room, one giant glass-fronted cabinet contained crystal statues of animals. The TV in the corner was playing a soap opera with the sound turned off. That was a common sight in El Sol houses. I saw a gun case out in the den. There were several mounted trophies on the den wall: a bighorn sheep, a mule deer . . .

"Hello," Havas called. "Anybody home?"

I pointed out the gun case to him. He'd already noticed it. The door was open and several racks were empty.

"They must be out. I guess we should go," I said.

"What's that?" Havas asked. He meant the noise that sounded like someone whispering. "Hush. . . ."

"Water?"

He walked out of the living room and pushed open the swinging door into the kitchen. The door swung shut behind him. "Oh, man," he said in a low voice. "Oh, no, man. You did it." The sound of water stopped abruptly as he shut off the tap. I went to the door and reluctantly pushed it open.

Havas was standing over the small body of Edith Munty. She was lying in a pool of blood on the bright yellow linoleum. She wore light blue slacks and a striped top, and an apron. She had been shot several times in the back.

Havas had a furious look in his eyes. "You were right. But we're a little late. What's the address here again?"

"Twenty-seven River Edge Road."

There was a green telephone on the wall next to a magnetic message board. On the message board itself was the article on Mulcahy's speech to the Kiwanis Club, clipped out of the newspaper. Havas dialed, waited a moment, then asked for a Captain MacNelly.

I listened for the next few minutes as Havas told the

police officer that: (1) he believed Elwood Munty had killed both Anderson and Hillal; (2) Mrs. Elwood Munty was lying dead on her kitchen floor at 27 River Edge Road; and (3) he assumed Elwood Munty had shot her too. "This man is a psycho, extremely dangerous," Havas said into the phone. "You'll want to tell your people to use extreme caution. I assume he shot his wife because he knows his time has come. He's probably suicidal. But I doubt if he's going to do us that favor." He listened for a while, then said, "No, I can't do that. No, Captain, I have no idea. Don't worry, I haven't touched a thing. One of my informants, yes. Father O'Neal down at Holy Innocents, if you must know. Yes, it was his tip. Sorry, Captain. I have to move fast."

He hung up and looked at me. "He wants us to wait around for Dorfman to show up. You don't want that and neither do I. Let's get out of here."

"But what about . . . ?" I looked at Edith Munty's body. "We can't just leave her."

"There's nothing we can do. They're sending an ambulance." He walked out of the kitchen. I followed him down the hall and out the front door. He told me not to shut the front door, to leave it just as we'd found it. We crossed the lawn to the white Cutlass.

"Where do you want to look for Munty now?" he asked. "You know any more of his favorite bars?"

"I can think of a few. Would you mind if we just stopped by my house for a second?" I hadn't spoken to Nancy since I left that morning. "It's only about a mile from here. Cottonwood Estates."

He nodded as he put the car into reverse. "You tell me how to get there."

I gave him directions as I tried to concentrate on looking out the window. I thought about Munty and why he might have killed Jamie. Perhaps Jamie had figured it out. Perhaps Munty had just thought he had. And what about

Johnny Attlee? Had Attlee known something about Aaron and Munty that nobody else had?

The Rabbit in my driveway cheered me up. "Well, at least she's here," I said.

Havas grunted something unintelligible and pulled to a stop at the curb. I jumped out and betrayed my anxiety by jogging across the white gravel. I could not help myself. I heard Havas' door slam and his own shoes hitting the gravel behind me. At least the front door was not open here.

I rang the bell as I dug for the keys in my trouser pocket. Soon I had the door unlocked and was standing in the sunny living room calling, "Nancy? Where are you?"

Havas went straight into the kitchen. "She's not in here," he said. I was already on my way back to the bedroom. Neither of us would admit it to ourselves, but we were searching for a body almost as much as we were for a live person. I would never forget the horror of Munty's kitchen.

Nancy was not taking a nap, as I had hoped. The bedroom was empty, the bed made neatly. I went to the window. Havas came in behind me. "I checked the garage. She's not in there."

The window was shut, reglazed since it had been blown out on Friday night. I opened it and called out her name. Although this faced the side of the yard, she could have heard me if she was sunbathing out on the back patio. There was no answer.

"A neighbor's house?" Havas asked. "A walk?"

"She didn't know any of the neighbors. She's hardly lived here. And who walks around here? There aren't even any sidewalks."

"Let's go look again. Maybe we missed something. Let's keep cool, Fernando."

I found the note a minute later. It was on a chair beside

the Formica-topped kitchen table. It was written in red pencil on the back of a junk-mail envelope.

> If you wish to help me, kindly bring Pointer's "Memo" to Father Ortega now. Or bring yourself alone.
>   Nancy O'Neal your wife

"This is weird," Havas said after he'd read it. "Does this sound like your wife?"

"She didn't write that. It's her handwriting. But she didn't write that."

"No?"

"Not in a million years."

"I'd better call MacNelly," Havas said. "Where are you going?"

"You call if you want. I'll take the Rabbit to the mission." I turned and went out the kitchen door.

"Okay, forget MacNelly," he said behind me. "Get in the Oldsmobile."

"What?"

"We're going in my car, Fernando." The next thing I knew, he had passed me, running across the gravel.

31

HAVAS RACED for the Interstate, careening through the moving cars on Desert Hills Avenue as if they were nothing but a few flags on a slalom course. He gunned up the entry ramp, then reached over and hit the switch on his glove compartment. A radio was concealed inside, with a microphone on a coiled black wire. He tried to reach the El Sol police operator down at City Hall, but the airwaves were jammed with calls. There seemed to be no way to get through all the confusion. He gave up in disgust after a minute, threw the mike on the seat between us, and switched on the AM radio in the dashboard.

I was still in shock. "He must be a monster," I said. "Edith Munty was one of the most likeable women in my parish. He just shot his own wife in cold blood. In the back."

"It looked like both shots hit her heart. She didn't suffer. Look at it that way."

"You look at it that way," I snapped.

He tossed me a look but said nothing.

"I'm sorry, Havas. I am very grateful to you."

"Bullshit. I'm doing this because I want to. Jamie Hillal was my friend."

"He was almost mine."

"Did you ever meet his father?"

"Yes, as a matter of fact."

"A good man. A wise man. When he arrived here with his brother over sixty years ago, they had nothing. Just a donkey loaded with rugs they'd brought all the way from Beirut to sell."

We were flying down the left lane of the Interstate into a fairly heavy flow of traffic. Havas drove with only one hand; the other tapped nervously on his leg. He kept looking over at me as he talked. "In the Twenties, they bootlegged. Jamie's uncle was shot for three cases of Scotch on the Gomez side of the river one night. Now Robert is the richest man in this town."

"I've heard."

"They treated me great. Arabs and Greeks aren't supposed to get along. Let alone Arab lawyers and Greek narcs."

"Who says?"

He laughed. "I told Robert I would find Jamie's killer. It sounds corny, I know. Tough shit."

"It sounds like you meant what you said."

"I did. Until you came up with Doll, I thought it was somebody hired from out of town. None of my informants could give me anything on what happened to Jamie. I was leaning to either Joe Moore or maybe somebody who didn't like the way Jamie had handled his case in court."

We were approaching the *barrio*: Sandoval Boulevard. Havas hit the brakes hard, jolting us down from ninety to sixty-five miles an hour, then flung us into the exit ramp.

A veil of reddish smog hung over the low rooftops of the *barrio*. A few blocks up the boulevard, flashing red lights turned in the gloom. Sirens were audible in the distance.

We passed few cars on these next streets. There were one or two low-riders slowly nosing around, some delivery vans, some older Detroit sedans on their last set of shocks.

Havas turned on the radio and moved the dial to the all-news station. An announcer was finishing his report on Wall Street's day back East. The Dow Jones was down three and a half points. Suddenly he was reading a strange bulletin:

> El Sol police report three of their officers have been shot dead along with one civilian at a warehouse on the western edge of the *barrio* this afternoon. Only preliminary reports have come through. We understand there is still shooting down there. Our source claims it involves a long-standing police "sting" operation designed to crack a stolen auto ring operating between this city and Mexico. We are waiting confirmation of this. In the meantime, according to our source, this ring has been responsible for hundreds of stolen cars over the past twelve months. It seems that shooting broke out when the police made their move to shut it down today. More on this as soon as we have it.

"Did you hear that?" Havas asked incredulously. We were cruising through the heart of the ghetto, passing broken-down tenements and abandoned wrecks that had been stripped bare. The smoke from the charcoal fires floated a mere fifteen feet off the ground. There was no breeze, and few people were out, despite the intense heat this afternoon.

"What does it mean?" I asked.

"It looks like Chief Almada got wind of Pasetti's plan to raid his department. So Almada beat him to the punch. It's brilliant. They've busted themselves and they're calling it a 'sting' operation. The person who's gotten stung is old Roger Pasetti."

"There's the Mission," I said. The adobe campanile and

the wooden cross were visible three blocks away above the low rooftops. "Something's going on."

"Yeah," Havas said.

We turned the corner and saw several cars parked at crazy angles in the street. Men crouched low behind the fenders. One man was aiming a rifle at the church. Havas came to a stop, and suddenly he had me by the shoulder and was holding me below the window level of the Oldsmobile. "This is a battle zone," he shouted. I could hear the gunfire on three sides of us.

"Get out this side," he ordered. He opened his door and slipped down to kneel on the road. I came bellying over the front seat and spilled myself out headfirst.

Havas told me to keep down and wait. He ran up to the low-rider parked nearest us. A young man, overweight, with long black sideburns, sat with his back against one of the doors. He had a revolver in one hand and a cardboard container of grapefruit juice in the other. He was drinking in long gulps. It was well over one hundred degrees and I was covered with sweat, although we had just been driving in Havas' air-conditioned car. Havas crouched beside him and spoke for several minutes. I saw how confidently Havas handled himself with these people.

I turned and stared at the Mission San Juan. Beyond the paved road, the front yard was mostly dirt, with a single concrete path leading up to the three steps in front of the doors. A body lay thirty feet away on the dirt: male, motionless. I heard bullets repeatedly slamming into the large bell up in the campanile. I assumed someone was firing back from up there.

People were spread out behind whatever cover they could find. There were perhaps thirty people altogether, many with guns. I saw the quick outline of a man as he raised himself from behind the false front of the main church and fired a pistol at the belltower. More gunshots. I heard a shout in Spanish.

Havas came running back and crouched beside me. "He's up in the belltower. He's got hostages. These people are furious because he's got Father Ortega up there. This is their turf, and Ortega is their man."

"Is Nancy up there?"

"Sounds like it. They say there's a woman hostage. He's got rifles and a lot of ammunition. They don't know what the hell he wants. He came here about an hour ago, took Ortega up in the tower, tied them up or something, and started shooting."

"This is hell."

"Do you have any ideas?"

"Are you asking me? You're the cop."

"I know but it's your wife up there. Let me try something." He opened the car door and edged across the front seat on his stomach. He opened the glove compartment again and turned a switch, then came out with the microphone in his hand. Suddenly the air was full of a high screech of feedback in the smoky *barrio*.

Havas' voice filled the battle zone. "MUNTY, I AM A FEDERAL LAW-ENFORCEMENT OFFICER. WE HAVE YOU SURROUNDED. A HELICOPTER IS ON ITS WAY WITH SHARPSHOOTERS. YOU DON'T HAVE A CHANCE UNLESS YOU FREE THOSE PEOPLE. LET FATHER ORTEGA COME DOWN HERE. AND THE OTHERS. DO YOU HEAR ME, MUNTY?"

There was no acknowledgment. A moment later, a young Chicano stepped out on the ledge that ran across the top of the false front of the Mission. He began to edge closer to the campanile. He kept himself flattened to the wall. At the corner, he would be able to look directly down into the arched window at the bell. He was very brave-looking up there—and very isolated. A shot rang out. The sound was buried under a wave of thunder from the other guns as the boy teetered, then fell. He hit the steps below, his legs spread out at a hideous angle, his head almost kissing the dirt.

Havas pushed the microphone into my hand, "You try it."

I held the mike for a moment, my mind a blank. "THIS IS FERNANDO O'NEAL. I READ YOUR NOTE AND I HAVE BROUGHT THE 'MEMO,' ELWOOD. I HAVE IT RIGHT HERE. DO YOU WANT ME TO BRING IT TO YOU? JUST GIVE ME A SIGNAL. YOU CAN HAVE IT. ALL WE WANT ARE THOSE PEOPLE, SAFE AND SOUND. ELWOOD, CAN YOU UNDERSTAND THAT? GIVE ME SOME SIGNAL."

"You're not going in there," Havas snapped. "No way."

"You've got a better way to distract him?"

He took his gun out of the holster at his waist. "This piece is good at twenty feet, not a hundred. I couldn't hit ten elephants from here to there. I've got to get closer. I couldn't cover you."

"It's my wife."

"He's a nut up in a tower with a rifle. You ever heard of that before? That's the American illness, buddy. I'm sorry, he's sick. I can't let you go."

Just at that moment Elwood Munty stepped onto the edge of the belltower window. He wore a white short-sleeved shirt, brown pants, and white loafers. Instantly the guns thundered all around us. Munty was hit. He did a kind of grotesque dance. I saw something flash behind him and then his head bent down and his body tried to fall to the ground. There was a rope tied around his chest and under his arms. When he was almost at the ground, the bell rang. He did not smack the earth, but rose again on the thin brown hemp, rose and rang the bell a second time. A third time. He bobbed on the end of the rope, and the bell rang furiously: four, five, six more times. At the seventh ring, Munty came to rest with his feet yards off the ground, his lifeless body beginning to show patches of red.

"*Padre?*" called a voice from the Mexicans around us. "*Padre Jose, está bien?*"

I looked at Havas. The DEA agent raised his eyebrows and said, "He killed himself."

"Like you said."

"Fernando O'Neal?" cried a voice in the belltower. "Are you there? Show yourself. That was your signal."

I put the microphone back to my mouth, absolutely astonished. "PROFESSOR SNOW?"

Havas tugged at my arm. "Who is that?"

"I think that was David Snow." My mind flashed a picture of the last time I had seen him: in the lot at McDonald's. Suddenly I felt my guts turn over with the truth.

"Are you sure?"

"I think so." I knew it was Snow. How wrong I had been about this "harmless eccentric" and his deadly academic babble.

"He must be a psycho. He's got to be," Havas said.

Snow's voice cried out, "Sacrifice, Father. We all must die. Father Ortega is waiting. Your wife is here."

"SNOW, I'M COMING INSIDE. I WANT TO UNDERSTAND THIS. LET'S TALK. I'VE BROUGHT THE POINTER REPORT. I WANT TO UNDERSTAND."

"Father, you will understand. I'm glad you're here," Snow called.

Havas had a fierce grip on my wrist. "I'm not letting you go anywhere, man."

"You have to. Use me to distract him. Run around the other way and get up behind him. It's not that high."

"Let's wait for help. We'll wait him out. You don't want to press him. He'd shoot you just as soon as he did Munty's wife. In a while he'll get tired, sloppy. We'll take him then."

"You saw these people shoot Elwood? I'm going in now. If I don't, he'll push her out on that ledge and they'll shoot her to pieces like Munty. The time is now."

"You know something? You're crazy too," Havas said. But I could see he was ready to go along with me.

"Do you have an extra gun or anything?" I asked.

"Nothing except this." He motioned with his own gun. "You want it? I'll give it to you."

"Bullshit. You take it. Start moving." I leaned low across the front seat and got the buff folder with the Pointer Report off the floor. Havas ran for the cover of the low-rider's Chevy. When he was three cars away, waiting for me to show myself, I stood up.

Each step I took across the small plaza in front of the Mission told me a different story. I had been wrong about Munty. Wrong about Aaron. Wrong about Snow. What had I been right about? I dared not look down at the dirt, just up at the campanile, from where my death would come, flinging itself down. I could imagine my death waiting for me beside that big old iron bell. I was walking on waves of heat. Any of the guns in the area could suddenly bark and I would go down. Never to rise again. Why had I chosen to leave the protection of the car? Each step told me there was one less step to take. I loved her this much.

Out of the corner of my eye, I saw Havas run around the far corner of the belltower as I reached the first step. I had to go around the dead boy's body. The blackened pine doors into the church were open. The Chicanos were holding their fire, but I could almost feel their fingers poised on their weapons. As I pressed inside the nave, I felt a surge of coolness. I was again out of range of Snow up in the top of the campanile.

His voice called eerily to me almost at once. "Father?" It was coming through an open door to the extreme left.

[304]

This led from the nave into the base of the belltower. "Father, are you safe and sound?"

He was using my words to mock me.

"Yes, Snow."

"Do you see the door?"

"Yes, I'm coming." A thought crossed my mind. "Can my wife speak to me? Just to show me she's all right?"

"I'm sorry, but she can't, Father. Her mouth is taped rather tightly. Sorry."

"That's okay."

"I would like to explain to you, Father."

"Please. I want to understand." I had moved into the shadows at the bottom of the belltower. It smelled of the plaster that was falling off in chunks and the old wood of the stairs that led up into the bell's chamber. I didn't want to climb those stairs, but I knew I was going to. "I'm right down here, Snow. But I won't come any farther until you explain."

I thought I heard scuffling noises. Was Havas trying to wedge himself up the chute formed by the adjoining walls of the tower and the church? I hoped it was Havas, hoped that he was a good and silent climber.

32

"Did you read my book?" Snow asked down through the darkness and smell of rotten wood. "My book on Aztlan?"

"Of course I read it. A great book, Professor."

"You didn't understand it."

"I tried to understand. It's very deep." Actually I had never tried to read his book, only skimmed it on several occasions.

"You remember the Fifth Sun? The Aztecs reigned supreme. The Fifth Sun ended when the Spanish, when Cortez, extinguished the reign of Quetzalcoatl. If you read my book, you know all this, O'Neal."

"Yes, I know it. Why didn't you mention all this when you called me this morning, Snow?"

He paused. "I was lying this morning, wasn't I?"

"I don't know." Did Snow even recognize the difference anymore?

"What you don't know is the Sixth Sun, the reign of gold, of despair. And now we stand on the verge of a Seventh Sun. No more tigers, birds, fish. No more men. We must look at the future, O'Neal. Do you know your own Bible at least?"

"Yes. What part of the Bible do you mean?"

"The Revelation, of course. The book with the seven seals. Who would open it but the Lamb? And we are going to be the seven horns of that Lamb, the seven eyes, Fernando. Did you hear the bell just now. Do you understand?"

"No, it's difficult."

"They say the Aztecs were the lost tribe of Israel. Aztlan is what St. John called the New Jerusalem. Why were you all so worried about the water? We aren't fish. The Fourth Sun was the Water Age. That's long gone."

"But you said Aaron and Jamie were right." The insanity of Snow's words kept me inching forward. Nancy was up there, at his mercy.

"I lied to you. I wanted you to come with me. But you made this necessary. I am grateful to you, Father. This is much the best."

"Why?" I had edged up four stairs to try to get a glimpse of the scene above. Snow's ravings were almost more terrifying than his murders. His voice sounded so sure of its own truth. For once, his words were far too easy to understand, if not to make any sense of.

"Jesus Christ is dead, Father. Just as Aaron Anderson and Jamie Hillal and Elwood Munty are all dead. We all must die. Seven deaths, seven sacrifices, and the blood the new gods need for their birth will be provided."

"Are you going to die, Snow?"

"I expect so. But first Father Ortega and your wife and you must die."

"But that is more than seven, Snow. Why don't you allow my wife to live? She's not involved."

"She's your servant. No, it will be seven. Some of the others did not count."

"But why must this happen now?"

"I am Yopi. You remember?"

"No, I forget." I was still moving up, step by step. I couldn't hear the sounds of anyone climbing outside anymore. But at least the more I talked to him, the calmer Snow's voice sounded above my head. "What is Yopi, Professor?"

"*Who* is Yopi," he corrected. "Yopi is the God of Spring in the Valley of Mexico. Our Lord the Flayed One."

"Like Jesus?"

"Those myths are not analogous. Not precisely. Yopi convenes the season of new growth. He is the God of Beginnings. The earth must cover itself with a new coat and exchange its dead skin for living."

"Snow, I'm coming up."

"You must come."

"Promise you won't shoot me?"

"I want you to see. Perhaps you can even help me. I am too old to be very good at this. The last one went badly."

"What do you mean?"

"Please come, Father. She will be difficult for me alone."

I had reached the last turning before the final flight of steps up through the trapdoor into the bell room. "Is 'she' my wife, Snow? I'm sure she won't be difficult."

"Not if you help me."

I stepped into the light that poured down from the windows of the bell chamber. As I walked those final ten stairs, I suddenly felt I had made a terrible mistake. It was too late to change it back.

Snow had chalked his face with red and yellow stripes. Horizontal stripes. Over this he wore his glasses. He smiled terrifyingly as he waved his rifle in my direction. I saw Father Ortega lying behind him, his mouth covered with thick white adhesive tape. His hands and ankles were also taped. His eyes were pleading with me. I didn't see Nancy.

"Where is she?"

"She's just over your head."

I looked up at the bell. This chamber was practically airless. I turned my head, and there Nancy lay. She was dead, I thought. Then I saw her eyes move. He had bound her wrists and ankles, taped across her mouth, and taped her around the neck, so that her head was held to the plaster wall. A long steel chef's knife lay on the floor about two feet from her.

"You see?"

"Yes, I see. I've got the Pointer Report." I held it out toward him. He looked so insane with the stripes across his face under his glasses.

"Yes, good, we'll burn that one too. Along with this." He reached into his back pocket and took out a piece of folded paper. It looked like Aaron's Denver ticket. He must have taken it off Jamie's body.

"Why did you kill Aaron, Snow? For Yopi?"

"I didn't realize at the time, but that's the way I came to understand. Aaron had to die. Aaron always had to die."

"Why?"

"He wanted to stop Aztlan."

"But how can you build Aztlan with no water?"

"Men need water. Gods don't."

I already knew the answer to the next question. Gods needed blood. He had already told me that.

"Tell me about Aaron."

"He called me up and said he wanted to show me something. He took me to those movies, thinking they would shock me. He always tried to shock me. He was a bad tease. But he went too far. I knew he would. He had found that Pointer 'Memo' which I hadn't found. When he teased me about it, about how it was right there under my nose, and why hadn't I been able to find it, well, I did what I had to do. He mocked me for the last time. He was the first."

"And Attlee?"

"A mistake, in retrospect. I wanted to take his living heart. But such things are not easy. The Aztec priests

[309]

were as skilled, as quick as our finest surgeons. No, Attlee was the sacrifice for Aaron, but I had to cancel that. Did you notice about the guns?"

"What about the guns?"

"I used a different gun each time. These criminals are so stupid. They leave a trail of obvious evidence each time they kill with the same gun. On top of that, they throw the gun away and the police find it. Then they are finished."

"What about my car?"

"Your car?"

"You managed to rig it so it would speed out of control."

"No, I never touched your car."

"Are you sure?" Something in his voice made me believe him.

"Of course."

"I saw you shoot at Nancy and me through our window."

"But you didn't recognize me."

"Not with your face like that." Now I realized the red and yellow chalk stripes had looked like an "orange mask" in the dimly lit panic of that moment in our bedroom.

"Yopi's face," he said.

"Why did Yopi kill Jamie?"

"He called me. He told me to come down to his office for a very important meeting. I knew the Arab was going to try something dangerous. I told you that when we had lunch. He said you and Munty would be joining him there. He said it was about this Pointer Report. He had good news. Well, I didn't want to hear any of his mocking lies either."

"The girl ran away."

"Yes, I forgot about her."

"But you didn't forget about Edith Munty. You shot her first?"

"Oh, well," Snow said, as if it was obvious why he had done this. "I didn't want to bring her along. Something had to give somewhere. One slave is all we need."

"What do you need a slave for?" I asked, straining to keep my voice sounding reasonable in the face of this confession.

"To flay, of course."

"Why a slave?"

"A slave can lend his skin to his master. The master dies, the slave's skin is used to cover him. You should have read my book more carefully."

"Yes."

"Aztlan will be reborn the new Jerusalem. From Indian blood and Spanish blood, Anglo blood, even African blood, a new generation of gods shall walk in this desert garden. But no Arab blood."

"Why not?"

"Another tribe of Israel. A jealous tribe. Why do you think they came all this way? To stop the new Jerusalem, of course. You can read that in the newspapers."

He smiled a horrifying smile, his face made up like a deathlike clown's. He believed he was the Aztec God of Spring. "You can help me flay her?"

"I can?"

"I asked if you can," he said.

"What exactly do you mean?"

"The earth must exchange its dead skin for a new one. In Aztec ritual, an earthly priest must be covered with the skin of a slave. We have two priests here now. You see the knife over—"

Havas had pulled himself up into the window of the belltower behind Snow. He held his .38 with both hands leveled at the psychopath's back. But Snow had seen my eyes move. As he turned, Havas fired. Snow threw himself to the side, firing the rifle from his hip. Plaster flew off the wall near Havas. Havas fired. The bell was hit, and I felt the ricochet burn the air near my face. Havas was firing to empty his gun. Snow was hit, but he kept shooting. Suddenly I saw a surprised look flash across Havas' face and he fell backward, off the ledge. I heard his body hit the roof below, and I presumed he was dead.

Snow lay bleeding on the floor not far from Father Ortega, who stared from him to me, terror-crazed. Snow had dropped the rifle by his side. He was reaching for it as I put my foot on the butt. The reddish stain was spreading quickly on his shirt front.

"I'll be all right," he managed to whisper. "If they take me to the hospital, I can live. And you can still help."

"Yes?" I picked up the rifle. "How?"

"You can take my place as Yopi."

"Of course I can."

"They'll say I'm crazy, won't they?"

"Yes." So they would indeed.

"You will do it?"

"Flay them, you mean?"

"Yes." He nodded vigorously, then coughed. His voice was just a hiss because of the wound in his chest. "Flay them."

I heard running footsteps below me. They hit the first of the wooden steps. Spanish voices, very excited.

"No, I can't do that," I told him. "Just this." I quickly pointed the barrel of the rifle at his face and pulled the merciful trigger. I wanted to turn my head but would not let myself. The bullet entered below his left eye, but it really did not make much of an opening in front. I threw the rifle down and moved away from the top of the stairs.

Nancy was staring at me from where her head was taped to the wall. I went to her first, ripped the tape off the wall and off her neck. I pulled the gag off next, and knelt to remove the tape from her wrists.

Outside on the roof of the Mission I heard Havas shout, "Fernando, are you all right?"

"Thank you," whispered Nancy. "Do you know what he was going to do to me? He was going to—"

I put my finger on her lips to keep her from finishing. The first of the young men reached the bell chamber and crossed to Father Ortega's aid.

"Thank God you're safe," I told her.

Epilogue

THREE WEEKS after my trial, on a hot September afternoon, Maggie came into my office with a thunderstruck
look in her eyes. There was a lady to see me.

"What lady?" I immediately thought of Nancy, who
had been gone since the day my trial ended.

Maggie wouldn't say. She just shook her head with an
expression that brought me quickly to my feet and
around the desk.

Doll was standing in the middle of the waiting area.
She looked radiant, her thick black hair cut shorter than
before, her eyes blue as deep water, dressed in a white
cotton frock embroidered with white silk thread. Maggie
had recognized her from Aaron's funeral four months
before. I hadn't seen Doll since I left her that evening in
the room off the fountain courtyard, since I drove down
the mountain with Aaron's briefcase.

"You're back."

"Inez said you came to the house," she said. "You
wanted to see me?" There was a distance in her voice, and
an appraising look in her eyes, that helped me to remember Maggie's presence. Otherwise, I might have simply
moved to embrace Doll.

"Do you want to come in my office?" I had another
thought. "Or why don't we take a walk?"

She nodded. I took her gently by the elbow and turned

her toward the door. "I'll be back soon," I told Maggie. She said nothing; she looked shocked.

It was too hot to walk outdoors. I took Doll down the corridor and into the nave of the church. It was dark and cool, empty, with just the faintest trace of last Sunday's incense in the air. At the entrance to one of the rear pews, she crossed herself and touched one knee to the tiled floor, then slid her hips onto the dark red seat cushion. She sat with her hands folded in her lap and her eyes on mine. I could see that Maggie had made her wary. But now that we were alone, she relaxed somewhat.

"Where have you been? Inez wouldn't tell me a thing."

"Mexico City. Oxaca. Acapulco. My country. I took your advice."

"My advice?"

"Yes, I went to travel with your money."

"*Your* money. Did you enjoy it?"

"Yes, very much. And you? How are you?"

"I'm fine."

There was little point in explaining to her. Because I had given Dorfman a truthful account of what had happened up in the belltower, including how Snow had died, the city attorney had indicted me on second-degree-murder charges. Our new mayor made sure of that. I knew that, in one sense, I was guilty. But I couldn't get over the other feeling. Being indicted for David Snow's murder was, I felt, almost a kind of honor.

Havas had found me a lawyer up in Salt Lake City: a brilliant young Mormon who had lost one leg in Vietnam and had a degree from Harvard Law. By the time I was free to leave the courtroom, my lawyer had reduced the jury foreman to tears—twice. By then the entire jury wished they could fire the prosecutor and impeach the mayor. What I had done up in the tower, in my rage, was illegal, even immoral. Yet I was only a man, and so were the jury: just men and women, not gods.

As for David Snow, Maggie was right. It was the water. During my trial, we learned that he had suffered several nervous breakdowns during his life. He had a history of clinical depressions. In 1949, in Phoenix, he had actually been arrested on a manslaughter charge. My lawyer had wanted to fly in a woman from Austin, Texas, who had once been married to Snow. She was prepared to testify to the fact that he had broken her arm in one of his insane rages. Along with everyone else in that courtroom, I came to believe that Snow had settled in El Sol because, without quite understanding why, the lithium in the water had soothed his psychosis. My lawyer did bring in a psychiatrist to testify about lithium, and a local geologist whose research showed that the lithium in the El Sol water was indeed less than it had been five years earlier. Why, he couldn't say. But the psychiatrist did say that when the lithium began to run out, so did Snow's sanity.

"Are you back for good?" I asked Doll.

She shook her head. "I leave tomorrow for Atlantic City. With a friend." She looked a little sad and yet excited too.

"Atlantic City?"

"The person I met in Acapulco . . . he was on vacation. He works in Atlantic City. It isn't far from New York, is it?"

"Not far, no. Your friend works in one of the casinos?"

"He has a very important job, yes."

It was not my place to ruin her excitement with my own opinions. I knew nothing. "Nancy and I have separated for good," I said instead.

"Yes, I thought so."

I wanted to ask her why, but let it go. This time Nancy had gone back East, not to California. Our love would remain, but it could no longer carry the burden of our everyday lives. I was grateful that Nancy had stayed until the trial was finished.

(We had found that gun she had packed in Colorado. It was in a box of her old photograph albums, not in with the garden tools as she'd thought. I had driven down to the police station the same day and turned it over to Dorfman. Of course the police lab confirmed that it hadn't been fired in years.)

"You said to Inez that it was very important I come see you," she said. "Why?"

"Aaron's will."

"His will?"

I explained. Aaron had left the bulk of his estate, about four million dollars, to the Church of the Holy Innocents. It was meant to found a school: a primary school that would concentrate on the fundamentals. Aaron asked that 50 percent of the students be "minority," meaning Mexican, kids on scholarships. The board of trustees were always to be chaired by the rector of Holy Innocents. However, for as long as they lived, Aaron had named two other "life trustees." One was Elwood Munty. He was deceased now.

"You're the other one," I told her. This was Aaron's last joke. I had to be the one to deliver it.

She covered her mouth with her hand, turned to stare at the stained-glass window, and finally asked, "What does it mean?"

"As long as you live, you will be a trustee of this school."

"But there is no school."

"No, but there will be one in another year."

"Do I get money for this?"

"Not really. If you come to meetings, your expenses will be paid. That's about all."

She thought some more, then nodded her head as if

she had reached a silent agreement. "Yes, I understand why Aaron thought of this. It's good, I think."

"Yes?"

"Yes. If ever I want to come back to the Border, you can send me a ticket. Or no?"

"Why not?" I laughed. "We'll just call a meeting for you."

She stared into my eyes. "Are you very lonely with your wife gone away again?"

"No," I said, no longer laughing. "Not at all. I also have a new friend."

Her eyes opened wide, and I knew she wanted to ask me more.

"She's a teacher," I said. "She only moved here in July. She came to one of our study groups one evening, at my house, and . . . we liked each other." I didn't continue, but thought of my friend's face with its simple beauty, her auburn hair and Kansas accent, flat as the plains. I was very glad she had not been in El Sol until long after the election.

Doll seemed to want to change the subject, and she must have read my mind. "What happened to your election? Did it go Aaron's way?"

"Yes and no. Mulcahy won the mayor's office. And Joe Moore won his Proposition 3. But, thanks to Aaron, Proposition 8 was defeated. They won't be tearing down the *barrio* for a few more years anyway." I reached over and took Doll's hand and brought it to my lips. She was a child of the *barrio*, and she watched carefully as I kissed her hand. "Was it Montoya who tried to kill me that night at the Rainbow?"

"I don't know," she said.

The mystery of who had tampered with my Fairmont was still unsolved. I suspected it came down to one of three men: Montoya, Joe Moore, or Roy, Aaron's stepson. I also had the feeling I would never know. It would remain an unsolved conspiracy—keeping me awake one night every month for the rest of my life. Unless I could learn to ignore conspiracies, even those designed to take my own life. That was something I doubted that I, or anyone else of my generation, could easily learn.

"Are you going to stay in El Sol now?" she asked.

"Now?"

I looked around the interior of the church: old adobe walls and modern stained-glass windows, the rich altar and the new kneeling cushions. I dropped her hand gently back on her lap. "The parish has asked me to stay here. Under the circumstances, I was quite surprised."

She didn't understand. She wet her lips with her tongue.

"Yes, I want to stay here for a while yet," I said.

There was a silence that drew out for several minutes. Finally Doll looked at me with regret and said, "My friend is waiting outside."

"Of course."

We rose and edged out into the aisle. She genuflected and we walked side by side to the large doors at the back. Doll paused. "Do you want to meet him?"

"I think I don't. Is that all right?"

"Yes. It doesn't matter."

"It does, but you're good to say so. Good-bye, Maria."

"Good-bye."

I wondered if we would kiss, and glanced for a moment at her parted lips. But she quickly put out her hand. I took it. We both looked away as we performed this last rite. I let her go out into the desert sunshine then, let her escape, with the light cutting into my eyes like a blade.

[322]